UNWANTED

UNWANTED

Book 1 of The Unfolding

D.W. ANDERSON

FIDELIS
PUBLISHING®

Fidelis Publishing®
Winchester, VA • Nashville, TN
www.fidelispublishing.com

ISBN: 9798993655048
ISBN: (eBook) 9798993655055
Unwanted
Book One of The Unfolding – A Novel

Cover designed by Diana Lawrence
Interior design by Lisa Parnell
Edited by Amanda Varian

Manufactured in the United States of America

10 9 8 7 6 5 4 3 2 1

FIDELIS
PUBLISHING

This novel is dedicated to my mom, Donna.

Like Sandy, her early life was difficult but she never used it as an excuse. She is with the Lord now and is dearly missed.

Contents

Prologue

Susan finished pressing the plunger down, the French press forcing the saturated grounds to the bottom and releasing a dark, rich, aromatic coffee.

She walked from the sideboard to the lone chair positioned near the modern linear gas fireplace that dominated the back wall of her office. The chair was a well-worn wingback. It clashed with everything else in the room, but it wasn't there for beauty. It was a reminder. A relic from the day her life split in two. The day she met Gustav. The day Addison Foster brought her to his home. The day she learned her parents were dead.

Susan Veil sat, cupping the mug in both hands as she took the first satisfying sip. She set it on the stand beside her and let her gaze settle on the flames. Her thoughts drifted back to 1930, the day everything changed. The day she liked to call the beginning of her greatness. Her mark on the world, still being etched into history, though almost no one knew she existed.

Slowly, the memory replayed. Addison Foster's cruel voice intruded first.

1930 NYC

"Gustav. Gustav. Where is that thickheaded boy I keep about, the big, muscled one."

Foster barked the question at the maid as she carried away his morning coffee tray. Startled, she replied, "I don't know, sir. I'll fetch him," and vanished through the doorway.

Gustav entered moments later, clearly just out of bed. His hair was disheveled. He wore trousers and a sleeveless undershirt, work boots already on. He was used to being summoned for errands.

Foster shot him a look of irritation, then launched into excited speech.

"I have just read some exhilarating news in this morning's New York Times. Davis and Merriwether Stockton were killed in a subway derailment last night. Good stock, both of them. They left behind a ten-year-old daughter."

He handed Gustav a set of keys.

"Take the Packard and fifteen hundred dollars in cash to this address. That should be sufficient incentive. I want the orphan girl here within the hour. No excuses."

Foster leaned forward.

"If the sitter refuses the money, persuade her otherwise. If she keeps the cash, she pledges her silence. Your intimidating stature will make that point. You will return with the girl. No loose ends. Do I make myself clear?"

Gustav said nothing. He turned toward the stairs.

"Leave the money and address with the maid, sir," he called back calmly.

Moments later he returned in a pressed driver's uniform, cap tucked beneath his arm. He slid the envelope of cash into his jacket pocket. It was a hot August morning. By the time he opened the garage door and started the Packard, sweat was rolling down his spine.

He arrived at the nanny's apartment at 7:22 a.m.

Just over twenty-four hours since the couple's deaths.

The timing was intentional. Foster wanted the girl removed before questions formed, before attachments complicated matters. Gustav had been sent with cash to avoid violence. If the nanny resisted, things would escalate. He hoped they wouldn't.

He knocked.

A young woman, no more than twenty-five, opened the door. Four children crowded behind her. Panic flashed across her face when she saw Gustav, and she tried to shut the door.

To be fair, Gustav thought, I am frightening.

He attempted reassurance, but his deep voice and German accent only made things worse. Finally, he tore open the envelope just enough for her to see the money.

The negotiation ended.

Within thirty minutes, Gustav left with ten-year-old Susan and her few belongings.

She showed almost no reaction to the news of her parents' deaths. They were often gone for months. Even the sitter hadn't known yet.

Susan climbed into the Packard and slid into the passenger seat beside Gustav instead of the rear. She looked around, wide-eyed.

"So where are we going," she asked brightly.

Gustav glanced at her, surprised.

"We are going to Mister Addison Foster's home. You will live there. He is very wealthy."

"You speak English well. Where are you from," she asked.

"Wiesbaden, Germany."

She smiled. "Meadow Baths. Near Frankfurt. Close to the Rhine and Schloss Biebrich."

Gustav was stunned.

Before he could respond, she continued. "Your accent is heavy but controlled. How long have you been here? Do you like Mister Foster. Will we be friends. I like you already."

She giggled softly.

Gustav barely heard the rest. All that remained was: Will we be friends. I like you already.

He was a good man in a bad position. Susan was water to a parched soul. He resolved instantly to protect her.

What he failed to recognize was that Susan's questions were calculated. She was not surprised by her circumstances. Her parents had been too absorbed in appearances to notice what they had raised.

Susan looked out for Susan.

By the time they arrived at Foster's townhouse, Gustav would have given his life for her. Not out of improper affection, but out of respect and honor.

He guarded himself carefully. Susan matured early; a genetic reality Foster prized for different reasons. Gustav never crossed a line. He never would. Yet as she grew, his devotion deepened, and Susan learned how to wield it.

If she ever developed a capacity for love, it did not come from her parents. It did not come from Foster. It came from the one man Foster believed possessed no qualities beyond muscle.

When they arrived, Susan took in the townhouse's opulence without fear or grief. She was exactly where she believed she belonged.

Foster descended the stairs.

"You are Susan. Simply Susan, never to take the name Susan Foster," he said. "Understand this. This is not charity. This is not affection. You are not my daughter. You are not my advisor. You are not my friend. You will do as I instruct, and in return, you will inherit what I leave behind. I have no heir. You will be that heir. Do you understand."

Susan nodded without hesitation.

The warmth of the fire pulled her focus back.

The heat radiating from the linear flame washed over her skin, and the memory dissolved. She lifted her mug and inhaled the aroma of the coffee, grounding herself in the present.

Young Susan had known she needed a new identity. Reinventing herself entirely had been exhilarating. Her new name needed to reflect secrecy.

How ironic, she thought, that day I became the first. The very first of the Unwanted. Now there are so many, and the numbers grow daily. I could not even guess closely. After all, I was purchased with cash, and I served in Mister Foster's house for the rest of his life.

The events of that day had given her the idea for the broader plan. Once it took root, it was obvious. A far better plan than Foster's. A patient plan, still unfolding after all these years, with decades yet to come before it was time.

She stared again at the smooth, consistent line of flame burning along the six-foot length. She did not carry Foster's eugenic ambitions as he conceived them before the war. She perfected them first. He had willed it. She had built it.

Her eyes smiled at the flame's unity. I have put together an organization that, by Addison's design, would have been led by four scholarly old fool's incapable of action and mired in secret meetings. They embraced a religious-like fervor for eugenics. Foster's will required a meeting of these men. She almost laughed remembering how she complied once. The group he called the TETRAD ended with a whimper. The whimper of cowards. Obligations met. Now the real work began.

She savored the last warmth of the coffee and the fireplace. Then she leaned forward. The aroma of the coffee carried her back deeper into her memory of that time.

Addison Foster's final day played out like a movie in her mind. The memory was so vivid it came with privileges. She could walk within it. Pause it. Step through it. She rarely indulged anymore, but this part was special.

Her eyes refocused.

When Foster collapsed on his drawing room floor in 1937, clutching his chest, she did not summon help. She simply stepped closer and watched.

She did not kill Addison Foster. She did not believe that counted.

As Foster often quoted, borrowing from Tennyson, it was simply nature, red in tooth and claw.

Susan rose with her coffee and sat at her antique pearwood desk, resuming the rigors of planning for a new humanity.

1

Chase POV 1: Even the Rain

SEPTEMBER 7, 1998 – COLUMBUS, OHIO

Sandy finished lunch at Taco Bell on West Broad Street, lost in thought. An involuntary smile crossed her face as Ruthy's words from eighteen years ago returned: "Child, I talkin' 'bout the good-good news. It gonna land right when and where He throw it, sure-sure."

She glanced at her watch, took one last sip of her drink, and pushed through the exit door and there it was: a blacked-out Chevy Suburban, perfectly positioned to follow her out. Was it the same one from the campaign rally? She decided to find out.

Adrenaline surged. She climbed into her Lexus RX 300 and pulled out east on Broad Street. Settling into the right lane.

The black Chevy snake slid into traffic three vehicles back, trailing behind a smoking Dodge Caravan. She nicknamed the van Cheech to keep her spirit's light. The light turned yellow. She slowed. The Suburban stopped behind Cheech, staying in the haze despite an open left lane. Why?

Sandy enlisted her Inner Crazy, a technique she had used since age eleven. When stressed, Sandy divided her mind into three advisors: Lefty, Mister Right, and Campus Hippie. Kids raised in isolation often learn to rely on internal voices. Sandy wasn't delusional. She simply reasoned things out verbally. Her humor did the rest.

Your paranoia is justified, Lefty said. Sandy nodded.

"Why stay in the smoke?" she wondered aloud. *More natural to switch lanes*, Lefty agreed.

She needed more proof. "Lord, help me. I need to know for sure."

The pursuit led to the Broad Street Bridge: a sea of red brake lights. Traffic had stopped. The Suburban halted a dozen cars back. Two men stepped out and approached on foot. Moving fast.

Time slowed, as it had for her the first time when her mother died in front of her. Bridge ahead. River below. Red lights. Sea of red. The Red Sea. Of course. A distant siren wailed: an accident ahead. At least she'd be closer to police if she couldn't break through.

"Time to part the Red Sea," she muttered.

She bowed her head. "God, I think I'm starting to understand that You are real. If You are, please don't let me hurt anyone. This feels like a plan, but I'm not sure if it's Yours or mine. I want to escape. Whatever happens, I will take it."

She dropped the Lexus into neutral and stomped the gas and the engine screamed. Confused drivers squeezed against guardrails, scraping metal, trying to avoid a perceived collision from behind. The chaos multiplied. The Red Sea parted.

As the Lexus rolled off the bridge, emotion hit. *These guys are going to kill me.*

Lefty chided gently. *You asked Him to intervene. He did. How much longer will you test Him before you accept the results?* Then Lefty fell silent.

One last trip home to grab her go-bag and her cat R2. Then she would vanish.

She pulled into the parking garage and into her parking space at the Leveque Tower, grabbed the brown paper sack from the glove box (her insurance), and entered the hotel lobby through the garage. Her reflection in the brass elevator doors showed raw panic.

Inside the elevator, she jabbed the close button repeatedly. As the doors slid shut, two men in suits and sunglasses entered the lobby. Agents.

She cupped her hands and shouted through the narrowing gap: "Gun!" The lobby erupted. Screams. People ran. *That should slow them down, but not long enough.*

The doors sealed. She pressed floor 3 instead of heading to the almost top of the tower to her apartment. R2 would have to wait.

On the third floor, she sprinted for the stairwell. At ground level she hurled the paper sack she called "insurance" against the wall. Roofing nails scattered across the landing. She burst onto Broad Street to the sound of a howl behind her. Campus Hippie taunted, *Tread lightly, boys.*

Rain fell heavy and cold, then poured as if in judgment. Two men pursued: one limping, one jogging casually. *Why weren't they running?*

Ahead, a man at the crosswalk watched her, rain streaking his glasses. Trap.

She turned down Pearl Street toward Gay, boxed into a dead-end alley. Brick walls. A black SUV blocked the exit. Confirming there was more than one SUV.

Exhausted, the truth hit her. "My soul is more important than my safety."

She ducked behind a dumpster, pulling trash bags over herself. The stench felt fitting. Maybe it wasn't the garbage that reeked, but her sins. No humor left to hide behind.

Minutes passed under the filth and darkness. Eighteen years collapsed into this single moment. Ruthy's promise, spoken over a frightened, pregnant teenager, finally landed exactly where He threw it.

"Okay," she whispered, tears mixing with rain. "I believe You now. What's next, Lord?"

Footsteps approached. Five men surrounded the dumpster: two from the SUV, two from behind, one from the crosswalk. Professionals.

"Sandy, come on," a gentle voice said. "Hiding in garbage?" She knew that voice.

He lifted her, chuckling. "You look like a drowned rat." Then his tone hardened. "You know me. My voice. My face."

"Your smell." She glanced at the limping man. "Ouch, puncture wounds hurt. Better keep that foot dry. They get infected."

"Sandy, we just want to talk. Come on over to the car. Let's get you dry."

"You don't chase someone down to talk," she snapped. "Last time I got in an EPS car, my life vanished. I am not that woman anymore." Her voice cracked on purpose.

"A mother knows. I knew when I heard his voice on TV. Why parade him like that?"

The agent sighed. "Sandy, you broke the rules. Almost twenty years ago, you signed a deal. We kept our end."

"He doesn't know anything," Sandy said.

"No thanks to you," he shot back. "Gabriel gave his security detail the note you slipped him. Good thing he did not read it."

He produced a syringe. "You are done. You are going to disappear. Either way, you can no longer be trusted. You are no longer useful."

She needed one point of recognition, something only he would understand. She put on a mocking face and said, "He can do anything, anything, anything under the sun."

He pierced her neck with the long, thin needle, applying slow pressure to the plunger and muttering so only Sandy could hear, "Thing Two and Thing One."

The rain surged as he pressed the plunger, then stopped the moment he withdrew the needle.

Greg stared into her eyes as she began to fade, holding her body firmly to prevent her from falling.

Sandy's last words, witnessed by the men, came faintly. "Forgive them." Then, louder, "So it begins," as her eyes, now expressionless, stared skyward.

Two of the younger agents lifted her body to the SUV.

Greg arrived back at his office after they dropped the body at North Fourth Funeral Services. He shut the door and locked it behind him. At the four-drawer lateral filing cabinet, he entered the six-digit code and waited for the mechanism to release.

He had not turned on the overhead light. Instead, he used his flashlight to scan the labels, pulling six hanging folders one by one and laying them across his desk. He switched on the desk lamp. The stack of surveillance files stood nearly eighteen inches high. He pulled the top folder free and began reading.

For hours he sat in the dim room, reviewing the surveillance of Sandy leading up to the day they first met. He turned to the section containing the dossier on their operative, Roger. Sandy's real story required a clear understanding of the directives Roger had been given by his handler. Greg settled in and refreshed his memory on the man who had set everything in motion.

As the night grew late, he continued. He saw every mistake he had made, both as Greg and as Agent Issachar when undercover. He combed through the records of Roger and the aftermath left for Sandy to clean up. He was halfway through the stack when he reached the file documenting her arrival on Saint Croix in 1979.

Greg stretched, remembering how his own timeline crossed these events and how many lives had changed because of this one woman. He smiled, or rather forced a smile to keep tears from forming. Everyone has regrets, but tonight the files brought them front and center and full circle.

He marked his place with a clean sheet of legal paper, returned the folders to the drawer, and locked it for safekeeping. That was enough for tonight. He would continue another time. Now he needed sleep.

2

Roger's Contract

APRIL 27, 1979 – NEW YORK CITY

Roger was wealthy. Wealth was not enough. Roger needed a hobby.

While some men played golf or painted, Roger toyed with women's hearts professionally. He lacked any normal hesitancy when manipulating people for money. His unseen employers paid him to date, investigate, and if directed, become intimate. *Their lucky day*, he often thought.

For Roger, every contract began the same way. A packet slid under the door containing the target's details: name, financial information, Enclave surveillance reports, likes, dislikes, favorite movies, foods, colors, books.

After reviewing the packet, he formulated a plan.

If the assignment fell within the scope of his charm, Roger accepted by walking to the newsstand roughly two minutes from his apartment. One choice to make: *Wall Street Journal* signaled acceptance; *New York Times* signaled rejection.

Roger, confident in his abilities, had never bought a *New York Times.* He knew one day he would overestimate his charm or underestimate the woman involved. It was only a question of when.

This packet intrigued him.

Tonight, he would finish his assignment with Angelina, and then he would fly to Columbus for the new assignment. Roger studied the photo of a green-eyed beauty captured leaving Café Brasilia Coffee Shop on High Street.

"Sandy," he said quietly, smiling to himself. "I look forward to meeting you."

Leaving to buy a *Wall Street Journal* at the designated newsstand, Roger then met his driver for the evening and his final moments with Angelina.

On April 28, 1979, Roger boarded an executive charter flight from New York to Columbus. He avoided commercial flights, when possible, to keep his profile low and indulge his taste for nice things.

The cabin attendant prepared everything exactly as requested: a decanted bottle of Heitz Martha's Vineyard 1974 Cabernet Sauvignon from Napa Valley, poured precisely ninety minutes ago. Next to the decanter sat a new Longines digital watch. It's red LED numbers showed five minutes remaining. A wheel of softened brie, sat next to a sliced sourdough baguette on a tray.

Roger insisted on precise wine preparation, in this case a 90-minute breathing time. In the past he had ranted more than once about failures. He requested no cabin service during the short flight, citing last-minute review items for a meeting.

Arriving on time, Roger checked into the Hyatt Regency and unpacked.

Donning an Ohio State University T-shirt, he filled a backpack with carefully selected books—a collection meant to present him as an introverted graduate student. His fictitious degree was an MS in computer science. With his role defined, Roger took a cab to Café Brasilia Coffee Shop.

This was how he fulfilled his contracts. This was how it happened with Sandy.

APRIL 28, 1979 – CAFÉ BRASILIA COFFEE SHOP, COLUMBUS, OHIO

Sandy was not in the shop when Roger arrived. He spent thirty minutes pretending to study. Then she walked in.

Within fifteen minutes, they were talking. Roger was very charming.

She was drawn to their shared interests, rough backgrounds, and similar philosophies about life.

"I can't believe I'm talking like this," Roger said. "I usually stay in the background, but you've drawn me out in a way I've never experienced. I'm not trying to scare you, but I've never met anyone like you."

He paused, staring into his coffee.

"Wow," Sandy blurted before her inner voice could intervene. "I was thinking the same thing. Almost exactly."

Campus Hippie spoke up: *Sandy, you don't know this guy. Don't open your heart. You will get hurt and I will have to remember it over and over.*

It was already too late.

She hoped Roger might end her loneliness. But when he suggested moving in together after only two weeks, her instincts snapped back into focus.

Too fast, she thought.

Roger was frustrated. Normally, assignments required only a few dates, the right emotional cues, and then intimacy. Sandy was different. She set rules.

Rules? She is mocking my charm, he thought.

His employer grew impatient. She was taking far longer than any of the others. This one felt like a higher priority than any other. The pressure to finish the contract grew by the day, and Roger could feel the scrutiny from his unseen employer.

Her rules were very clear.

"We can date and share expenses," she told him. "But I get the couch. You get the floor. I'm not ready for more. Agree, or we keep things as they are."

Inwardly furious, Roger agreed with practiced respect.

A few nights on the floor and she will crack, he thought.

After it became apparent, she was never going to bend to his charm, he tried a different approach. Mister Good Guy went away, and distraught Roger took over. He drank whiskey, rubbed some into his clothes, and picked a fight. He claimed she had driven him to drink, that her rejection was unbearable.

That night, he shook her and shoved her against the wall.

She locked herself in the bathroom until he left.

The next morning, he arrived with an expensive Siamese cat and begged her to give him one more chance.

Sandy loved cats, but her Inner Crazy warned her not to accept it. In the end, the cat won her over. His personality overcame her caution.

She gave him one more chance. And Roger knew it was his last.

His orders were implicit. Rejection meant failure. Failure meant the end of his dream job.

On July 1, he feigned drunkenness again, forced himself on her, and fled to New York within the hour.

The money was in his account when he arrived.

He sent someone with an unauthorized key to retrieve the television they had purchased together, that hid a camera and recording device.

That darn cat kept staring at the lens and sniffing at it. He thought it best not to risk her curiosity.

Unlike other targets, he did not worry about Sandy pursuing him.

She sees me as a drunken abuser now. She will not chase me. She will not report me.

He felt safe. At least in the short term. *She will move on.*

What Roger did not know was that Sandy, once a fourteen-year-old girl plotting her escape, had already mastered the long game.

3

Life After Roger

AUGUST 8, 1979 – COLUMBUS, OHIO

Sandy approached the front door of her ground-floor apartment, a small part of a larger old brick home. The house had probably been quite something in its early days, but its proximity to campus had earned it an ignoble fate: being chopped into smaller apartments.

She loved her little place. It was a small one-room efficiency carved from what was most likely the original full kitchen. It would have been large even by the standards of the day it was built. But when you pack an entire apartment into those four walls, the description changes from large to efficient.

The kitchen ran along the front exterior wall. A small closet stood in the corner to the left of the door. Between the two was a large old window with a deep ledge on the inside and a slightly rippled, single-pane of glass. The imperfection and age of the gifted glazier's handcrafted window created a slight distortion of the outside world. The placement of this large single pane of glass had obviously been placed to provide ample natural light for the once-fine kitchen.

A small bathroom occupied the opposite corner, and between the bathroom and the kitchen stood two end tables flanking a single roll-out couch that served as both couch and bed.

This was the only place Sandy could really remember calling home after her parents were gone. She refused to call any of her foster placements by such a normal, happy word—unaffectionately referring to them as foster prisons. The last one was in Marion, so Sandy called it MCI, referring to the Marion Correctional Institution, not far from her last stint on East Church Street.

On her eighteenth birthday, April 7, 1978, at exactly 12:00 a.m. The bedside clock's fell in unison clacking softly as they fell. Sandy pulled open the front porch window. Wearing her one pair of thrift-store Guess jeans and her purple Goody comb, its handle visible in her back pocket. Sandy slung her JanSport backpack on. Now she was ready.

Softly she stepped onto the rotting porch roof, then jumped to a nearby tree. Sandy climbed down and ran, putting Church Street far behind. She stopped, breathing hard, at the Greyhound station on West Center Street. Sandy had been planning her Freedom Day since her fourteenth birthday. Today no one had any right to stop her from leaving. Taking the bus to Columbus, she picked up a COTA bus and went to the apartment she had circled in the *Dispatch* ad. That is how she arrived at her apartment on West Starr Avenue.

Sandy enjoyed the irony of moving to West Starr Avenue. She liked thinking she had followed a star to her freedom.

Sandy was a slim young woman, standing at five feet ten inches tall. She had always been tall and slim. However, she was what polite ladies called an early bloomer. Her dusty blonde hair was cut fairly short, and her rare emerald green eyes gave her a striking look. She tanned very easily, which contributed to her somewhat exotic appearance. Due to her physical appearance, especially at an early age, she almost always dressed practically.

She worked hard not to be noticed. Two rules from foster homes had kept her safe: travel light and make yourself plain. First rule, pretty was a blessing and a curse. Pretty privilege had a dark side and seemed to invite more trouble than benefits. She had learned how to navigate both sides, but she did not enjoy it.

Funny in a dry way, Sandy possessed a well-developed sense of humor. They say humor is born in pain; in Sandy's case, they were probably right. Good looks and humor were not all she possessed. In addition, she had a smooth and captivating singing voice, a very quick wit, and a survivor's mindset.

All of this fell at odds with the single most important rule Sandy had placed in her life: be a window. Something someone looks past or through but never at, even if they stare directly at you. Windows are a lens and a frame allowing you to focus on the picture beyond. It is what you see through them that catches your interest. No one cares about the frame that holds the glass in place. Sandy had done a pretty good job of being a window, or at least so she thought.

She unlocked the door and knelt to gather the mail pushed through the slot. Roger the Siamese cat sat on the windowsill, his piercing blue eyes unconcerned, licking a paw.

"Roger, why do you always knock the mail everywhere? Can't you leave it where it falls?"

He stared and kept grooming.

Roger the cat was her only companion, friendly on his own terms, but still a comfort. And yes, she named him after her ex-boyfriend, a choice that surprised even her. The Siamese was a gift from Roger before he disappeared, and she'd resisted naming the kitten right away despite his urging. After he fled, she made a bold decision. Rather than relive the trauma every time she heard his name, she would give it to someone who brought her joy instead. That day, she began replacing the memory of that night with something gentler, something she chose. Roger the cat.

Giving Roger (the cat) an exasperated look, she began gathering the brightly colored envelopes that dominated most of her mail that day. In fact, the scolding envelopes started about two weeks after and almost every day since Roger Senior had disappeared.

Roger wove around her legs, purring. She gave in. "All right, Rog, but there isn't much left. Eat slowly."

She poured the last of the kibble into his bowl. Her heart sank as she felt how light the bag of kibble had become. While he ate, she sat with the mail. Past-due notices glared up at her. Electric. Credit card. Threats disguised as polite reminders. "You're a bad person." Of course, the bill did not say that in words. She took every past-due notice as a personal accusation.

The last envelope was different. It came from a pregnancy center on High Street, just blocks away. She stared at it. It was a friendly pastel pink and blue themed envelope with an elegant font. The letter was long so Sandy skimmed it. "In trouble? We can help you navigate this difficulty and find the solution that is right for you. Stop in for a free consultation at our campus location." The remainder of the letter was just information about the address and acceptable insurance coverage.

"How do they know?" she muttered. "Well, that's just great, Rog. Now even the mailman knows I'm pregnant."

She chuckled at her own joke. The laugh faded into shaking shoulders, first gently and then harder, more pronounced, then tears. She cried harder than she had in months. Roger padded over and curled beside her.

Why did she get this letter? Maybe they mailed it to everyone? She had taken three tests, all positive, but she kept hoping for a mistake. That hope was gone now.

"Come on, Rog. Let's get the bed out and sleep."

They pulled the couch into a bed. She checked the deadbolt, brushed her teeth, and climbed in. Roger settled next to her.

"Well, Rog, tomorrow I'll go see what those pregnancy center people have to say. I can't even take care of you and me properly. What am I going to do with a baby? I don't really know what to do. It can't hurt to get info. Besides, I don't have insurance so that will slow things way down, I am sure. Yes, tomorrow we get information. That is what we need the most."

"Meow," said Roger.

"Do I hear skepticism in that Meow?" Sandy remarked sarcastically. "Good night to you too."

She rolled over to face the bathroom wall. While Roger the cat slept soundly, her mind wandered to Roger the boyfriend.

He was not aware of her full story. He knew she was bounced around, but Roger had no idea how hardened she could be when attacked. He didn't know her as the fourteen-year-old plotting her escape. After all, Sandy's Freedom Day took four years to execute, waiting patiently until she turned eighteen. Only then did Sandy make her clean break.

In the end, after she had left her foster wardens behind, she knew they would continue to collect the checks sent by the State for her care. Sandy waited, allowing the checks to continue flowing in and be cashed by the greedy Kincaid's. She waited long enough to let the dollar amount rise to a felony. Then she used the very system that failed her to bring them down. A single anonymous call backed by precise background knowledge was enough to light the fuse.

They likely knew it was her.

Sandy didn't care.

When the time comes for Roger the ex-boyfriend, he will know it was me too. With that oddly comforting thought, she eventually drifted off to sleep.

4

A Familiar Lie

For Sandy, the next morning arrived with a familiar lie.

Her mother used to say, "Everything always looks better in the morning." Sandy dismissed it. That saying ranked right up there with "All's well that ends well." A past coworker had shortened it to "All's well that ends." That felt more honest.

Sandy dragged herself out of bed after a fitful night: bad dreams, a brain that would not shut off, and the occasional Siamese kick to the face. She went to the fridge and pulled out the last bit of half-and-half for Roger Junior, hoping to head off the inevitable.

Too late.

He began complaining before the bowl hit the floor, yowling sharply as she set it down and asserted his dominance.

"Yeah, you're the man, Roger," she said dryly.

While Sir Roger the Magnificent lapped at the bowl, Sandy hopped in the shower and cranked up the hot water. She let it beat against the back of her neck until the tiny bathroom turned into a sauna. After drying off, she cracked the door to let the steam escape and dressed, savoring the warm, moist air drifting into the main room.

Normally she would never use that much hot water. The effect on the electric bill was too great. But after yesterday's scolding red envelope, she felt rebellious.

She grabbed her keys and her small, functional purse, took the pregnancy center letter from the end table, folded it in half, and plunged it into her bag. After a quick goodbye to Roger and a warning to leave the incoming mail alone, she exited the apartment and locked the deadbolt behind her.

Heading down the sidewalk, She turned left at the end of West Starr Avenue, and walked north on High Street toward the Pregnancy Center, just a few blocks away.

A white van with no back windows sat parked near the end of West Starr Avenue, on the opposite side from where she crossed the street.

Wow, what an obvious surveillance van, she thought, amused. Just like in the movies. *Wonder who they're spying on?*

Inside the van, it was hot and cramped. Surveillance and recording equipment generated constant heat despite a reinforced cooling system. A running van with no windows near a university campus would draw attention.

These were not local police or federal agents. They were employees of Enclave Protection Services, a private contractor staffed by former law enforcement and military personnel specializing in surveillance, background investigations, and protection services. Many agents suspected EPS was more than it appeared to be, but no one asked questions.

"Man, I'm sweating so much my suit is soaked," Rookie Agent Max said, watching Sandy pass by on the monitor. "My fiancée asked if I worked out at the gym in my suit. I lied and said the bus ride was hot, with no good seats near the air conditioning. I hate that I can't tell her what I do. Honestly, sometimes I don't even know what I do."

When his partner Steven did not respond, Max refocused on the screens.

"She's crossing the road at the clinic," Steven said. "Stand by. She'll be inside in a minute. I'm beginning the verification background now."

"Copy that," Max replied. "I'm checking financial and foster records for final screening."

"Sylvia," Steven said, "she's entering your lobby very soon. Do not proceed until we re-confirm background eligibility. Stay tuned for the green light. If you copy my instructions, glance at the clock on my mark. Three, two, one, mark."

Sylvia glanced at the clock to the left of her desk, then back.

"Message received," Steven said.

While Sylvia waited, she slid the file onto the keyboard tray so she could still read it without drawing attention. She reminded herself she was on camera. Every movement mattered. A misfiled memo had been tucked into the back pocket of Sandy's overview brief. It was not about Sandy at all. It was about a foundation Susan had formed in 1940.

Her first instinct was to leave it alone. Lately she had begun to suspect that ignorance might truly be bliss. But she also knew she might never see this memo again, and she needed reassurance that her work was as altruistic as Susan claimed. Something had been gnawing at her for years. She wanted answers, and she knew they would not come easily. The memo landing in her hands felt like divine intervention, if she believed in such things.

She leaned closer and read as quickly as she could before she had to slip back into character. Whether this was a loyalty test or something else entirely, curiosity pushed harder than caution.

5

Origins: Memo Addison-Foster Foundation

MARCH 1940, NEW YORK CITY

The Addison Foster Foundation was introduced to the public as the Addison-Foster Foundation. That single hyphen was a quiet stroke of genius. It suggested an old family lineage and neatly disguised the truth: the two words were simply a first and last name.

The name was presented to the public to honor a real woman named Addison, who had died in Florida from Huntington's disease. This genetic stalker, Huntington's chorea, killed her twice. First came the living death: onset in the thirties or forties, then a relentless march through body and mind, stripping motor control, speech, and finally the will to live. Only after that did the body follow. Yet the disease's cruelty did not end there. Its 50 percent inheritance rate cast a generational shadow, poisoning marriages, discouraging children, and sentencing entire families to lives of dread. Every spilled coffee, every forgotten name became a possible omen. In every sense, it was a family killer.

This is Addison's story, along with the press release issued by the Addison-Foster Foundation at its public launch in January 1940:

> Addison lived her life head-on. From a young age she understood that her future, and her little sister Lyndsey's, came down to a single coin toss. The same toss that decides who bats first in

> baseball or which end zone a football team defends. Heads, you live. Tails, you begin the long, narrowing walk into darkness.
>
> Addison, who preferred "Addi," was strong. She split that strength between caring for her mother and shielding her sister, "Lynds," from the worst of the fear. She extended that same fierce loyalty to her friends, stepping in whenever anyone was bullied or treated unfairly. That is how she lived, and that is what we at the Addison-Foster Foundation intend to do in her honor.
>
> The Addison-Foster Foundation will continue the fight she started. We will work tirelessly to eliminate this genetic coin toss, devoting all our resources to its causes. We will end the passing of this misery from one generation to the next. Addison lost her battle, but her tenacity lives on through our namesake. We will not rest until genetic defects are no longer inherited. We will lift these weights from the scales of human life and create a future free from Huntington's and all other forms of genetic evil, so that everyone can live as fiercely as Addi did.

Susan herself was the architect of the Foundation. She said the quiet parts out loud: the simplest path to eliminating Huntington's was to identify carriers early and eliminate them. No carriers, no inheritance. Problem solved.

To keep the true work hidden, the Foundation established two public-facing entities: Enclave Protection Services and LIFE, or Lives Invested for Excellence. They became the visible hands of a much larger design, following the old bureaucratic rule that the left hand never knows what the right hand is really doing.

Sylvia barely finished and pushed the file back under the keyboard tray when the young lady made her way to the reception window. Sylvia suppressed the rising nausea and had barely enough time to place her receptionist's smile on before the young lady's arrival at her window.

6

Operation Baby Moses

AUGUST 9, 1979 – COLUMBUS, OHIO

Layers of need-to-know-only protocols could be confusing. Dr. Mills who today was playing the role of Sylvia the receptionist did not enjoy this type of field work. Today's subject required her involvement directly. Pretending to be someone of lesser skill or importance did not come naturally to her, although when on assignment she performed well.

Normally there were ten or twelve potentials at a time. Today there was only one. No other invitations were sent. The word *Potential* was also misleading. The decision that Sandy would be presented was rhetorical.

The other agents today assumed Sylvia was a junior EPS operative close to their rank, possibly lower. Neither Steven nor Max had ever met Dr. Mills in person. If they had known, it would have made them nervous based on her rumored reputation.

During this confirmation process, EPS rules stated firmly that at minimum an audio, and whenever possible video, record of the confirmation and a redundancy must be archived. The other solid rule of the process was no real names. Botching a final report would lead to immediate termination. The agents often nervously joked about the exact nature of that termination. Suffice it to say, you do not break protocol on purpose or even by accident when it comes to an official record.

In this case, Max would operate under his code name Levi, and Steven would be referred to as Simeon for the official record. Sylvia was to remain Sylvia, since that was already a code name.

The Pregnancy Crisis Center was wired for sound and video, with RF transmitters sending hidden feeds back to the van on High Street. Two Panasonic time-lapse VCRs and two Nagra reel-to-reel audio machines, paired redundantly, recorded on separate frequencies to mitigate equipment failure or signal interruption.

Steven sat before the console dual monitors and checked his watch. Then he pressed the master record button. Both screens flickered to life, showing the clinic's interior, and both audio tape recorders began to spin.

"Time is 9:24 a.m.," he said. "Subject Sandy Vanover approaching the Pregnancy Crisis Center from the High Street entrance. Official record re-verification begins now. Simeon on console one. Levi on console two. Location seven-one-nine. Agent code name Sylvia acting as receptionist Sylvia. Subject about to enter. Reminder: code names only for the duration of the re-verification."

The rule was now absolute.

The front lobby door opened, marked by a brief burst of ambient street noise of High Street traffic noise into the quiet reception area. A young, attractive woman stepped inside and approached the desk.

Dr. Mills, as Sylvia, flashed a rehearsed receptionist's smile. "Hello, dear. My name is Sylvia. How can I help you?"

Sandy produced the folded letter from her purse and showed it to the receptionist.

Levi and Simeon were no longer listening. They had moved on to other tasks.

In the van, Simeon began speaking for the record as Levi worked beside him. Two Lanier Advocate four-cassette decks recorded their voices through wired microphones. Their purpose was to re-verify surveillance facts before any offers were made. Due diligence was critical. Selecting the wrong subject could jeopardize everything—even they did not know today was not about a choice.

Levi spoke evenly for the record. "Tracking background on the father, known as Roger."

Simeon interrupted sharply. "Strike that sentence from the record." Simeon flipped the toggle marked mute to temporarily disable the mics. "Miss Veil called me this morning and told me and I mean *told* me, to leave any info of the father out of the record. She will handle his documentation herself. And stop giving me that look. I don't know why she didn't call you. I just know she did call me." With that, he flipped the toggle back and the mics were live again, cutting off any chance at further discussion. "New orders. Leave the boyfriend alone. Drop all background collection on him. He is not to be included in tonight's record. The male associated with this subject is to be excluded entirely. Confirm understanding.

He replied, "Yes sir, Simeon. Roger that."

Simeon rolled his eyes at Levi's dramatic reaction to the redaction of his report on Roger. Miss Veil had called. She had given a direction. That was the extent of it. As far as Simeon was concerned, none of this was his problem.

He leaned toward the microphone and spoke for the record.

"Accessing previously accessed ARPANET nodes information stored in the A-FF CompuServe storage account to verify collected data.

Parents deceased. High debt. No inheritance or insurance. Foster care since 1970. Left foster care at eighteen. No high school diploma. Valid driver's license, no vehicle. No close friends. Never married. Non-smoker. Non-drinker. No substance abuse. Hobby: singing when alone under surveillance. Reported last foster parents for fraud, resulting in arrest. No phone. IQ recorded at 130. ACT composite 31. SAT total 1410. Risk level 5 out of 50. Strong upside.

Baseline indicators: Subject presents with negligible social footprint. No durable friendships, no family stability, no adult advocates capable of sustained inquiry. Academic profile remains anomalously high across all testing environments. Consistent top percentile performance without external support. Behavioral pattern shows marked self-containment, avoidance of attention, and persistent refusal to pursue advancement opportunities. Financial trouble documented across all guardianship placements. Subject carries personal debt and demonstrates heightened anxiety around institutional authority. Emotional posture suggests chronic vigilance and a learned reluctance to trust. This produces compliance under pressure and minimal outward resistance. Subject is effectively unanchored. Brilliant, isolated, and unprotected. No structural barriers to redirection.

Suitability for Operation Baby Moses: Profile aligns with all operational criteria. High cognitive value, low relational entanglement, and no foreseeable search effort in the event of removal. Absence of meaningful attachments ensures clean extraction. Subject withdraws rather than escalates, reducing operational noise. Psychological markers indicate she internalizes distress, limiting disruption and preserving mission integrity. Subject avoids visibility, which makes her movements easy to obscure. She will not self-advocate or challenge procedural authority. All indicators confirm she will transition without incident and without generating administrative or community-level scrutiny. Recommendation stands. Proceed. Subject is an optimal intake candidate with no anticipated complications."

"With Simeon's affirmation, Sylvia, you are authorized to evaluate the subject and, if appropriate, move to the offer phase. Please confirm receipt of responsibility with a visual check of the clock on your left. On my mark. In three, two, one, mark."

Sylvia glanced at the clock, then back to Sandy.

"Visual confirmation received," Levi said. "This concludes Levi and Simeon's involvement. Operation handoff to Asher and Issachar is now in effect. Asher, Issachar, are you in position?"

"Affirmative," came the reply. "Asher affirms. Issachar affirms. All agents confirmed. Handoff complete. Simeon and Levi are now ten-six."

With the transfer finalized, Steven climbed through the narrow hatch separating the overheated surveillance compartment from the driver's area.

Max slid into the driver's seat, started the van, and cranked the window down as fast as he could.

As Steven buckled in, Max checked his mirrors and began cutting the wheels and easing forward preparing to pull into High Street traffic.

Steven was just starting to speak when Max spotted a gap and pulled out into traffic aggressively. The tires chirped as the van merged into the lane. Their raised voices could be heard fading as the van rolled down High Street.

Back at the pregnancy center, Sylvia called out in a clear, lilting voice, "Miss Vanover, why don't you come on back?"

She stood, opened the door to the exam hallway, and gestured for Sandy to follow.

Sylvia's cheerfulness caught her off guard. Her Inner Crazy stirred.

Mister Right spoke first. *This feels wrong. Why is she so cheerful? She's not the one making the decision. I don't think she is as happy as she sounds?*

Okay, Sandy, knock it off. Are you really judging someone for being nice?

Her instincts, sharpened by years in foster care, disagreed. Something was off.

Campus Hippie whispered: *This feels exactly like a new foster home. Sandy, you did not think this through.*

As they moved down the hallway, Lefty's urgency spiked. *Why aren't you running?*

Mister Right piled on. *Be logical. There's no one else here. Near campus? There should be a waiting room full of girls.*

Sandy. Stop walking!

She forced her focus outward, pulling the voices back. Either she was wrong, or they were.

She realized she was already inside the exam room.

7

The Exam Room

Once inside the exam room, Sandy forced herself to focus. She had big decisions to weigh. Her life had been a chain of disruptions and hard choices, but this felt heavier, like something she could regret forever if she did not give it her full attention.

Sylvia also was struggling to focus. Her mind was still processing what she had just read. Sylvia was a professional, she broke through her thoughts and began to speak. "Now, dear, sit right here in this chair. We'll begin with some written tests."

"Written tests?" Sandy let out a nervous laugh, but Sylvia pushed ahead.

"Yes, dear. This process can be overwhelming for young ladies. We need to make sure you're strong enough to handle the mental strain. It's routine." She handed Sandy a sealed test booklet. Its blank cover reminded her of the guidance counselor exams she had taken so many times before.

Sylvia passed her a pencil, pulled over a rolling lap desk, and set a timer for fifteen minutes. "Begin, dear. Your time is ticking." She perched on the exam stool, pretending to review a chart. Sandy wondered why a receptionist would need a chart at all. Yet Sylvia was doing some research of her own. Inside the dossier there was a single-page memo.

She tore open the seal and breezed through the test. Six minutes later, she handed it back. Sylvia blinked, assuming the results would be terrible. But when she compared Sandy's answers to the key in her folder, she froze. Every score hit the top of the scales used to identify ideal candidates.

Trying to hide her shock, Sylvia cleared her throat. "Thank you for completing this so quickly. We can review it later."

The folder was not just a medical record. It was a surveillance dossier and as Sylvia just learned it contained more than she wanted to know. Had Sandy seen the surveillance photos inside, she would have joined Sylvia in being sick.

Sylvia broke the silence. "Hop up on the exam table."

"Wait. Where's the doctor? The nurse? Any other patients?" Sandy's voice rose. "Something's not right. I'm leaving. I'll figure this out myself."

Sylvia dropped the act. The test results told her the deception would not hold much longer. Her face hardened. Her voice sharpened. "You are going to want to sit down and listen."

The shift caught Sandy off guard, though she had half expected it. *My Inner Crazy was right. Mister Right and Campus Hippie tried to warn me.*

"What's going on? Never mind, I'm out."

She grabbed the door handle, but it locked with a soft click. No one had touched it. Instinctively she snatched the nearest object, but the pencil felt pathetic in her hand.

The corner filing cabinet swung inward. Two large men stepped through. The cabinet closed behind them.

Sylvia spoke before she could react. "My name is Doctor Mills, and you are right. Something is wrong, but not in the way you think. I am happy to tell you that you qualify for a unique, incredible opportunity."

Anger surged through Sandy. "You clearly don't know me. Threats and intimidation are the fastest way to make me say no."

"Sandy," Dr. Mills said, hearing her advantage slipping, "listen for five minutes. If you are not interested, you can leave through the door you came in. But I think you will find this opportunity, with these gentlemen's assistance, is far better."

Sandy pressed her back to the wall, fear and fury rising. She pointed at the wind-up timer. "Set that timer and hand it to me. You have five minutes."

Impressed, Dr. Mills obeyed.

"Well, get going," Sandy said. "Your time is ticking."

Her sharpness was a survival tactic, a way to seize control. No moment in her life had ever felt this consequential.

For five minutes, Sandy stayed silent as Dr. Mills recited details of her life no one should know, ending with her pregnancy and Roger.

As the timer ticked away, the offer finally came.

"These men can help you pack your belongings and your cat, Roger. They will take you to a private plane waiting at the airport. You will be flown to a tropical island with a hospital equipped with the latest technology and the best doctors. You will live there until you have your baby. We will cover all expenses, pay you fifty thousand dollars for the baby, and return you to America with a new name, clean credit, money in the bank, a new car, and a mortgage-free home.

"Before you ask why, let me explain." Sandy felt a chill as the doctor continued. "We are part of a behind-the-scenes university collaboration. We call our organization LIFE, Lives Invested for Excellence. We believe every person deserves a chance. Though not religious, we share pro-life values. Our sociology experiment aims to prove that babies aborted nationwide have value and dignity. We follow their lives to show how society benefits when babies on the brink of abortion are allowed to live, raised in stable homes, educated, and trained to tackle society's greatest threats."

She leaned in. "You have no money, no family, no involved father. This is your chance to escape your struggles and give your baby a life with real potential. The difficult part is that you must decide now and leave tonight. What is keeping you from an offer that could change your life and you're the future life of your baby's?"

Just as the word "baby's" left her lips, the timer bell dinged. Soft, resonant, final. The moment etched itself into Sandy's memory forever.

8

Fight or Flight

That soft ding from the wind-up timer became the trigger for the most significant turning point in Sandy's life. From that moment on, the sound of any bell would remind her of her baby, leaving her to wonder where and how they were doing.

Something isn't right, she thought.

Aloud, she said only, "Let's go."

This is how the foundation grew. One unwanted baby at a time starting in 1940 and accelerated during the Second Great War. During this time period, unwed pregnancies grew a documented 6–10 percent in the United States. Many families sent adult children away to have babies and give them up for adoption. The only real difference between that and what the A-FF did, or its front organization LIFE, is where the children ended up.

Sandy remembered little of what followed, but the echo of that bell stayed with her.

Through the filing cabinet's hidden entrance, She was guided into a large black SUV.

Her next clear memory was eating a Charburger and fries from Charbet's near campus. The meal sat waiting for her on the private jet at three o'clock, courtesy of a phone call from Issachar. She ate faster than she meant to, realizing after the first bite how hungry she was. She had skipped both breakfast and lunch while with Thing Two and Thing One.

In true Sandy fashion, she teased the stoic men, singing a childhood memory from watching *The Cat in the Hat* with her mother.

"They can do anything, anything, anything under the sun. Thing Two and Thing One," she sang.

They remained unfazed, referring to one another only as Issachar and Asher. Sylvia had been right. Their help was efficient and undeniable.

Sandy watched Roger in his roomy carrier as he was presented with a can of expensive cat food she could never afford. Exhaustion finally claimed her, and she fell into a deep sleep, snoring softly through most of the flight.

Roger, though thoroughly bribed, remained alert. He sniffed the expensive cat food, performed an exaggerated show of excited interest, then nudged it into the back corner of the carrier once the gloved hands withdrew and the door clicked shut. Settling in, he fixed his piercing blue eyes on Sandy as she slept.

When she fell fully asleep, Glove Hands rose quietly, adjusted her pillow to ease the snoring, and pressed a small syringe into her neck. She glanced briefly at Roger, who appeared calm and sleeping, then returned to her seat. Roger did not sleep, groom, or fuss. He watched Sandy without moving for the remainder of the flight.

In the rear seats of the Cessna Citation III, Issachar and Asher rested after Sandy was sedated. Issachar, however, struggled to sleep. His thoughts returned again and again to the young woman. Not inappropriately, though he found her attractive, but with something closer to paternal concern, despite being only ten years older.

Her resilience troubled him. She had endured an ordeal that would have broken most people and yet remained polite, sharp, and quietly humorous. *She is still piecing this together*, he thought. Her instincts were practical and fast, even under pressure. In eight years with Enclave, he had never seen a reaction like hers. They were dismantling her life and rebuilding it at her request, rushing her toward an undisclosed destination, and she had not collapsed.

The thought made him snicker aloud.

Asher shifted in his seat. Issachar paused until the movement stopped. Then he stood quietly, careful of the low ceiling, opened an overhead bin, and retrieved a blanket. He adjusted Sandy's neck where the pillow had slipped and draped the blanket over her.

Feeling watched, he glanced back. Asher and Glove Hands remained asleep.

Roger lay still, eyes wide open.

Is he guarding her? Issachar thought. *I don't even like cats, but this one thinks it's a lion.*

He knelt beside the carrier and rested his hand against the bars. Roger slid forward and licked his fingers. Their eyes met, and for a moment there was an understanding that required no words.

Concerned the pilot's voice might wake the others at any moment, Issachar returned to his seat.

If she ever heard me say "would not, could not" like Dr. Seuss, she would never let it go, he thought, smiling.

Her "Thing Two and Thing One" song had nearly cracked his composure. Her voice, clear and warm like Karen Carpenter's, was another surprise. With that thought, he drifted into uneasy sleep.

The pilot's voice woke him.

"Ladies and gentlemen, we have landing clearance. We'll begin descent in fifteen minutes. Please fasten your seat belts and prepare for landing."

Thing One, Thing Two, and Glove Hands rose, checked Sandy and Roger's seat belts (both still asleep), and prepared the cabin.

As Issachar settled back, doubts resurfaced.

LIFE. Enclave's role in all of it.

Something was wrong. This feels bigger than it used to.

Sadly, for everyone involved, Issachar had not yet put the pieces together.

And that delay would cost more than one life.

9

Doctor Who?

Dr. Mills exhaled, shedding her Sylvia façade. She had maintained it through the entire Baby Moses protocol until the handoff to Asher and Issachar. She admired the young woman's quick thinking and defensive posture; Sandy's abrupt shift in attitude had likely changed the course of her life. Dr. Mills was still trying to decide what to do with the memo. She decided she would put it back where it belonged in the file and return the folder, as is, to the clerk. She knew she would not forget the substance of the memo or its implications for what she had now participated in. What could she do about it, she rationalized? She knew the babies were taken care of and that the mothers were well compensated. She tucked the file under her arm and decided to move on.

She walked back down the long corridor, now heading toward the reception door and main lobby. The sterile hallway invited unwelcome thoughts. A competent physician from a reputable school, hiding behind layers of deception. *Which one am I?* her conscience asked. Dr. Mills? Sylvia? Josie?

Passing through the lobby, she removed the temporary sign from the window and replaced it with one reading "For Sale or Lease." She exited through the back door into the alley parking area and climbed into her nearly new white Mercedes. She let the engine idle while the interior cooled, savoring the wave of new-car smell. Adhesives, plastics, vinyl, leather. One of her few indulgences. She traded cars annually, accepting the depreciation to renew it. Money had never been a concern.

At forty, she was still striking. A child prodigy, noticed by LIFE at thirteen after her parents died in a car-train collision. Guided into the organization's orbit, recruited by a now-deceased member, she began reporting to Miss Veil at fifteen. High school at fourteen, pre-med at fifteen through Miss Veil's influence, Ohio State College of Medicine at eighteen, graduated with honors at twenty-one, internship complete by twenty-three.

Now in her seventeenth year with LIFE, she wondered when or, more concerning, *if* she would ever be allowed to retire.

Gratitude and obligation bound her tightly. Marriage, children, a normal life. All of that seemed impossible. Her life had not been normal since thirteen.

Her face paled as a realization struck. She had not once thought of Melanie, the name her parents gave her.

"Why include it?" she said aloud. No one used that name. No children, nieces, nephews, siblings. Parents gone. Work consumed everything. If someone called out "Melanie," she doubted she would turn.

She pulled onto Lane Avenue, passing Tommy's Pizza and Harrison House, and pressed play on the Becker cassette player. Beethoven's "Moonlight Sonata" was the first track and its expression filled the car. The Sonata allowed her to cry without condemnation, attributing the tears to the music's genius rather than her own sorrow. Often times she would click rewind and listen again. It was the only piece she ever listened to.

Is it a masterpiece, Melanie wondered, using the name deliberately, *or a painkiller?*

She merged onto 315 North as tears streamed down her cheeks. Grateful for the tinted windows, she let them fall.

The gated, tree-lined driveway opened with a click of the single large button clipped to her visor. She always called it "the house" never her home. The distinction mattered.

The modern glass-and-steel structure rose from the property, striking against the natural landscape. Sunlight moved through the structure as if a welcomed guest being taken on a tour. It passed through the front of the house in the morning, crossed the living and dining areas, then lingered in the afternoon along the rear glass wall overlooking her neighbors wooded horse farm. Horses grazed beyond the fence. A pond reflected the trees. Adirondack chairs sat unused on the deck.

The house would never hold happiness. It existed only to conceal her.

Inside, no one greeted her. It was the beginning of a four-day weekend for her. She poured a glass of wine and settled into an oversized chair with her newest escape, Danielle Steel's *Season of Passion*. Romance novels let her imagine that she was being chosen, desired, loved.

She fell asleep with the book in her lap, remaining there for over an hour in an awkward position.

Waking suddenly, she resumed reading and finished the novel in one sitting. The clock read 5:00 a.m.

Dragging herself from the chair, she went to the kitchen, removed a liter of Stoli from the freezer, and headed upstairs. Within two hours, lights off and alarm set, the vodka had done its work. The clock read 7:00 a.m.

Silence settled over the house, broken only by Melanie's quiet cries as she dreamed fitfully of the woman she had sent away. Her conscience ruled her sleep.

Who are these people?

Doubt had begun to bend her inward, though she had not yet embraced it. She had missed a call from Miss Veil earlier, which was never acceptable. A small thing, but it lingered.

A day would come when the truth pressed in with clarity. Divine appointments are not written on calendars. They are set for you by the unchanging Organizer. His plans unfold. His promises hold.

For now, Melanie wept in her sleep.

10

An Opulent Cage

AUGUST 10, 1979 – SAINT CROIX U.S. VIRGIN ISLANDS

When Sandy woke, she was startled and immediately concerned. She was no longer on a plane. She was in a bed.

Her first instinct was to call out.

"Roger! Roger, where are you!"

"Yowl," he opined. Roger had leaped onto the bed out of nowhere, making virtually no sound when he landed. Then he lay down beside Sandy and began to purr.

He had feigned sleep through removal and transport from the airport. After Glove Hands left, Roger ventured out. Cats are known to be curious, but Roger was more concerned than curious.

She reached out to pet him, but her motor skills were not fully restored and still slow. What was intended as a loving stroke landed as a poke in the face. With that, the moment was gone. Roger jumped down to explore.

"What's the matter, Rog? You can dish it out, but you can't take it? You kick me in the face while I sleep all the time!" she said playfully as the drugs from the plane ride started to react to her waking state. "You can explore the room too. We'll compare notes later."

Sandy looked around and was blown away. It was more than one room; it was a luxury suite. She could hear waves crashing and smell fresh air, so she tried to sit up for a better view. Her head swam, and a series of beeps and chimes pierced the peace.

Within seconds, a dark-skinned nurse burst in. She appeared to be in her late forties or early fifties, with a graceful demeanor and a local accent that was almost Creole-like, rhythmic and lyrical.

"Are ya alright, ma'am?" she said.

Sandy couldn't pull herself together quickly enough, so the nurse repeated, "Are ya alright, ma'am?"

The nurse was already touching buttons, silencing the beeps one by one. Sandy noticed the IV taped in her arm.

She was groggy but had not completely lost her edge. "No, no, I'm fine, but I'm a little confused about what's going on around me right now, Miss . . ."

Catching the cue, the woman said, "Meh name Ruthy," pronouncing it Ruty, "ya know, jus' like de woman in de Bible, dat faithful Ruth who end up right in de line a King David an' Jesus Christ Himself! Ya can call me Ruthy or Nurse Ruthy, whicheva roll off ya tongue sweet. But leh me tell ya, when I haffi give a shot an' dat needle flash, dem same patients start callin' me Nurse Ruthless quick-quick!"

She laughed a bold, bright laugh, impossible to ignore.

"And it Ms., not Mrs. Mi lose mi husband years back, so Mister Right Two still out deh somewhere! But mi open for di possibilities, ya hear? Now hol' on a sec. Leh mi unhook all dis stuff so ya can move free-free. Careful, eh? Ya prob'ly still woozy from di flight. I haffi tell ya up front, dem knock ya out pon di plane wid some lorazepam after ya drop asleep. Di doctor pon di flight give di dose sheself. But leh mi apologize for dem! I chew dem out good-good, doctor an' all. When I first see ya, ya look so harmless, an' dem had ya jumbied out proper, but dem was worry ya go freak out 'cause a di long-long flight."

Sandy gave a confused look. "What does jumbied mean?"

Ruthy laughed again. "Oh, right ya pon Saint Croix. When we say jumbied out, it jus' mean di drugs mek ya look like a jumbie, dat's a ghost, mi love. Ya was up in di air over six hours, but ya tough, an' dem shouldn't a do dat widout ya consent, plain an' simple."

She leaned closer and lowered her voice. "For tell ya di truth, mi dear, I t'ink dem afraid a ya. Ya intimidate dem proper.

"I can tell ya kitty cat care 'bout ya true-true."

"Yowl," interrupted Roger.

"Now don't go get mad wid me, eh? I mean no offense at all. I jus' don't know ya name yet, so I cyan call ya proper. You an' I go be good-good friends, watch an' see. I love all animal, but especially dem handsome cats, dem sleek, dem proud, dem know dem worth!"

"Meow," he exclaimed, appearing to accept her apology and agree with her assessment. With that, Roger showed his tail end and resumed exploring.

The women shared a smirk at Roger's indignation.

"As I was sayin'," Nurse Ruthy said, "dat cat know! Like he stand up tall an' say, 'Don't gimme no six for a nine!'"

She interjected, "What does that mean, 'Give me no six for a nine'?"

Ruthy laughed a hearty, joy-filled laugh, and Sandy thought, *I need to make her laugh as often as I can while I'm here. That's a laugh I want to remember.*

"I wasn't t'inkin'. Ya ent from 'roun' here. It a common island sayin'. Mean ya cyan fool 'em, no way.

"Dem try di same trick pon him like dem do ya, 'cept his was in di food. He mus' smell di sleepin' pill dem crush up in dere, jus' a simple sedative. But ya know, he outsmart all a dem. I know 'cause after he come out for explore, I determine for clean di carrier. I ent want him uncomfortable an' yowlin' all night. But when I stick mi head in dere, dat crate clean-clean. No mess, not'in'! Pretty amazin' for a cat lock up six hours or more!

"Ya know, I t'ink he skip di food so he could stay awake an' watch over ya!

"Yeh, dat cat got plenty goin' on, an' real handsome too, but he already know dat.

"Look at me jus' runnin' mi mout'. Dere ya go! Now ya off di electronic leash an' ready fi roam.

"I hafti go check pon mi other patient now, mi love. See dat pendant 'roun' ya neck? If ya get lost or need any kine a help, jus' push dat button. I or somebody closest go come runnin' fi rescue ya quick-quick. Check out di place an' di beach. It beautiful an' peaceful ya so till! I born an' raise right here whole life, an' I still t'ink it di best. Most people cyan say dat!"

"You got that right," Sandy said. "Thanks, Ruthy. I'll buzz you if I need you."

Sandy glanced around again. First, she would join Roger in a little reconnaissance.

The bedroom was light and airy, separated from the next room by a half wall fitted with slatted shutters. They could be opened to invite the breeze or closed for privacy.

The bed, though clearly clinical with side rails and wheels, was surprisingly comfortable. Its extra height made getting in and out easier, and a remote allowed it to be lowered. She suspected she would appreciate that feature later. The bed was dressed in Egyptian cotton sheets and pillowcases, topped with a light bamboo blanket in a soft island blue.

The room itself was large enough to accommodate doctors or emergency staff if needed.

Opposite the bedroom wall was the front door, which opened onto what she would normally call a patio, though here she thought it might be referred to as a lanai. Large potted trees surrounded a wicker sectional sofa with bright orange cushions.

The living room's exterior wall, including the lanai doors and adjoining side wall, was entirely glass. Floor-to-ceiling panels ran from the lanai to the kitchenette. They appeared fixed but were not. Inside the glass rested retractable sunshades, controlled by a switch labeled "Shades."

She flipped the switch. Electric motors hummed as the shades rose in synchronized elegance, disappearing into the frame.

Sandy opened the glass door and swung it inward, letting in the breeze and ocean sounds.

Next to the shade switch was another labeled simply "Walls."

She flipped it toward Open.

Motors engaged again, followed by a series of clicks that initially sounded like cracking glass.

Roger yowled in alarm and leapt from behind the sofa.

With the panels unlocked, they began moving in sequence toward the kitchenette, where a storage cabinet had opened in anticipation. One by one, the panels pivoted, squared themselves, and slid silently into the cabinet. When the last panel entered, the cabinet door began to close. Sandy thought about the brooms marching to the music in the classic *Sorcerer's Apprentice* cartoon. She could almost hear the music as the walls danced toward the cabinet.

Roger panicked and attempted to jump inside the closing space.

The mechanism paused. A light above the cabinet flashed red in sync with a soft but insistent warning tone.

Confused, Roger bolted back to the couch.

After a few seconds, the sensors reset. The cabinet door resumed closing and latched with a quiet click. In place of the glass wall remained a nearly invisible but durable screen.

This was the coolest thing Sandy had ever seen.

She decided to leave it open until bedtime.

Roger, now recovered from the trauma, planted himself behind the couch with his nose nearly touching the screen, assuming his sworn role as protector. He sniffed the air with seriousness, as if saying, never fear. I will keep watch.

"Looks like we're both going to enjoy that feature, huh, Rog?"

"Meow," came the reply.

The kitchen shared the back wall of the living room.

"Well, at least that's familiar," Sandy said aloud.

The appliances were commercial grade, including an espresso machine similar to the one at Brasilia Coffee Shop.

"Probably not cooking much on that stuff, Rog."

"Meow."

He circled her legs.

"Oh, I see. You're starving. Such a gallant young man, skipping food and rest to guard me."

"Meow."

"Let's see what they gave you."

Before opening the cupboards, Sandy paused. "Before I feed you, I want to know where you were hiding earlier."

Roger glanced away from the end of the couch. A diversion.

She walked behind the sofa to the end table near the window switches and spotted a wooden enclosure that matched the room's décor. On closer inspection, it revealed the fanciest litter box she had ever seen, complete with a filtered fan humming softly to control odor.

"Wow. Fancy."

"MEOW."

Sandy came back and opened the next kitchen cupboard. It was stocked with premium cat food, tuna, salmon, chicken, shrimp, neatly stacked.

She pulled down a can of shrimp. "How about shrimp, to celebrate our ocean view?"

Followed by a terse "Yowl."

She found a can opener, then a cabinet containing engraved bowls labeled by meal periods. Grabbing the one marked Breakfast. Sandy wondered out loud. "How do I know it's breakfast? I have no idea what time it is. There are no clocks ."

She shrugged. "Breakfast it is."

Roger's impatience escalated into something that no longer resembled patience.

She set the bowl down. His whiskers were already in it.

As she stood back up, she swooned with a light-headed swirl of the room that washed over her. Guess the meds aren't fully gone yet.

More questions surfaced.

Why did they drug me? Why did Ruthy admit it so easily? Ruthy seemed genuine. Sandy was confident she could get answers from her soon.

While Roger ate, Sandy opened the refrigerator. It was packed with fresh produce and pregnancy-friendly foods.

"There's more food here than I could buy in a month," she said aloud.

Lefty finally surfaced. *They drugged us. Hello.*

Mister Right judged. *Of course, we should be concerned.*

Campus Hippie stayed quiet.

She raised her voice. "Why can't you both be more like Campus Hippie? Calm down. I'm doing reconnaissance. When I know the answers, you'll know the answers. We share a brain."

Silence.

She decided to explore the beach and pool.

First, the restroom.

The bathroom was massive and fully accessible, clearly designed for medical care and childbirth. Everything was thoughtful. Everything was prepared.

She exited the bathroom and called out, "See you later, Junior."

She closed the door behind her, listening for the click.

Roger did not respond.

He was already asleep by the screen, stretched out on the cool tile, soaking up the sun and catching up on the sleep he had lost guarding her.

11

Slow Waves

Sandy stepped out of Suite 18 and was stunned into a kind of paralysis. Not physical, but deeper. The view from the lanai arrested her.

The resort's pool dominated the foreground, and beyond it the ocean stretched wide and endless. Together they formed a seamless panoramic so beautiful it felt unreal.

Her world slowed.

This had happened before. As a girl of barely ten, she had stood helplessly as her mother suffered a fatal heart attack while she held her hand. It had happened again years later when Roger overpowered her, the moment that led to her pregnancy.

The doctor who arrived thirty minutes after her mother's death had called it tachypsychia: the mind accelerating perception during trauma, flooding the body with chemicals so it could process what the brain could not. Stress or drugs could also trigger it.

This time felt different.

No fear. No violence. No trauma. If anything, it felt like joy. Or wonder. Or awe.

It began when she focused on the waves crashing against the white sand. Her vision softened. The rhythm of the surf slowed, aligning to a steady internal tempo, like the pendulum of a grandfather clock.

As the ocean slowed in her perception, patterns emerged. The waves formed a hand, made of water, long fingers stretching toward the shore. At their fullest extension, those fingers splayed wide, releasing wet sand gathered from the ocean floor. Each grain seemed deliberately placed.

When the extension was complete, the hand withdrew gently, retreating into the cool sea from the hot sand. As it receded, it gathered new grains, selecting them carefully before drawing them away.

The motion repeated. Purposeful. Ordered.

The scene overwhelmed her.

How does this beauty just happen? How do my eyes know how to see it? Why is my heart beating normally while the ocean slows? Who controlled those watery hands? Who decided where the ocean stopped and the beach began?

All her senses converged: the clean ocean air, the warmth of the sun, the cool breeze on her skin, children laughing as they chased one another, the steady cadence of the waves.

Tears threatened.

As Sandy contemplated the vision, she did not notice the brief glimmer across the far side of the pool, a surreptitious telephoto lens half-hidden in the bushes, tilting slightly as it adjusted focus.

"Well now, look who out and about today!"

The voice snapped everything back to full speed.

The slow motion vanished as quickly as it had come. Sandy felt an unexpected sadness at its passing. She turned to see Nurse Ruthy approaching, smiling warmly. Ruthy had emerged from what looked like an outdoor bar attached to the resort.

"How my favorite patient doin', eh?" Ruthy asked, her smile genuine and open.

Though annoyed at losing her private moment, She was glad to see a familiar face.

"I'm fine," Sandy said. "Maybe a little hungover from that neck jab on the plane, but feeling pretty privileged to be standing in your slice of heaven."

Ruthy paused, suddenly serious.

"Oh no, chile. I love it here, I do, but we cyan be callin' it heaven. Heaven goin' be far grander dan dis. No pain. No sorrow. No tears. Jus' sweet fellowship wid de Father, de Son, an' de Holy Spirit forever. I love it here, but I still cyan wait fi heaven."

The earnestness of Ruthy's correction caught Sandy off guard.

Seeing her reaction, Ruthy chuckled. "Ahh, I see ya face. Ya t'inkin', 'Don't sell me no six fi a nine,' ain't it?" She laughed softly. "Now hush. Dis ain't no sales pitch. God serious business. Every one a we gon' face Him one day, whether we choose to or not. Anytime ya wanna talk, dat my favorite topic."

Sandy gathered herself. "I'm really confused. Would you come inside and talk with me? Also, I already need the bathroom again."

Ruthy laughed. "Yeh, ya pregnant, alright!"

12

Evening and Morning

She remembered her questions just before Ruthy left for the night.

"Ruthy, can I ask you a few things that have been bugging me? Nothing major, just confusing."

Ruthy smiled. "Sure, chile. Shoot."

"Why are there no clocks here?" she asked. "Not outside, not in the common areas, not even in my room."

Ruthy nodded, as though she had been waiting for it.

"Ya see, mi dear, pon St. Croix we livin' pon Island Time. Di sun pop up 'roun' six-thirty dis season. Dat mean time fi rise an' shine. Den she ease down 'roun' seven in di evenin', time fi slow t'ings down."

She gestured toward the open lanai. "Stores an' business dem run pon Island Time too. Ya cyan set ya watch by dem. Dem take break when dem feel, close when dem ready. Clock an' calendar? Dem only bring frustration. Most a we leave di watch home an' jus' go wid di flow."

She smiled again. "Look now, di sun settin' pretty-pretty. So we doin' evenin' ting. Eat a likkle somethin' good, den we tuck ya in nice-nice."

Roger woke to the smell of eggs and yowled as he stretched, announcing himself like room service had arrived. Sandy and Ruthy laughed.

Ruthy hopped up, opened a can of chicken, washed Roger's shrimp bowl, and placed it on the floor. She refreshed his water dish.

Roger offered a loud "Meow" and dove in without hesitation.

"Hey, Roger," Sandy teased, "no tip for your server?"

Roger ignored her completely, burying his face in the bowl in open disdain.

As Ruthy helped her settle back into bed and reattached the monitors, she spoke again.

"About earlier," Ruthy said gently. "Ya in any trouble besides di pregnancy? Mi other patient fly in pon di same plane three weeks back. Dat plane come an' go regular. Ev'ryt'ing alright?"

Sandy put on her best poker face. "I'm fine. I probably just needed to eat and rest."

She knew she had to give Ruthy something believable. "I'm ashamed of being an unwed mother," she continued. "Most people with your beliefs wouldn't approve. That's why I'm here, to have the baby in secret. Like they used to, to avoid family scandal."

Ruthy's warm smile confirmed it had landed.

Ruthy adjusted the IV fluid bag, watching color return to Sandy's face. "Dis ya mobile," she said, patting the IV pole. "Ya can roll it 'roun' easy-easy 'til I come back in di mornin'. Tomorrow big day, ya hear? I bring di baby heart monitor. Ya go hear di baby heartbeat. Sweet-sweet sound."

She pointed toward the pendant resting near Sandy's hand. "Ya should be good fi di restroom, but use di pendant if ya need help. No shame. I got a permanent room right yah. Five minute from dead sleep. Call me anytime."

Ruthy paused, then added softly, "I not here fi judge. One sin ent worse dan another in God eye. I admire wha' ya doin'. Dat baby go have a lovin' home an' a chance. Most people take di easy road. Ya honorin' di life God mek. I proud a ya."

Before Sandy could respond, Ruthy smiled at the cat on the floor. "Good night, Roger."

The breeze cooled as the sun fully set and the moon rose. Ruthy pressed the wall control, and the glass panels slid back into place with smooth precision. Then she lowered the blinds, and the outside world disappeared. The door closed with a soft hotel *thunk* as Ruthy left.

Sandy lay quietly, Ruthy's words echoing in her mind.

I'm proud of you.

She had not heard those words often.

Tomorrow she would hear the baby's heartbeat. The realization unsettled her, yet she found herself waiting for it.

As she drifted off, Roger offered a small "Meow."

"Meow to you too, buddy," she whispered.

This sleep came naturally. The ocean waves folded into her dreams.

Roger, having napped most of the day on purpose, stayed alert. He roamed the suite, sniffing corners and pawing quietly, like a spy sweeping for threats. Finding nothing, he eventually climbed onto the back of the couch, positioning himself where he could see her sleeping through the shutters.

For good measure, he pushed his dinner bowl in front of the door. If it moved, he would hear it.

Satisfied, he settled in facing her, keeping watch through the night.

Sometime in the middle of the night Sandy woke to the sound of metal sliding on tile. It was faint, and she had a hard time placing it at first. Then she heard the front door quickly shut and latch. All was quiet again. Sandy was so exhausted she could not stay awake long enough to investigate. She faintly remembered a strong and chilling cat hiss from Roger, but she could not tell if it was real or a dream. Before she could reason it out, she succumbed to sleep again.

13

Heartbeat

AUGUST 11, 1979 – SAINT CROIX, U.S. VIRGIN ISLANDS

Sandy woke early though she could not be sure exactly when. Island Time made that difficult, but she guessed it was around six o'clock, perhaps an hour and a half before sunrise. She found she did not mind it. The absence of an alarm clock felt gentler, less invasive.

She carefully unhooked herself from the monitors, leaving only the IV in place. The bag was empty, but she chose not to remove the needle herself, wary of infection and unwilling to risk anything that might jeopardize her baby's safety. That thought stopped her cold.

My baby.

She stood still, staring at the IV line.

Just days ago, she had referred to the pregnancy as "it" and blamed "it" as part of a sequence of unfortunate events. Now her internal language had shifted without permission. Now she was using words like *jeopardize* along with *my baby.*

She did not like that the change had happened so quietly.

Shaking off the thought, she prepared for Ruthy's arrival. As she stepped out of the bedroom, she noticed a single cat food can in the entryway. No food had been eaten. *Rog, I know this is upsetting, but you have to eat. Next time I will watch you eat your dinner.*

Today was the fetal Doppler, and to her own surprise, she found herself eager to hear the heartbeat.

She freshened up in the bathroom and slipped into a robe, sweatpants, and flip-flops. Clothes waited neatly in the closet, her size, matching her usual preferences. That detail unsettled her more than it should have. After dressing as far as the IV allowed, she fed Roger and refreshed his water. Once Sir Roger was fully satisfied, she turned her attention to herself.

She ate a banana and some pineapple chunks from the refrigerator and drank two glasses of orange juice. Mostly she was thirsty. She wanted coffee, but the espresso machine looked complicated.

Is caffeine bad for my baby?

There it was again.

Ruthy returned just before seven, as promised, knocking politely on the lanai door and waiting. Instead of calling out, Sandy opened the door herself. She stood there looking rested, robed, wearing sweatpants and slip-on beach shoes.

Ruthy paused, startled.

This isn't the same woman I tucked into bed last night, she thought.

Sandy smirked. "Good morning, Nurse Ruthless. Can you unhook this empty IV bag? I can't finish dressing until it's gone."

Before stepping inside, Ruthy lifted a small device with a flat handheld sensor attached by a coiled wire. "Look wha' I bring. Fetal Doppler. We hear di heartbeat today."

She slid it into her back pocket, entered the suite, and removed the IV needle in seconds.

Ruthy turned politely while Sandy changed into a blouse that lifted easily for the exam. She asked Ruthy casually, "What about caffeine? And orange juice. Is that actually good for the baby, and why?"

She avoided possessive language as best she could.

As Ruthy prepared the Doppler, Sandy's thoughts returned to the same uncomfortable question. How had her language shifted so quickly, from distance to concern? She did not have an answer.

Roger announced Ruthy's arrival belatedly with a stretch and a loud yowl, hopping down toward the litter box.

Ruthy laughed. "I half expect him fi tuck a newspaper under him arm 'fore he head to him upscale facilities."

With Roger occupied, Ruthy nodded toward the bed. "Lie down pon di bed, mi dear. Pull up ya blouse an' relax."

Sandy complied, suddenly nervous.

"I puttin' gel pon ya belly," Ruthy warned. "It colder dan ya like, but it warm up quick."

"Got it," Sandy said.

"Sorry, forget di towels," Ruthy said, returning quickly. "Here come di cold stuff."

Despite the warning, Sandy gasped when the gel touched her skin.

Roger ran in, assessed the situation, found no threat, flicked his tail in offense, and strutted away.

Both women laughed.

"If he wasn't a cat," Ruthy said, "I swear dat tail gesture ent polite."

"At least I know he loves me," Sandy said.

Then, smirking, "Meanwhile, back to my cold jelly belly."

Ruthy laughed, muttering, "Holy cat woman," before positioning the Doppler. She checked the recorder. "Dis might tickle, Sandy so don't move too much. I go count di beats an' tell ya when I done. Relax an' enjoy."

Within thirty seconds, despite her squirming and Ruthy's stern looks, they heard it. Faint at first, then strong and steady. A heartbeat.

Ruthy held the Doppler steady and clicked on the recorder.

Sandy heard nothing else after that.

Boom. Boom. Boom.

Faster than she expected. Tears rose before she could stop them.

Roger leapt onto the bed with a joyful yowl. Not alarmed, not angry. Just present.

The moment broke. Sandy wiped her eyes. Roger had done it again.

Ruthy clicked off the recorder. "Pretty amazin', eh? I love dis lil device. Sound like ya did too, Roger."

Ruthy did not comment on Sandy's tears.

As she cleaned off the gel, she returned to find Roger curled contentedly in Ruthy's lap. Watching them, she felt an unexpected sense of trust.

If Roger trusts her, I will too.

She opened the blinds, letting the light pour in, then opened the walls. The glass panels folded away as the breeze filled the room. Roger leapt from Ruthy's lap and resumed his post behind the couch, scanning the outside world like a tiger disguised as a housecat.

With the air flowing through the suite, Sandy sat across from Ruthy, her expression intent.

"Sandy?" Ruthy asked gently. "Wha' gwan?"

Sandy spoke deliberately. "I need fresh air and exercise. How about a walk on the beach? Would that harm the baby?"

Ruthy understood without asking more.

"A walk good fi ya an' di baby," she said. "I come wid ya. We keep ya hydrated an' don't overdo it. I grab water. Put some out fi Roger."

"See you later, Roger," Sandy said. "Mommy's going for a walk."

Together, nurse and patient stepped out toward the beach.

14

Waves and Whispers

Ruthy and Sandy did not speak as they left the lanai, passed the pool, and walked toward the surf. Ruthy sensed something was wrong but trusted Sandy enough not to press. She slowed her pace, feigning exhaustion, allowing Ruthy to offer support. When Ruthy slid her arm around Sandy's waist, she leaned in and whispered, "Alright, wha' gwan?"

Sandy answered softly, her lips barely moving. "Let's sit by the waves, near the chairs under the cabana on the left. Don't speak louder than necessary. Don't turn around. Keep your mouth covered when you talk. Trust me. We are being watched, and I want to keep you safe. Can you do that?"

Ruthy answered quietly, "Yes," careful not to nod.

They reached the cabana closest to the water and sat facing the ocean.

"What I'm about to tell you," Sandy began, "I don't fully understand myself. I'm not proud of some of it, and I would appreciate it if you listened until the end. There's a lot I don't know, and I'm still figuring out what I've stepped into. Please hear me out."

She told her story. The loneliness. The foster homes. The choices made from survival, not malice. She shared every detail she could remember, filling the gaps with careful guesses and instincts honed from years of watching her back. The conversation lasted nearly forty minutes, long enough to raise suspicion if anyone was observing.

When she finished, Sandy said quietly, "Okay. I'm done."

She stared at the water, heart pounding, waiting for rejection. This was the first time since Roger that she had let her guard down completely. Mr. Right screamed at her to stop. Her Inner Crazy begged her to protect herself. But Sandy ignored them. She needed to speak to someone, or she would unravel, and Ruthy was the only person she thought might be able to be trusted.

Ruthy finally spoke. "Wow. Dat a whole heap fi take in. But since ya share ya story, I feel ya should hear mine too."

Ever practical, Sandy said, "Maybe we should walk. If we sit too long, whoever's watching might get curious."

"Good idea," Ruthy replied.

They stood, letting the water cool their feet, and began walking along the shore.

"I don't wanna be preachy," Ruthy began, "but imagine ya got a glass a water, an' unlimited clean, cool water anytime ya need it. Den ya meet somebody dyin' a thirst. Ya go wait fi dem ask? Mek dem squirm? Or ya offer di water free-free?"

"Of course you offer it," Sandy said. "I don't see the point you're making."

"It same wid spiritual t'ing," Ruthy said gently. "Ya racked wid guilt. I got di equivalent a cool water, somethin' fi help heal ya. I sharin' it wid ya now."

Ruthy shared her story and her faith. Sandy listened politely, asking few questions. She had heard versions of this message before at soup kitchens, on television, from campus preachers who shouted condemnation through megaphones. While she appreciated Ruthy's sincerity, what Sandy wanted now was something practical, not spiritual.

When Ruthy finished, they turned back toward the lanai.

They agreed, without saying it directly, to distance their familiarity once inside. Suite 18 might be monitored. Roger's strange behavior, stalking corners and swatting unseen threats, made Sandy wonder if he sensed something she could not.

At the lanai entrance, Ruthy spoke barely above a breath. "Now ya tink bout what I said. I go t'ink how fi help ya. One ting I can tell ya for sure, I go help ya. I ent afraid fi dead. I know wha' come next."

There was no hug. No outward sign of affection.

Sandy turned and went inside. Ruthy returned to her room.

That was the last time Sandy ever saw Ruthy.

15

Is Happiness Allowed?

AUGUST 11, 1979 – DELAWARE, OHIO

Dr. Mills woke around 11:00 a.m. on Saturday feeling very poorly. She went to bed too late thanks to another Danielle Steel novel and now she felt worse than she had in a long time. Dr. Mills was not an alcoholic, as far as she knew. After all, she was able to function well in her important role at LIFE. How could she be an alcoholic? But as a doctor, it made her reconsider the veracity of her self-diagnosis.

Dr. Mills decided today was another good day to sleep some more. She grabbed her bottle of choice, Stoli vodka from the nightstand and poured herself a solid two fingers, pushing three, into her empty rocks glass. She tossed it back like a cowboy and replaced the glass on the nightstand. The large bottle of Stoli went on the floor next to the bed. She would need to give the idea she might be an alcoholic some more serious thought. But later. Right now, more sleep.

She woke again to the obnoxious electronic ringing of her bedside phone. As she gathered the strength to answer it, she wondered what was wrong with the actual bells they used to put in phones. "Ugh, I feel like I just fell asleep."

She mustered her Dr. Mills personality. Who could be calling her? Her number was unlisted, and very few people had this number. As her eyes struggled to adjust, she spoke out loud. "Who could be calling me at home so early on a Saturday morning? She rolled over to face the clock as she reached for the phone. The display read 7:45 p.m. She composed herself and answered.

"This is Doctor Mills speaking."

"Hello, Doctor Mills. I'm sorry to bother you. This is Agent Issachar with Enclave Protective Services. I have updates for you. I was instructed to deliver them in person."

She was already at a disadvantage based on the amount of vodka no longer in the bottle.

"Can't this wait till later in the day? It's only 7:45 in the morning" If a pause were a sound, the one on the other end of the line would have resembled a scream.

"No. I am sorry, it cannot wait. Sounds like you might have had a power outage or something if your clock shows a.m. The time currently is 7:45 *p.m.*" Dr. Mills recovered her composure while saying, "Forgive me for misspeaking. Yes, of course it is 7:45 p.m." Next, Dr. Mills did something she had never done before and had no choice, since she was clearly not safe to drive.

"You will have to come to my house. I'm not available to drive into the city right now."

This decision required another breach of her personal rules. She gave him her address and invited him over. To complicate matters further, she was not at her best. She was still mildly intoxicated and her façade faltered.

Issachar was concerned. He had never met Dr. Mills and was nervous about going to her home. Still, the report had to be delivered in person. He would not break protocol by going around her to Miss Veil. They both unsettled him but Miss Veil more so.

He jumped into his brand-new Oldsmobile Toronado and hit the road. The car seemed built for the winding, tree-lined route out of the city. The roof opened. The upgraded Delco GM, AM/FM radio also boasted a built in eight-track player. As he drove the cars cabin was filled with the sounds of WLVQ FM 96. Sun-dappled pavement rolled beneath him as he pushed the car a little faster than he should. Not because he wanted to arrive early but because he loved to drive. This road brought out the best in the car.

He arrived earlier than intended. It was only 8:30 p.m. He drove a few miles farther, then doubled back, enjoying another six minutes along the Olentangy River. He turned around in a driveway and returned, pulling up precisely at 8:45 p.m.

At the gate, he shut off the stereo and searched for a call button. A metallic click sounded. The gate began to swing open. *She must have a camera*, he thought.

Unease crept in as he followed the driveway. The seclusion impressed him, but that feeling faded when he reached the clearing. The house stopped him cold.

Then his attention shifted to the woman stepping out the front door.

He knew her as Josie. Or Sylvia. Processing what he saw, the conclusion landed hard. Josie, Sylvia and Dr. Mills were the same person.

She stood awkwardly in the doorway. Outside the structure of an active operation, she felt exposed rather than in control. Unsure which version of herself to inhabit, she hesitated. The man in her driveway was confident and handsome. I see these agents as code names and muscle. I never really see the person. I wonder if they would say the same.

Issachar was Greg Johnson. Thirty years old. Never married. No living relatives. Almost a prerequisite for EPS contract work.

She looked different than she had days earlier. Light streamed from behind her through the glass, framing her figure. Her hair was down. She wore slacks that fit well and low heels.

She brushed her hair quickly, letting it fall straight to her shoulders. A departure from the pinned, proper style she usually wore. Her blouse was light and flowing, untucked, hanging comfortably over her slacks. To Issachar, she was pretty.

They greeted each other with mutual awkwardness.

"Doctor Mills."

"Agent Issachar. Please come in. We can talk in the living room."

He took one of the Vladimir Kagan chairs. She sat on the nearer end of the matching sofa. He removed his notebook and began.

"Subject Sandy Vanover was flown to secure location VISC 18. She was administered a light dose of lorazepam via syringe prior to departure. Transfer to Suite 18 was completed before she regained consciousness.

"I wrote the next portion verbatim: 'She is being cared for by Nurse Ruthy, who is not a contracted agent and does not appear affiliated with either organization. Care provided exceeds expectations. Earlier today, the subject tested the nurse for information, assuming greater awareness than exists'. The result is a confused nurse who may become curious. She is assigned to another case as well. We return to Suite 18 in two weeks. Video surveillance is active in key areas, though the cat appears adept at locating cameras. I am concerned the subject may violate agreement terms and expose herself to consequences.'

"My recommendation to the EPS agent was continued monitoring of all subject/nurse interactions over the next two weeks unless behavior warrants immediate action. Given the subject's child is a high-value asset, we did not want to overreach and disrupt your broader plan."

He looked up.

"Are you in agreement or should I revise the directives?"

He continued without waiting.

"The questions requiring your decision are these. Do we accelerate the visit to assess the nurse's awareness? If she is compromised, do we replace the nurse only? Or do we relocate subject and child and scrub the site? If so, do we mothball the location temporarily?"

He closed the notebook.

"End of report."

Dr. Mills leaned back. Once again, Issachar noticed how attractive she was compared to his memory of the prior mission. The furniture encouraged proximity. He was aware of it. He suspected she was too.

"I'm not on a time schedule," he said carefully. "We could take time to game-plan before I submit your response. Removing two acquisitions, especially this one, could create complications with both our superiors."

She showed strain but the delay appealed to her. So did his presence. Alcohol still softened her judgment. She was not eager for him to leave.

She stood. His eyes followed her before he caught himself. He rose as well, the angle of the chair forcing him forward. Their proximity surprised them both. They paused, aware and unsettled.

"Your caution is wise," she said. "Do you have time or do you need to get home to your wife?"

"No one to go home to," he said, smiling. "Just me and my new car. And you?"

"No," she said too quickly. "No one."

They ordered carry-out from a nearby Mexican place. He opened the moonroof as they drove and turned on the radio to the local rock station. Together they botched the lyrics to everything from Elvis to the Beatles while they enjoyed the fresh air and the company. They sang loud and unguarded and for both of them, unknown to the other, were having the most fun they could remember.

Returning with the food, they ate by the pond in Adirondack chairs. The decision to wait until the scheduled visit came easily.

The evening passed with conversation and laughter.

They agreed it had to remain secret, though neither fully understood why.

Before he left, he told her the one thing that could undo them both. He wanted her trust. He wanted this to be different.

Walking to his car, he blurted, "My name is Greg Johnson." He steadied himself. "I'm glad to have met you, Doctor Mills."

At 2:00 a.m. on August 12, he slid back into the car. She rested a hand on his forearm through the open window.

"My name is Melanie Fields," she said. "It was nice to meet you too."

She placed a slip of paper in his palm. Their fingers lingered longer than she intended. Then she turned and walked back to the house.

Greg smiled at the paper. No name. Just a phone number.

Melanie closed the door and paused. The house felt different. Is it possible this could become a home? She dismissed the thought and went upstairs.

She went to bed without the vodka.

She did not cry in her sleep that night.

16

Decisively Deceitful

After Greg left and before sleep, Dr. Mills picked up the slim touch-tone phone on her bedside table and dialed her supervisor's private line.

The phone rang once. Miss Veil, the head of the LIFE project, always answered quickly.

Her voice came through worn and husky.

"Are you alone?"

The question caught Dr. Mills off guard.

It's after two in the morning. When do I ever have company?

Does she know something?

No. Play it calm. There's no way she knows about Greg.

A smile crept across her face at the thought of his name. She suppressed it immediately, aware that even smiles could be heard if you weren't careful. She had been in the field long enough to know better.

"Yes, I am at home," Dr. Mills said.

"Report," Miss Veil said.

Dr. Mills slipped into professional cadence without pause. She had delivered countless reports like this.

"Female subject, eighteen years old, slightly less than two months pregnant. Control DNA for fetal assets confirmed. Subject accepted the LIFE offer and signed all documents without close review. Signed copies should have reached your drop point yesterday.

"Follow-up at the Saint Croix birth-care facility is scheduled for two weeks from induction date. Subject assigned to Suite 18 to ensure compliance. Transport delivered via our jet by EPS agents Issachar and Levi.

"The subject is exceptionally intelligent and resourceful. Due to this, I ordered precautionary monitoring and a low-dose lorazepam injection prior to flight, along with a sedative for the feline companion. These precautions appear effective."

She paused only long enough to breathe.

"One area of caution. EPS senior agent Issachar reports is as follows:

'The subject is being cared for by Nurse Ruthy, who is not a contracted agent and does not appear affiliated with either organization. Care provided exceeds expectations. However, earlier today, the subject tried to manipulate the nurse for information, assuming the Nurse has greater knowledge then she possesses'. This interaction confused the nurse, who may now, become curious. The same nurse Ruthy is handling another case for us as well. We are due to return to Suite 18 in two weeks. Surveillance is in place, but the subject's cat appears to have a knack for locating cameras."

Dr. Mills continued evenly.

"My conclusion and direction to EPS was to continue monitoring all interactions between subject and nurse and reassess at the next scheduled visit, unless new behaviors warrant immediate action. Given the subject's visible, though still unexplained to me, high-value status, I advised against escalation that might disrupt your larger objectives.

"Do you agree with this assessment, or would you like me to modify the agents' current directives?"

There was no hesitation.

"Your directive is affirmed as you have reported," Miss Veil said.

After only six minutes the conversation was over and the phone line went dead.

Dr. Mills completed her professional obligation to report. She felt the update was accurate and was satisfied she successfully convinced Susan to delay any reactionary response. She was not sure what the alternative would have look like, but after reading the memo about the secret layer of the Foundation, she was afraid to find out. At least she could rest easy knowing her report diverted immediate consequences for this remarkable young lady.

17

Dreadful Debbie

Miss Veil did not put the phone down. She flicked the receiver button and dialed another number.

"Debbie?" she said.

"Yes, Debbie speaking," the other voice replied.

"Eliminate the nurse assigned to VI-18 and VI-27 immediately. Assume duties. Confirm whether the objective remains immediately executable. No further contact between nurse and patients is permitted."

"Affirmative. Confirmed," Debbie responded.

Both hung up without hesitation.

It was 2:18 a.m. on August 12, 1979, in both Ohio and Saint Croix.

Back on Saint Croix, Debbie forced her way quietly into Ruthy's bungalow at 3:47 a.m. Ruthy was sitting in her recliner chair.

"Hey, Debbie. I know you was coming. I been waiting pon you. You always quick-quick fi pick up dem shift when people disappear off island, eh? But I see you, girl. I see exactly what you really doing dere," Ruthy said.

Debbie pulled the front door closed with her gloved hands at 4:08 a.m. and went home to shower.

18

Paradise Lost

Sandy woke to blue and red lights flashing on the ceiling of her bedroom through the window. She resisted the impulse to investigate or appear curious. It didn't really matter anyway; she knew Ruthy was gone. This truth became palpable when Ruthy failed to arrive to care for her.

Based on when she noticed the police lights that morning, the call must have come in recently. Sandy assumed Ruthy was most likely killed sometime between the time she left last night and 8:30 this morning.

Less than fifteen minutes later, a new nurse arrived at Suite 18.

Nurse Debbie.

Debbie was efficient.

"Where is Ruthy?" She asked directly.

"She's visiting family," Debbie replied. "Her mother fell ill, so she had to take a flight off the island rather suddenly." Then, for good measure, she added, "Nothing more important than family."

Sandy knew Ruthy's family lived on the island. She also knew Ruthy's mother had died years ago.

Debbie did not react. She simply nodded and said, "That is true," playing her role politely and moving on.

She tried another angle.

"What was all that noise earlier? The police and everything? Is there a hurricane coming or something?" she asked, playing dumb. "I don't think we have those in Ohio."

Sandy knew she was lying.

Her Inner Crazy began trying to put the pieces together.

Lefty started. *Debbie knows something.*

Campus Hippie invoked the Emergency Survival Protocol they had relied on for years. *Trust no one.*

She felt the weight of Ruthy's absence settle in. She felt responsible, and yet something else stirred beneath the guilt.

Ruthy had told her the day before that Saint Croix was not her home.

"But you were born and raised here," Sandy had said.

Ruthy had smiled, then laughed softly. Her gaze drifted past her, focused on something unseen. She had turned, thinking she must be missing something in the distance.

"This is only a temporary home," Ruthy had said gently. "My real home is with God. Someday, I don't know when, I will go there. I am not afraid."

Then she had said it. The words that stayed.

"I have been waiting most of my adult life to hear His voice say, 'Hello, dear Ruthy. Well done, My good and faithful servant. Come and enter into the joy of your Master.'"

The memory settled.

Sandy felt a small, unexpected smile rise and disappear just as quickly. *Good for you, Ruthy. Enjoy eternity in Paradise.*

Instead of tears, Sandy felt peace. Even in death, Ruthy had created beauty.

All suspicion about Debbie solidified moments later.

Debbie opened a can of salmon slowly to coax Roger from hiding. She replaced his water and called for him softly.

Roger answered with a sound she had never heard before.

A long, chilling hiss.

The reaction was immediate. Debbie set the bowl down and said sharply, "I'll come check on you later," and left.

Roger's warning sent a shiver up Sandy's spine. He sensed something she could not.

Campus Hippie spoke first. *We need to know more about LIFE. We can't do anything from here.*

She closed her eyes to reset her thoughts. It had been a difficult morning, but now she resolved her confusion and settled on a strategy: keep her head down, eyes and ears open, learn what she could, reveal nothing, and wait until she was off the island.

Patience was her friend.

19

Born to Lead

MARCH 23, 1980 – ST. CROIX, USVI

Since Nurse Ruthy's disappearance, Sandy played it straight.

She let Nurse Debbie do her job and followed the rules, knowing how to play the long game. Sandy learned that skill well before Freedom Day in Marion. Months passed in uneventful repetition, echoing her days on Church Street.

She lost track of time on the island but her growing belly told the truth. She was nearing seven months on the island. With two months already behind her before arriving on Saint Croix, her due date was close. When Sandy asked Debbie about it, the nurse replied flatly, "You'll know when I tell you. Stop fretting."

The pretense of kindness was gone.

Roger hissed every time Debbie entered Suite 18. Sandy kept the windows and blinds closed and stayed reclusive to protect him. She could not bear losing him too, so she operated in protection mode. Debbie did her job. She complied. That defined life in Paradise.

Now it made sense why Ruthy corrected her. Heaven was not this place. Ruthy would never have allowed that confusion.

That night, Debbie helped her clean up and prepare for bed. Roger hissed again and Debbie left. Sometime after dark, Sandy's water broke. *When she realized the bed was wet and understood why,* She pressed the pendant button around her neck.

The hours blurred into pain, pushing, and Debbie's clipped instructions. Someone brought in an incubator. Wall panels slid open, revealing hospital equipment hidden in the room all along. Lights. Plugs. Switches. She focused on one thing only.

Her baby.

After four exhausting hours, the baby was born. Sandy collapsed, barely conscious. Then she realized something was wrong.

The baby was not crying.

A woman in surgical garb entered and moved quickly to the incubator beneath its padded, warming light. She cried out, "My baby! Why isn't my baby crying?"

The doctor worked efficiently. The baby gasped. Then cried.

Relief flooded Sandy.

Behind her bed, Debbie injected something into her IV port.

Sandy felt the sedative coming and made a decision. She went limp on purpose, pretending to lose consciousness. She knew Debbie would assume the drug worked immediately. The baby was breathing. That was enough for now.

As she lay still, she heard Debbie ask, "Doctor Appleton, how is he?"

He.

Sandy woke the next day in a different bed. She was cleaned, dressed, and alone. Roger meowed in relief, then hissed, and fled to the litter box as Debbie entered carrying a cat carrier.

Panic surged.

"What is going on?" Sandy demanded. "Where is my baby?"

"The baby is healthy," Debbie replied evenly. "But the baby is not yours. Remember the deal?"

From outside the room came two voices. One was Sylvia from the pregnancy center. The other was familiar.

"Don't make a fuss. Everything will be fine."

It was Issachar or Simeon. Sandy did not care which.

Glove Hands appeared and grabbed the carrier. Roger fought wildly, hissing and scratching from behind the couch.

"Leave him alone!" Sandy cried. "Don't hurt him!"

Roger was caged quickly, furious and humiliated.

Sandy forced herself upright. "At least tell me, was it a boy or a girl?"

Only Debbie answered.

"You lost that right when you sold the baby. Start your new life and forget this ever happened. Read the fine print next time. Or you will end up like Ruthy."

Pain flared at her neck.

Sandy turned to see Sylvia standing beside a wheelchair.

Later, as the room tilted and Roger slept unnaturally still in his carrier, Sandy slurred, "Thing Two. Is that you? You came back for me."

Issachar's voice answered softly, "Don't worry, Sandy. I'll take care of everything."

As consciousness slipped away, she spoke quietly, each word deliberate despite the drug.

"I need to know whose plan this is. Who killed Ruthy. And what is really going on."

Roger slept on.

"Now I get answers," she whispered.

The weakness in her voice didn't blunt the menace beneath it.

20

New Identity: AKA Sandy

MARCH 24, 1980 – COLUMBUS, OHIO

After landing in Columbus, she said nothing.

As she prepared to leave the plane, the tall man known as Issachar handed her a thick clasp envelope.

"Your new identity. Don't let anyone see the contents," he said. "Keep it close."

Then he noticed. "Oh, right. You don't have a purse. Wait!"

He jogged back, dumped his briefcase onto the seat, and handed her his Dooney & Bourke soft leather messenger bag.

"No," Sandy said reflexively, trying to refuse it.

"You'll need it," he replied. "I'll get another one."

Sandy didn't thank him.

Entering the terminal, she realized how sore she was from labor. *Once the baby is born, the mother is no longer welcome in paradise,* she thought bitterly. She wasn't sure what "life" even meant anymore. Anyone who employed Dreadful Debbie couldn't be as empathetic as they claimed. No white sandy beaches here. Just reality.

What she needed first was privacy and a restroom.

She spotted the women's restrooms near the baggage claim and made her way across the concourse.

The bathroom was fairly empty, and all the handicap stalls were available. She chose the one farthest from the door, at the end of the row.

She set Roger's carrier down in the extra floor space and removed the clasp envelope from the messenger bag. The outside simply read *Sandy Foster*. She opened it and pulled out her new Ohio driver's license first.

She pulled out another card. A Bank One debit card in the name of Sandra R. Foster. *Middle initial R?* She glanced back at the driver's license and it clicked. Ruth. Her middle name was now Ruth. Sandra Ruth Foster.

"Who did this?" she whispered.

Issachar.

Her throat tightened. Guilt over her lack of kindness toward him hit hard.

Pushing that aside, she reached deeper into the envelope. One item was thick and probably contained neatly bundled cash. She left it tucked inside for now. The last item was a smaller envelope containing a key ring with four keys: two for a vehicle and two for a door. A temporary tag on the car keys read "Long Term Parking – Lot B, Space 4."

She snorted despite herself. She could almost hear Groucho's voice: *"Course you need not worry, folks. I parked where I would remember. Same place as B-4."*

She found the car exactly where the tag promised.

It wasn't a Crown Vic or a boring sedan. It was a brand-new 1980 Jeep Grand Wagoneer.

She tried the key. It worked.

Inside the glove box was a dealership envelope from Bill Swad AMC Jeep. The title was in her name, purchased over a month ago. MSRP: $20,380.

Stapled to the sticker was a crooked green business card, hand-cut from construction paper. Written in bold black marker, it read:

Dealing Bennie – *My cards are green because I can save you so much green!*

She laughed softly. *I wonder how long this guy will sell cars.*

A TripTik sat beneath it, already mapped to Timberbrook Lane.

She buckled Roger's carrier into the passenger seat, looping the seatbelt through the handle, and climbed in. The odometer showed only fourteen miles. The new-car smell filled the cabin. She liked it.

Her new place was at least a forty-five-minute drive from the airport. She was starving. Roger still hadn't woken up, which worried her.

Please perk up soon, she thought.

She ignored the TripTik and followed I-270 toward West Broad Street. As she exited the freeway, she spotted a Sisters Chicken and Biscuits.

The smell finally woke Roger.

"Yowl!"

She laughed out loud. "Oh, thank God."

She set the food between them and headed back onto I-270. Twelve minutes later, she turned onto Timberbrook Lane.

A brick ranch house. Two-car garage. Space. Distance. Quiet.

The porch light was on. A SOLD sign leaned in the yard.

Inside, everything was ready: food, clothes, toiletries, and Roger's setup.

She checked every room with a kitchen knife in hand, then finally ate. Roger demolished the chicken like he had never been fed.

In the master bedroom, she locked the door and slid the knife into the nightstand drawer.

A Post-it note waited inside.

Me. In case of emergency. For your eyes only. A phone number followed.

She closed the drawer without reading further.

Roger claimed her side of the bed. She rolled him gently away.

"Yowl," he protested.

The light went out.

For the first time in months, Sandy slept.

Two houses away, an older man sat in his home office.

Along the far wall stood a heavy shelf lined with color televisions, each with a labeled remote. The desk below was littered with papers, scribbled notes, and three clipboards filled with log sheets. At the center sat a microphone pedestal with a single wide button.

Snacks were everywhere: a bag of Sour Cream & Onion Doritos, a box of Nabisco Swiss Cheese Crackers, two cans of Aspen soda (one empty, one open), and a wicker basket overflowing with candy bars. Marathon, Choco'Lite and Reggie! bars.

The man was heavyset but not obese, just large. He had a white beard and mustache and would have made a decent Mall Santa. Even with his size, he seemed non-threatening but serious. He wrote on the logs, then glanced at the monitors.

All the images showed Sandy's new home. Only exterior views. Every inch of the one-acre lot was covered.

The night vision cast a greenish glow, making the scene feel eerie and dangerous.

He pressed the microphone button.

"Lights inside all out. No movement anywhere. I think we're safe for tonight."

A male voice answered, "Let's hope so. Keep an eye out and make sure your relief person understands to pay attention. No one in or out without my approval until morning. Hopefully she just sleeps."

21

Not Known / Knot Right

JULY 10, 1983 – DELAWARE, OHIO

Greg and Melanie sat quietly in the Adirondack chairs by the pond behind Melanie's house. This had become their unofficial refuge over the past several years when the weather was nice.

Melanie broke the silence. "Greg, we have been holding on to this secret for years now. What do we do with this?"

"Which secret are you referring to? The one that protects our forbidden love and would probably put us both in a grave if whoever we work for finds out? Or the secret protection of the second most valuable asset to our employer, whose importance we still cannot explain? We continue to help her stay safe and hunt for her son. The same son who, based on the security around his location, everyone agrees is being trained, educated, and groomed for some undisclosed purpose."

Melanie did not answer right away. "Honestly, we are doing the best we can. Gaining trust and influence from the inside out. Sandy has been digging ever since she returned. She flies under the radar and I have someone watching her home around the clock."

"I know you are walking a tight line. But I do not understand. Her location is known by LIFE and therefore by the A-FF as well. They know where she works. So how exactly have you kept her off their grid?"

"I haven't. And before I tell you, are you sure you want to know? I have never brought this up because I don't want you becoming a target." He paused. "I feed them video. Lots of video. Sandy at work. Sandy at home. Sandy at the park. Sandy with her cat. Sandy shopping."

“I still don’t understand.”

“What is the best way to make someone lose interest in something? You provide it so often and in such volume that eventually they stop paying attention. I control the flow of information. Steady stream of long-winded reports. Pages of dry surveillance language. Hours of footage of the most boring activities imaginable. So when Sandy is out investigating, they see Sandy playing with Roger or learning to make stir fry from the cooking channel.”

Melanie stared at him. “If they ever figure out what you have been doing, your life will be in danger.”

“I haven’t really done much.” He said this with a smirk. “I placed a few similarly worded addresses on different forms in her file. Phone numbers off by a single digit. Oh, and I may have had the file labeled under a Spanish woman named Juanita Cabrera.” He let that land. “But I made it right. I fired the fictitious employee who created her file.”

Melanie blinked. “You fired someone who does not exist.”

“Immediate termination. Very satisfying.” He leaned forward. “Besides, honey, I am the hardest-working, most effective agent they have. Earl relies on me to clear just about every important investigation. So the plan is simple: keep a constant flow of boring intelligence moving. When she is out running operations, we ratchet up the flow. Dual purpose. Desensitize and alibi. Sandy is not aware of any of this. As long as we maintain that loop, she is safe.”

Melanie was quiet for a moment. “Greg, I think that time is coming to an end. Sandy has been back for three years with no trace of her son. She will escalate out of frustration. Unless she gets some help in the search, she will not stay quiet much longer. We need to think that through soon.”

Greg nodded slowly. “Our two agencies have gathered information on both adoptive and foster parents but were told to leave the genetic parents entirely out of the reports. Then there is the issue of the baby’s biological father, a known person. Half the genetic material for that child came from him. Why was I never asked to review it?” He paused. “Sandy is clearly exceptional. Adaptive. Highly intelligent. She turns hardship into leverage and conceals her thoughts and conclusions with remarkable skill. So what did they see in that combination we missed?”

“It all comes down to one question,” Melanie said. “What are they up to?”

She hesitated, choosing her words carefully. "There is research emerging about non-coding DNA. Some scientists believe critical information is buried in the parts of DNA we do not yet understand. What if they believe the combination of Roger and Sandy produces something rare? Something hidden in what most dismissed as unimportant strands?" She stopped. The weight of what she was saying settled over her. "Greg. What if this was never about the babies at all? What if it is about what the babies carry?"

He let that sit. "Have you noticed every child fits the same physical and racial profile?"

Melanie swallowed. "I thought I knew what we were involved in. Now I'm not sure. Greg, I'm scared. I don't know what has happened to those children."

They sat in silence, watching the pond reflect the late morning light.

Greg glanced at his watch. Then he made a decision.

He stood to his full height and stepped in front of Melanie as she sat in the low Adirondack chair, his shadow drawing her full attention. He knelt slowly, locking eyes with her the entire way down. Her world narrowed. She could not speak.

Greg reached behind his back and produced a small, dark blue velvet box.

"Melanie," he said softly, "I don't understand our work anymore. I don't even know who we work for. But I know this: I love you. We can figure out the rest."

He paused, visibly struggling, then smiled through it.

"Will you be my lawfully wedded, fully secretive, double-undercover spy wife? Till death but not unemployment, do us part?"

She blinked. "What?"

Then, "Yes! Of course. Yes!"

They kissed.

Greg laughed. "That might be the strangest proposal in history. Want to see the ring?"

"It's perfect," she said quietly. "You know I can't wear it."

"I know. Neither can I. But we'll know."

He had already arranged everything.

A pastor and his wife approached across the grass. The backyard neighbors' two Appaloosa horses stood quietly at the fence, as if aware of the gravity of the moment.

Greg Johnson and Melanie Mills were married beside the pond, witnessed, lawful, and secret.

Later, as they packed for a brief, untraceable road trip, a helicopter passed overhead.

"Negative. No sign of activity. Mercedes parked as usual," came the report.

"Copy. Returning to base."

They drove away, moonroof open, music blasting from the eight-track player.

They were right about one thing.

Everything that mattered now traced back to Sandy and her baby.

22

The Last Roar

DECEMBER 13, 1991 – COLUMBUS, OHIO

Sandy had built a quiet life on the outskirts of Columbus. She liked her brick ranch on Timberbrook Lane. With the money left for her, she had added a tall privacy fence around the backyard so she could enjoy the outdoors without feeling watched. While living in her new cage, she began investigating. She gathered information wherever and however she could find it. So far, the trail to her son had been cold, but she had never given up the pursuit.

LIFE and Enclave were not the only subjects she researched. Sandy needed to understand more about what Ruthy had believed so thoroughly that she had faced death with courage. She still could not trust people, at least not yet and not most of them. So she turned to what Ruthy had called the "good-good book," not every day but more frequently than she had expected. She was fascinated by its layered quality, by the fact that it had been written by so many different authors over a long period of time and yet remained so consistent, and by how it had retained its relevance for more than two thousand years and still provided clarity for so many. She was not convinced yet, but she was learning.

Ruthy's life had proved to her that the end could come at any time. That created an urgency she tried to ignore. Her early life had taught her to be slow to trust, and the one time she had not, Roger had happened.

Her quiet house came with quiet neighbors, retirees on both sides. She worked several jobs after relocating, and when a Meijer Supercenter opened minutes away, she found something steady. Meijer was open twenty-four hours, and Sandy preferred the overnight shifts when the store was calmer. She started at customer service and returns. Management quickly noticed her ability to handle difficult customers, and before long she was promoted to nighttime assistant manager. The pay was good. She liked her coworkers. From the outside, her life looked normal.

Sandy was pulled from her thoughts by an overhead page. "Assistant manager to Hard Lines, please. Management assistance needed near Hard Lines."

The familiar click of the intercom followed.

Sandy headed toward the far right of the store, past jewelry and into Hard Lines. As she rounded an aisle, she heard a giggle.

She stopped cold.

Two people stood there, holding hands, sharing a private joke. People she had believed were long gone from her life.

Something was wrong.

Greg spoke first, smiling broadly. "Are you the manager?"

Sandy could not speak. Why were they together? Why were they here? What did they want?

The woman she remembered as Sylvia spoke next, but her voice was different now, gentle and unrehearsed. Sandy found her own voice first. "Sylvia? Issachar? I don't understand."

Greg smiled. "Can we talk somewhere private? Your place after work?"

Sylvia smiled warmly. "We are not here to hurt you, dear. I can prove it. I will tell you two secrets that only a handful of people in the world would understand the importance of."

"Go on," Sandy said, finally finding her assistant manager voice.

Greg nodded. "My real name is Greg Johnson. This is my wife."

The woman smiled. "Melanie Johnson. Most people still know me as Doctor Mills."

Sandy steadied herself. "Those are two secrets that could be used against you. If you're here to cross me or harm me, you may find it far more difficult than you think."

"Oh, I doubt you could surprise us further. You have proven highly resourceful," Greg said. "Sandy, we are not here to hurt you. In fact, we would like to help. So how about giving us a chance to talk somewhere other than the aisles at Meijer?"

Sandy pulled a small notepad from her waist apron. "I'll give you the address. I think I can trust you because you're the one who created my new name."

"Yes," Greg chuckled. "I did give you the name. I'm glad you approve. I won't need the address, though. I bought that house for you. Remember?"

"Right," Sandy said, managing a tight smile. "What time?"

"In an hour," Melanie said.

They ended the conversation publicly for appearances.

"Thank you, Manager Sandra," Greg said loudly. "I agree that the price is fair now that you have explained it. But I think we will check The Andersons store over by Sawmill first before we commit."

Sandy replied, "That's fine. Check them out. I'm certain I will see you sooner or later."

Sandy walked away. A minute later, Greg and Melanie did the same.

When Sandy arrived home, they were already waiting in the driveway. It was midnight. The neighborhood was asleep.

She unlocked the door. "Make yourselves at home," she said awkwardly. "You bought it."

Roger appeared, puzzled by the extra people. Greg knelt, and Roger immediately approached, winding around him.

Sandy laughed softly. "You traitor."

Greg frowned. "He has lumps. Is he okay?"

"No," Sandy said quietly. "Good days and bad days. The bad ones are winning."

Roger meowed once and wandered off to his recliner, asleep within minutes.

They talked until after two-thirty in the morning. When Greg and Melanie finally stood to leave, it felt as if she had known them her whole life, though she had learned their real names only hours earlier.

She knew they were not there to betray her.

At last, Sandy realized she was missing her opportunity to ask the questions that had haunted her for years. "Wait, I have some more questions. The kind that will haunt me if I throw this opportunity away. Melanie, I need to understand. I have holes in my life."

Melanie looked to Greg. He nodded. They both sat back down.

"I will try," Melanie said. "But some truths carry risk."

"When I agreed to the deal," Sandy said, "you told me you, well, you as Sylvia, worked for a group trying to prove babies had value. Was that true? Did my son grow up safe? Loved?"

Melanie exhaled. "I believed that at the time. I worked for what I thought was LIFE. I was recruited young. They paid for medical school."

Sandy leaned forward.

"For reasons I still don't fully understand," Melanie continued, "you and your baby mattered more than any other case. LIFE has made offers to a lot of young mothers in similar situations, but you and your baby seemed to carry a heightened importance. As for where your son ended up, all I know is he is genius-level smart and doing very well."

Melanie paused. "How well did you know the father?"

Sandy laughed softly, pain barely disguised. "Not at all. He took advantage of me. When I hear a bell, like that timer in your exam room, I think of my son and know letting him live was right."

Melanie's expression shifted. "Do you mean you were forced? That's not what I heard. This doesn't make sense compared to the others I've worked with. Why is your baby different? How would they even know he'd be a genius? You're bright, but so are many people. And a child comes from two parents. They only had you."

The realization hit them all at once.

"Unless they already knew the father."

Melanie asked quietly, "How did you know the baby was a boy?"

Sandy told them about Debbie. About pretending to lose consciousness. About listening.

Greg interjected, "Until we know what is in play here, you should probably keep this to yourself. Keep your head down. Let us do some recon."

Melanie spoke gently. "Greg and I will see what we can find out. You must never look for him. Let us try first."

Sandy replied, "I can try, but I can't promise."

Melanie smiled. "We would expect nothing less."

Greg went to check on Roger. Melanie produced an all-white business card with a single phone number.

"This is my car phone. Call anytime. Never leave a message. I will return it when I am alone."

Sandy slipped it into her pocket.

Greg returned, hugged Sandy, and whispered, "Roger is in pain. It's probably time. Do you want me to take care of him?"

Sandy nodded.

Greg lifted Roger gently. He put Roger's cheek next to his and gently scratched his other cheek, being careful not to hurt him. The effect was evident. Roger remembered Greg and trusted him. They must have bonded during those troubled times. Then Greg whispered in Roger's ear. "It's okay, Roger. Thing Two has got you."

They left.

Sandy closed the door, sat down in her chair, and cried.

23

The Sequel

DECEMBER 14, 1991 – COLUMBUS, OH

The next morning, Sandy woke up startled. She thought she heard Roger moving around near his litter box. Was that all a dream? No, not possible.

Clank.

There was another sound from the kitchen.

Sandy crawled out of bed and pulled on her bathrobe. She grabbed the kitchen knife she had kept in her drawer since the first night she moved in, then quietly made her way to the kitchen.

There it was: the source of the noise, a young Siamese looking just like a young Roger the day they met. There was also a note sitting on the kitchen table.

Roger was brave. This little guy seems to be similar. Though nothing can replace Sir Roger, we hope that this little guy helps. Love, G & M. P.S. We will be back in touch when we can. P.P.S. I still have a key, in case that was not obvious at this point.

She did it again. She started crying, partly because of Roger and partly because of this new beautiful Siamese. He was purring while sitting on the floor. She scooped him up and looked straight at him. He met her gaze without even flinching.

"Well, that settles it. I will name you."

Then she changed her voice to match the movie commercials she saw on television.

"Roger Two, the Sequel."

"How about for your shortened name I just call you R2, or, to mix it up sometimes, R2 C2? Do you like that, little guy? It stands for Roger Two, Cat Two, and it sounds cool like that *Star Wars* movie."

"Meow," said R2.

"Yowl," said Sandy.

From that point on, they were best friends, and he picked up as much as possible where Roger left off, keeping a watchful eye on Sandy. He did not replace Roger (no cat ever could), but he was certainly a welcome substitute.

They played and had fun getting to know each other better for the remainder of the morning. For lunch, she grabbed the keys to her newly purchased 1991 Ford Explorer.

They hit the road toward West Broad Street. She picked up a meal at Sisters Chicken and Biscuits to honor the tradition she had with the first Roger. Sandy decided to take the back way home and enjoy the ride with R2.

She headed farther west on Broad Street and was approaching Rome Hilliard Road. Sandy carefully drove through the short stretch controlled by the Village of New Rome. The place had a reputation, and she did not want the drama. She set her speed just under the limit and white-knuckled through, reminded how stressful that stretch always was.

She arrived home, thankfully without incident, and then she and R2 enjoyed their meal and watched some television.

There was something still bothering her about Greg and Melanie's visit. As nice as it turned out to be, including the kindness Greg showed with Roger and his sequel, the visit was still concerning. He still had a key.

If he had a key to the house all along, then who else did?

Even though both Greg and Melanie had assured her that Greg was the only one assigned to her surveillance detail, she could not trust her life to that assurance. She was not sure what to do. What she did know was that she must remain in survival mode.

While R2 C2 took another nap, Sandy had more time to sit and think.

In the small house nearby, the older man sat in his office. He was munching on crackers and summer sausage set on a plate on his desk. He had a chilled bottle of Welch's sparkling grape juice in an ice bucket and a wine glass sitting at the ready.

The radio interrupted his repast as he watched several monitors. He had recently placed a camera in the living room, being careful not to put it somewhere that would embarrass him but intrusive enough to understand the pulse of what was happening at Sandy's little house on Timberbrook.

"Base to SV1. Report, SV1."

"Subject seems to be enjoying her new companion. Nothing else to report other than she seems somewhat depressed or maybe not feeling well. Hard to tell through cameras."

"Keep me posted, SV1. Base out."

The old man made a cracker with cheese and summer sausage with a drop of brown mustard and propped his feet back up on the desk to settle in.

24

Origins: Fortune Builder

JULY 1932, THE GREAT DEPRESSION, NEW YORK CITY

The vision of Addison Foster was ambitious. The documents he bequeathed to Susan upon his death laid out a worldview that would have intimidated most people. Susan was not intimidated. She was invigorated.

Mister Foster's philosophy did not shock her. She understood the framework immediately. It made sense to her.

Believing that Addison Foster represented a superior breed of human was not difficult. In her mind, he possessed all the hallmarks of superiority.

When the Great Market Crash arrived in October 1929, there was no panic in Foster's household. Susan had arrived in 1930. By then there was no evidence of hardship. By 1932 she had already proven her usefulness and was ready to push forward with her financial plan to advance this grand vision. She was beginning to master the neurolinguistic techniques required to manipulate both Gustav and Addison Foster.

The only person in the house who saw through her charm was the original maid.

Susan framed her for theft and had her dismissed within months of arriving. When Gustav questioned the cruelty of firing someone during an economic collapse, Susan replied calmly, "She should have thought of that before she challenged me."

Susan liked to learn.

One afternoon, she asked politely, "Mr. Addison?"

"Yes, child?" he replied.

"This market crash everyone is speaking of—has it affected you?" she asked, smoothing her skirt with her palms. She knew this gesture soothed his ego while minimizing her perceived threat.

"Of course not!" Addison blustered. "My father, Fletcher, worked hard to build his medical practice so his children would be well provided for. That is precisely why I never married and never had children. I have greater ideals than parasitic offspring. I am trying to save the world!"

"As for the crash," he added impatiently, "why do you ask?"

"I ask to learn," Susan replied. "If others are losing money and you are not, would this be a good time to acquire property? Commercial buildings? Residential apartments?"

Addison frowned. "Get to your point, girl."

She lowered her eyes and tilted her head slightly, another gesture she had learned calmed him.

"You mentioned last week that Mr. Roosevelt has spoken of a New Deal. Government projects. Infrastructure. Employment."

"Yes, yes," Addison snapped. "What of it?"

"So if the government plans to seize land through eminent domain for these projects, would they not be required to pay fair market value? And if property values are currently depressed but expected to rise with economic recovery, would this not be an opportunity?

"If one quietly worked through others to acquire land or buildings sitting in the way of progress, would that not create a large return? Do you not have the high-level connections to identify those spaces most likely?"

Addison dismissed her with a wave of his hand. "Leave me. Gustav, meet me in my office."

Within minutes, Addison Foster was on the phone.

"Hello, Gifford. Addison Foster speaking."

The conversation that followed was routine. Conservation concerns. Urban planning. Public works. Addison took notes carefully.

The next day, he met with his bank and a real estate associate.

Susan was not invited.

She did not mind.

There was a microphone hidden inside Foster's desk, concealed within one of the antique puzzle boxes built into its frame. Addison knew the boxes existed but had never bothered to solve them. Susan worked on them late at night. When she succeeded, she installed the microphone. Hiding both transmitter and receiver required creativity. Gustav helped.

That single insight transformed Addison Foster's modest fortune. His wealth grew from roughly ten million dollars to over four hundred million dollars in real estate value by the time of his death in 1937. When the holdings were liquidated in 1938, the foundation controlled more than four hundred fifty million dollars.

She learned many things from this series of events. The most valuable tip came from understanding that knowledge is power and information fuels knowledge. She learned that the best most useful knowledge came in the form of timely secrets of others. Her recorder in the desk made her realize that access to others secrets yielded big dividends.

As Susan reviewed the objectives, she recognized the truth immediately.

This plan would outlive her.

The real problem was succession.

Most people, Susan observed, do not pay attention. She would not announce the foundation publicly until it was necessary.

With World War I still a living memory and the Great Depression unresolved, Susan understood the scale of the work ahead of her. She also had just learned that knowledge is power, or more accurately, inside information is both money and power if you obtain before others. It can always be used to gain advantage. She carried this lesson forward almost her entire life. She valued information over money. This would serve her well in the future.

She would need time.

Why she felt compelled to do this, she did not know. It was not love for Addison Foster.

She decided to leave the question unanswered. The who, what, when, and where were sufficient. The why, she concluded, did not matter.

25

Johnny Keys

DECEMBER 23, 1991 – O.S.U. CAMPUS, COLUMBUS, OHIO

Johnny worked the padlock combination on his roommate's bedroom door. It was almost Christmas, but his buddy Pete wasn't going home to Mom and Dad. Pete was going to party through the New Year with his friends.

There it was, right in plain sight. *Real smart, Pete.* Johnny was searching for Pete's student credentials, lab access, and lab key that were hung on a lanyard. His roommate Pete was a computer science major. Johnny considered Pete a lazy person but a good programmer. Not as good as Johnny, of course. But pretty good.

Johnny hated having to pretend he was ignorant of computers. He was a genius posing as a guy who came to campus and never left. Pete constantly made fun of him. Things like, "Hey roomie, you need me to show you how to set that digital watch?"

Johnny laughed to himself as he slid the lanyard into his pocket and pulled out an identical padlock, dropping the old padlock into his coat pocket and replacing it with the new lock, securing Pete's door as if he were never there.

Slipping the lanyard around his neck, Johnny stepped outside onto the King Avenue sidewalk, then turned east on Neil Avenue, heading toward Dreese Labs.

Johnny entered the campus building and stopped in the restroom. He straightened himself up, wiped the sweat from his brow, and then headed straight for the computer lab.

He approached the check-in desk for the lab. Johnny planned this specifically for today based on the guard-on-duty schedule. He expected to see "Bobble-Head" Bobby at the security desk, and to his relief, there sat Bobby. Pete and his friends referred to him as "Bobble-Head Bobby" because Bobby napped deeply and often on the job. This assignment could not draw attention to itself, so Bobble-Head Bobby was a gift.

"Hey there, Bobby. Working right up to Christmas, I see? Seems like you're always here when others are celebrating. You must have made someone mad." Johnny added a slight smirk at the end to ratchet up the sincerity.

However, the micro expression on Bobby's face hinted that he was suspicious. It appeared as if he did not recognize this person who was addressing him by name. *Kudos to Bobby*, Johnny thought, since he had, in fact, never been here before.

Bobby had his own tricks to play after years of dealing with tricky students. He glanced down at his own lanyard that included his name. Bobby thought, *I don't know this kid. He probably learned my name from my ID on my lanyard just now.* However, when Bobby glanced at his own lanyard, it was face down on his ample stomach, making Bobby's name not visible.

With so many students coming and going through these doors daily, Bobby began to distrust his own memory. And so Bobby did what lots of people do in that situation: he pretended. This is also what Johnny was counting on.

Bobby said, "Oh hey there, good to see you again. Working late tonight yourself, I see."

"Yep. Professor wants it done tonight, and you know what that means. As a grad student, you say 'yes, professor' and get it done. You certainly don't argue. Anyway, I have my key with me. Do you have a logbook started so I can sign in and out?"

"Nah, I didn't start one tonight. I didn't expect anyone to come use the lab tonight. Most students are off campus for Christmas break," said Bobby.

"Okay then, Officer Bobby. No need to get up. I'll check back in when I lock up and leave."

The fact that this kid had his own set of keys made Bobby more at ease. This kid was probably a harmless teacher's pet. *Harmless* was the wrong word to describe Johnny. It would be more accurate to use its antonym: *dangerous*.

Johnny sat down at a workstation midway back in the lab. The CPU at this station was positioned between one green and one amber phosphor monitor. A beige keyboard and a single mouse were attached to the CPU. One of the monitors displayed NSFNET, and the other displayed terminal access to the newly provided CERN WWW academic gateway. Both monitors blinked in anticipation.

Johnny took a second to revel in the amber and green glow of these monitors and enjoy his moment in the sun.

Dopamine began to flow as he began to type. His approach was methodical. He first looked for a way to exploit a weakness in the gateway's login ID protocols, switching back and forth to each monitor and watching code scroll by as quickly as he could edit.

He assigned himself higher login access, then moved on to the system directories and modified the startups. Next, he added hidden entries into the initialization files that would run tasks not initiated by the user or their knowledge. This all worked through assigning a nonstandard port that would activate every time the system restarted.

He created a privileged user account with a modified authentication path, thanks to a .rhosts file injected into his code from the 1.44 disk he brought with him to save time. He grinned wider when he encountered a forgotten ownership stemming from a legacy permission.

The click of the keys ramped up faster as he pushed his way past these annoying but not unexpected setbacks, finally granting remote shell access through carefully modified daemon configuration files. He hesitated for half a second, then left a single comment buried deep in the daemon config: "elegant enough for now jokey" before moving on.

All of this coding provided a very simple entry point for EPS. The access point Johnny created allowed continued and undetectable access to what was being called the World Wide Web.

Johnny was sweating from the exertion. He imagined himself on a grand theater stage conducting a symphony. The sound of clicking keys could be heard throughout the room. This was his music. But like a tree falling in the forest, no one but Johnny could hear it.

Johnny created the perfect way in and the perfect way out. He was intoxicated with hubris and began to feel invincible.

Bobby was asleep at his desk, and Johnny was in the zone. Johnny took another half hour to complete his task, and when he had finished, he leaned back in the chair. The amber and green glow coming from the monitors softly confirmed his handiwork.

Johnny leaned forward and gave each machine a benign task to cover his activity from the next user of those terminals.

Johnny finished by standing and stretching like a marathon runner. Then he let out a loud yawn purposefully to wake Bobby up. Johnny left by locking the door and saying, "Good night, Bobby. Have a Merry Christmas!"

To which Bobby replied, "You too! Did you get done what the professor wanted?"

"Well, Bobby, I have always been an overachiever. I got it done, and since it's almost Christmas, I wrapped it up real pretty with a bow."

Bobby chuckled, and Johnny walked out of the wing and into the night.

Johnny went home and put Pete's ID and key back where he found them, then swapped the locks back to remove his own. He went to the kitchen and placed a phone call. The voice on the other end of the phone, a woman's voice, responded on the first ring.

"Report."

"Finished. Back door installed," was Johnny's clipped response.

"Good. Stand down and return," was the response, followed by the sound of the line going dead.

Johnny hung up and looked around the kitchen. Dishes in the sink, and the room was full of odd smells.

"Ah, the campus life. I won't miss this."

He walked out the door, turned onto King Avenue, and picked up a cab on High Street.

26

Punctuality

DECEMBER 24, 1991 – COLUMBUS, OHIO

The phone rang four times and went to voicemail. Sandy hung up and put the kettle on for tea, content to wait. She started a packaged fire log in the fireplace, not for warmth but for comfort. The tea was for the same reason. R2 seemed to enjoy the fire as well. It was close to Christmas, and she had done no decorating, as in years past.

She had a single framed piece on the mantel, bought on clearance at Meijer's last post-Christmas sale, that read . . .

The phone rang.

Sandy picked it up cautiously as she turned the kettle off. The tea could wait. This could not.

"Hello, Sandy. I saw that you called. I am in my car as promised, in the garage. There is no one here, so our privacy is intact. How is R2 fitting in?"

"R2 is wonderful. Thank you both for that kindness. I could not have done what Greg did for me. As for R2, although he is not Roger, I think they are related in ways beyond breed."

They both laughed, the sound fading into a pause while Sandy gathered her thoughts and her courage.

"It is my fault she is dead. Ruthy, I mean. I just couldn't keep my mouth shut and my curiosity in check. I was hoping you might know more about the details. I am almost completely sure it was Debbie but I could be wrong. No matter who killed her it was my fault. I should have kept my questions to myself. I knew we were being watched. I knew it was dangerous. Yet I did it anyway." Her voice paused as her throat tightened to restrain the tears.

Melanie spoke kindly and clearly, but with an emphasis Sandy had not heard from her before.

"If you are thinking you caused it, honey, you can leave that in R2's litter box where it belongs. No offense intended."

Melanie continued. "I do not believe I have told you how my parents died. I was fourteen when a train struck their car."

"Oh no," Sandy said softly. "I did not know."

"Bear with me. This story matters. They were driving to pick me up from a friend's house. It was the first time I had stayed away overnight. Young prodigies do not get many sleepover invitations. My parents did not like the friend. They thought she was too permissive, too boy-crazy, and not careful enough. They were worried about scandal and how easily it could derail my future.

"I begged to go. They finally relented with one condition. I had to be dressed and ready at exactly eight a.m. They were punctual to a fault, so I agreed. That night I had fun. Popcorn. Scary movies. Things my parents would never have allowed. For the first time in my life, and to this day I don't know how, I overslept by ten minutes.

"I called my mother and asked her to delay the trip. I did not want them arriving early or discovering how late we had stayed up by chatting with my friend's parents. My mother delayed their arrival by exactly ten minutes. They left ten minutes later and reached the tracks ten minutes later."

Melanie paused.

"So, the questions became these. Did I kill my parents? Did I cause their death? Did my sin play a role? Or was it the train engineer? Was he tired? Was he careless? The truth is, I do not know. And I do not know who killed Ruthy. But I promise you this. If I ever learn the truth, I will tell you."

"Melanie, thank you for trusting me with this. I am so sorry you went through it. I have always believed that beauty can come from pain. You are proof of that to me.

"Ruthy's death may have to stay in that category for now. My interest in who God is and the truth He represents came from my time with her. I am not giving up, but Ruthy always talked about Joseph in Genesis, chapter fifty. What man meant for evil, God used for good."

They ended the call amicably, and Sandy felt settled, at least for now.

As she hung up, her eyes returned to the mantel art. It was a simple calligraphy piece with a papyrus-like scroll unrolled and an image of the earth seen from above. The scripture read Matthew 5:5: "Blessed are the meek, for they shall inherit the earth."

She had never noticed before that the earth was not shown from the usual angle. At the center of the image was St. Croix.

Melanie, however, wondered. Had she herself played any role in Ruthy's death? The timing was unsettling, though not necessarily causal. She decided to leave it for now, but she needed answers. Sandy deserved the truth.

27

Know-It-All Paul

JANUARY 1, 1992 – COLUMBUS, OH

"Know-It-All Paul" was, in fact, Paul Adio Matthews. His late-night AM show occupied the 2:00 a.m. slot, aimed squarely at hackers, phone phreakers, and conspiracy theorists. Management always opened with the standard disclaimer, which Paul liked to mutter under his breath.

Paul had been born on Saint Croix, but years at Ohio State had worn his island accent almost completely away. He could turn it on and off at will. Most days he kept it off. When it suited him, though, he dialed it back in, thick and easy. The conspiracy crowd loved it on the radio. Strangers tended to lower their guard around it too. He also found the double superlatives really helped set people at ease and loosen their lips. It was one of the simplest interrogation tricks he had.

"Hey out there, all you big-brain show-offs. It's me, Know-It-All Paul, your favorite loudmouth host. Tonight, on *It's Not Random*, we're talkin' major events of 1991. And lemme tell ya, good riddance to that year, man. Two hours in the rearview here in cold, cold Columbus. Let's hit the phones, but first, lemme set the table."

He leaned into the mic.

"You know how it goes. Military boys, universities, think tanks, them fake charitable research outfits. Same circle, same dance. Tight as ever. Now some geeks like Dark Dante got burned in April, and then to round out the year we got Phiber Optik practically walkin' right into Operation Sundevil's cousin for a Christmas takedown. And right on cue, here come the big toys. ARPA fading out, World Wide Web stepping in. Triple W, man. Two cans and a string turned global spider web. Question is, this thing real? Or just another toy for the eggheads?"

Paul chuckled.

"Gopher gone. ARPA pulled the plug back in '90. Now we all caught in one big web. Old English Tim mighta got it right this time. Anybody pokin' around out there? Phone phreaks still ghostin' and dumpster divin'? Any of you 414 kids lurking? I wanna hear from you."

The call-in number lit up.

"Well, "Remember now, no real-name business, just your hacker's name. Big Brother always listenin' in on the Know-It-All Paul Show." "Hey deh, caller you our first caller for the show. You on the air. What's your handle?"

"Love the show, mon. My hacker signature is Spider Monkey. First-time caller. Yep, I've been all through the new internet."

Paul perked up. "Well, do tell."

"I work for a charity foundation. Genetic research. We hack other systems all the time. This new Net makes it easy. Faster than ARPA ever was. Never been caught."

Paul said. "Well, Spider Monkey, keep climbin' them trees. Shake somethin' loose for ol' Know-It-All Paul."

The next caller came on.

"Name's Paw Bell. Phone phreaker. ARPANET was a joke to crack. And there's a back door y'all ain't talkin' about. Same one Spider Monkey's folks put in."

The line went dead.

Paul noticed immediately. Red light out. Not static. Not a drop.

He covered smoothly. "Thanks, Paw Bell. Call back anytime."

Commercial break.

The business line rang.

Paul answered, irritated. "Know-It-All Paul speakin'."

No one replied but he could hear someone on the end of the line. Just as he began to say something the lights in the studio went black and all he could see was the glow of the exit sign.

Paul left the studio carefully, stayed under streetlights, and took a cab to Soussy Market instead of home. He walked the rest.

Inside his apartment, he swept quietly. No lights. Heart pounding.

He went to the window. Keeping low to see if he was followed.

The bullet shattered the glass inches from his head.

Paul ran at a crouch toward the door and in the landing between apartments.

He flung the front door open and entered the landing between apartments. His neighbor Lori was standing in her doorway with the door wide open. Paul spoke in a loud whisper, "Get down and come with me if you want to live! They are coming and if they don't find me, they will take it out on you."

Lori looked around before she turned back into her apartment. Heading straight through to the back wall she flung the window open that led to the back wall fire escape.

Within seconds, panic pumping adrenaline, they were down the fire escape.

Once down, they stuck to the shadows and fled into the nearby Iuka Ravine. Lori suggested they head to Buckeye Donuts on High Street. It was a 24-hour bakery and there were always people inside. At least there would be witnesses and it would buy time to think.

Two men followed them. They radioed ahead.

A white van collected them minutes later.

The sign on the fence behind the parking lot where they left the van for the night read:

Enclave Protection Services LLC

Paul would later reflect on the mistake they made.

They underestimated him. They forgot why his nickname was Know-It-All Paul. Curiosity, once awakened, rarely goes back to sleep.

28

Paul Calls Sandy

JANUARY 1, 1992 – COLUMBUS, OH

About three p.m. that afternoon, Sandy's phone rang, her phone only rang from work so it nearly made her jump out of her skin. Probably a wrong number. Best to answer it in a deeper voice, she thought.

"Hello," she said, trying to sound more like a man than a woman.

"Hello, Miss Sandy. My name's Paul, and I'm a good friend of Greg and Melanie, eh."

"Look, what was your name again? Paul?" she snapped. "I don't know how you got my number, but if you value your well-being, you should forget it."

The phone rang again almost immediately. When she answered, she barked, "WHAT!"

"I'm Ruthy's son!" he blurted out, panic sharpening the words, knowing this was probably his last chance to get them out.

They made arrangements to meet the next morning at eleven a.m. at Westland Mall, near the Tinder Box, beside the mall information desk.

Before she hung up, she said, "Bring your birth certificate and your driver's license. If I can't verify what you're saying, it will be a very short meeting."

She ended the call and turned her attention back to R2.

After sitting together on the couch, a little longer, she said, "Well, R2, let's grab a snack."

R2 didn't move. He just stared at her with those bright blue eyes.

"What?" she said. "You're not hungry?"

"Yowl," R2 replied, and it clearly meant no.

Sandy studied him for a few seconds. "You're sure you're not actually a nephew or some close relative to Roger? You're worried about me, aren't you?"

"Yowl."

"Aw, buddy. I'll be careful. And if this isn't what it's supposed to be, I'll ditch fast and make sure I've got a parking spot for a clean exit. How does that sound?"

"Meow."

He hopped down and headed toward the kitchen for his snack.

"Well," she added, "since the chicken place is right across from the mall, maybe we'll have that again tomorrow?"

"Yowl."

She smiled. She knew that one meant yes.

29

Westland Mall

JANUARY 2, 1992 – COLUMBUS, OH

Sandy arrived twenty minutes early to the meeting with Paul. She parked near the mall entrance closest to Chi-Chi's. Part of her survival skill set was never parking near the door she planned to use. Most people parked close to where they entered; anyone watching would assume the same. If she had to run, they would be looking in the wrong lot. It was not perfect, but it bought time. She also carried her pepper spray.

The mall was no longer the bustling place it had been when she moved near here in 1980. It had lost anchor stores and dozens of smaller shops as newer, larger malls drew traffic away. City Center downtown had done particular damage. Westland now felt hollow, which made it useful and dangerous at the same time.

She chose the area near the Tinder Box deliberately. Three access routes fed into it from different parking lots, and it sat directly across from the mall information kiosk, which had a direct line to security. The cigar shop itself drew a narrow, self-selecting clientele; anyone lingering there without looking the part stood out immediately. It gave her visibility, witnesses, and options. That was all she needed.

She arrived early and took a seat that did not advertise where she had entered, giving her a clear view of the approaches before anyone could see her. If something felt wrong, she could walk away before the meeting ever began.

Sandy was surprised to realize she was nervous. No one on the planet had affected her life more than Ruthy or "Ruty," as she would have pronounced it. Sandy smiled just thinking about that simple word, Ruthy. She had known her for less than three days, and yet the impact lingered years later. Sandy found herself remembering conversations about the beach, about the limits of the water, as if they had happened yesterday. Ruthy was the reason Sandy had sought out a church at all, even though fear had robbed her of the joy of getting to know what she imagined were genuinely kind people. People like Ruthy.

She was drifting through memory when her inner voice snapped her awake.

Lefty: *Wake up, daydreamer. You're not paying attention. I think he's here.*

Campus Hippie chimed in. *Yeah. And he's got a woman with him.*

Mister Right added calmly. *He looks nervous and scared. That tracks.*

Then her inner noise went operationally quiet. Or as close as it ever got.

Sandy watched him for a few minutes. There was no reason to give up her positional advantage yet. He could have a tail. What's the deal with the woman with him?

As she watched him, she speculated. The man *could* be Ruthy's son, although Sandy had not known Ruthy had a child—she really didn't know her that long. He had an easy, healthy build not gym-made, just naturally solid. That tracked. He wore a white Alfred E. Neuman for President T-shirt. His skin tone echoed Ruthy's, slightly lighter but unmistakably related. The woman with him was red-haired, striking, and visibly nervous, wearing faded jeans and a Teenage Mutant Ninja Turtles shirt. She clung to his arm. Whether it was affection or fear, Sandy could not yet tell.

They were both scanning the area. They were getting antsy.

Sandy stood. Paul spotted her immediately. They converged near the information booth at the same moment Sandy moved toward the clustered seating. The rounded Naugahyde benches were common in public spaces like libraries and airports. Sandy used the moment to manufacture awkwardness, making it look like she had not intended to sit with them as she took the seat opposite.

The woman's arm remained entwined with Paul's. Dependence. Fear. Possibly both. Something was there, but Sandy could not read it yet.

Slow down, Mister Right advised. *You don't get everyone in thirty seconds.*

Sandy spoke first. "We can talk politely, but keep arm movements and gestures to a minimum. Did you bring the documentation I asked for? If not, I walk away now."

Paul handed it over. "I brought it. I ain't givin' you no six for nine."

She looked up at him.

That smile.

It was Ruthy's. Unmistakable. And the phrase did not hurt.

Don't get sloppy, Lefty warned. *Suite 18 was probably bugged.*

Sandy kept her face neutral and reviewed the documents.

Paul Adio Matthews. Born January 12, 1960. Charles Harwood Memorial Hospital, Christiansted, St. Croix. Mother: Ruthy Esther Matthews Father: Jonathan James Matthews.

His Ohio driver's license matched.

Lori, flustered, produced her own license without being asked. Sandy scrutinized it, suppressing a smile. Nervous people overcompensate.

Sandy handed everything back discreetly.

That was when she noticed the two men entering the Tinder Box.

Long hair. T-shirts. Jeans.

Not cigar men.

They were pretending to browse.

There it is, Sandy thought.

She waved as if greeting a man entering near the Chi-Chi's entrance. The man walking in caught the gesture and waved back, clearly delighted. Sandy motioned "one minute" and pointed to her watch. He sat down to wait.

Sandy leaned in and whispered, "We need to move. I'm walking out with that man. I'll get my Explorer and pull around to the back Sears exit. You two go into Sears. Paul, tell the cosmetics counter those two men tried to grab your girlfriend in the restroom. When security gets called, you run. I'll be waiting outside."

She slid her pepper spray across to Paul. "If they get close, use this."

Then Sandy stood, slipped on her flirty dumb-blonde smile, crossed the distance, kissed the confused man on the cheek, and laughed loudly. "Oh, Harold, you are so bad."

They walked out arm in arm.

Paul and Lori followed the plan. It almost happened clean.

The shorter man was fast.

Paul sprayed him fifteen feet from the doors. It bought just enough time.

They piled into the Explorer.

The second man stumbled out wheezing. Sandy muttered, "Guess he was a smoker, after all."

She drove away and took a looping route that avoided the traffic light directly in front of the mall.

From there they reached Timberbrook without incident.

Inside the garage, Sandy moved fast. She retrieved her Galco shoulder holster, her Sig Sauer, spare magazines, and ammunition.

R2 saw the weapon and vanished into his carrier, alert but calm.

They did not speak much.

Paul finally broke the silence. "I see why my mom liked you."

Sandy nodded. "We're bugging out for a few days. I know a safe place to think."

She packed. Paul gathered supplies. Sandy swapped plates again. Surveillance monitors were checked.

No movement.

They pulled out.

A heavy-set older neighbor with white hair was pruning his fruit trees in his front yard. Appearing to take advantage of the winter peace.

Paul frowned. "Why is this guy trimming trees in January?"

Sandy did not answer.

Behind them, the white-haired man turned, pulled out a phone, and pressed redial.

"They made it out clean."

"Affirm," came the reply. "Issachar out."

30

Emergency Road Trip

JANUARY 2, 1992 – COLUMBUS, OH

Sandy stopped at the Meijer gas station and filled up the Explorer, then asked the fuel station manager if she could borrow the internal phone. She needed to call the store manager.

"Hey Alice, I'm sorry I have a bit of an emergency here. I have some old friends in town and one of them was in trouble with her boyfriend. I'm going to take them out of town and help cool things off for a day or two. I know it's short notice but would you mind if I called Valerie to see if she can cover me for a few days?

"Sure, that is fine. I think you cover more for everyone else. Let me know if Valerie can't cover it and I will see what I can do. Hope everything gets worked out. Stay safe sometimes couples can turn on the one trying to help. Do me a favor though, please. Call me and let me know your home safe. Don't forget, ok?"

"Thanks, Alice will do. Thanks, By."

She dialed Valerie's number next. Sandy could have called her first but wanted to make sure everything was done the proper way. Less drama and suspicion that way.

Valerie picked up on the second ring. "Sure, no problem. You have covered me so many times I couldn't count them."

"Thanks, Valerie," Sandy said.

Paul and Lori waited in the Explorer, talking quietly. Lori's voice carried more flirtation than fear. *Interesting*, Sandy thought.

Sandy climbed into the driver's seat, started the Explorer, and pulled out. They took the freeway north, exited near Dublin, then followed side roads toward the Scioto River. After a left on Dublin Road, the tension eased. It was late afternoon, and once they hit the back roads, even R2 relaxed.

Sandy pulled over at a construction site along the river. She lifted R2 and whispered, "I know this isn't your litter box, buddy, but I need you to work with me."

R2 complied, shooting her a look that clearly said she owed him.

After the situation was negotiated to a satisfactory conclusion for all parties involved, Sandy scooped him up and returned to the Explorer. R2 settled onto Paul's lap, much to Paul's awkward discomfort.

Sandy shot him a look that said let it happen. R2 did.

Lori leaned forward from the back seat. "I wonder what they're building back there. Looks like it's going to be some giant awkward house or something."

She reached into the bag. "Anyone want a can of coolish pop or some snacks?"

For a while, the Explorer filled with crunching, chewing, and the occasional embarrassed "Excuse me."

R2 answered each one with a polite "Meow."

He received people-food he normally did not get and was having a very good road trip.

Paul and Lori told their story, starting with the radio station phone call two nights earlier. They had spent the rest of that night at Buckeye Donuts until sunrise. Still needing a place to hide, Lori called a coworker from Gumby's Pizza, who let them crash for the night. They had not mentioned to Lori's friend that they had been shot at and chased. Lori said, "I was fairly certain that detail would have ended the hospitality."

Sandy asked clarifying questions and logged the answers away.

By the time they finished, she understood what was happening, though not why. She would take it to Greg and Melanie later. Not yet though. She was not convinced they were safe yet and she did not want to complicate it further.

Sandy folded the unanswered questions into her inner voice, where doubts and facts could sit side by side until they resolved. That part of her never slept. It only worked. Whether that was a gift or a curse depended on the outcome.

They turned down a gravel driveway around 4:30 p.m. Lori spoke up, "Where are we?" "Somewhere near the intersection of Nowhere and No Clue." Paul quipped.

Snow covered the ground. Old snow. It did not snow anywhere along the way.

Trees closed in around the drive, branches interlocking overhead. It was not dark or eerie. It looked more like the trees were holding hands with friendly affection. Like kids playing a game on the playground. In summer, the canopy would have blocked the sun entirely. Now, in winter, it still felt like a tunnel.

They pulled up beside a large brown pole barn.

Then things got lively.

Two large dogs charged the Explorer from somewhere near the house. R2 was unimpressed but unwilling to appear weak. Gathering his courage from the ignoble shelter of Paul's lap, he leaned against the window and hissed.

It sounded like air escaping a slashed tire.

A friendly-looking man emerged from the house. The dogs immediately disengaged, trotting back to him and hopping into his truck without hesitation. They sat and waited, as if to say the excitement was over.

R2 declared victory with a triumphant "Yowl" and reclaimed Paul's lap.

Sandy stepped out. "Hey, Dave. Sorry to drop in on short notice."

Sandy turned back to the Explorer. "Paul the keys are in the ignition if you get cold. I'll be right back."

Minutes later, Sandy returned, hugged Dave like a brother, and watched him drive away with the dogs hanging their heads out of the pickup truck ears flapping in the wind.

"Let's get this stuff inside," she said. "We can stay here a few days."

They unloaded and went in.

Lori opened her mouth to ask questions. Sandy's look shut it down.

"Two bedrooms down, one up," Sandy said. "Lori, take upstairs. Paul, couch first shift. We swap around four."

She paused. "Lori, not to be sexist, but you work at a restaurant, right? You know how to cook?"

Lori lit up. "Finally, something useful. Is there a grocery store nearby?"

"Not really," Sandy said. "But the pantry and freezer are stocked."

Lori headed upstairs.

The house was an A-frame with a glass front wall overlooking the road and driveway. In winter, visibility was excellent. In summer, it would be nearly impossible to see anything beyond the trees.

Sandy moved the Explorer behind the house, lining it up with the laundry room exit in case a fast departure became necessary.

Upstairs, Lori found a claw-foot tub and called down, "Anyone mind if I take a bath before dinner?"

"No," Sandy and Paul answered together.

"Just don't fall asleep," Sandy added.

R2 explored the beams of the post-and-beam interior, eventually climbing to the highest supports. From there, he padded across to the upper windows and absorbed the last of the daylight.

Warm, fed, and content, he watched the road until sleep claimed him.

31

Nails in the Night

As the house grew quieter, with Lori upstairs enjoying her warm bath, Sandy and Paul finally had a chance to talk. Ruthy hung between them like a storm cloud. Sandy spoke first. "There is so much I want to learn about Ruthy and about you."

Paul began, "I was born on Saint Croix. Mom was eighteen when she and Dad tied the knot, and not long after that, she ended up pregnant. Dad was a good man, a theologian, an author, a public speaker, and a part-time lecturer at colleges all over the world. Brilliant mind. Gentle, tender heart. He and Mom were truly in love. I mean, I was only old enough to know him for the last five or so years of his life. He died from pancreatic cancer when I was ten. What I remember the most though was the two of them always found both the time and the reason to laugh and praise the Lord for His goodness. As a kid I was angry. What's so funny about Dad suffering from cancer? I was old enough to remember that it was painful. I also remember hearing things like 'I love you,' and 'I'll miss you,' and an abundance of tears."

Sandy gently asked, "There is something I have to ask. I am concerned you might take it the wrong way but here goes. What happens to your accent? It comes and goes, mon." She finished with a smile.

"I have been in the States for almost five years now exclusively. I occasionally went back for visits but not enough to fall back into the dialect. I still could talk sweet-sweet when I wanna set people at ease. I use it pon the radio too. Folks like it, and it keep dem listenin', ya." He smiled. "Think of it like a nice fancy business suit. I put it on when I am going on the air or trying to investigate something. People love the accent and the friendly-sounding nature tends to loosen lips."

"Ah, very clever," Sandy said. "You think I could get 'way wid dat? You know, if I could set people at ease wid my lil' sweet-sweet island patois I does do so good-good?" They both laughed a carefree laugh and then they heard, "Hey there, what are you guys laughing about? Hope it's not me." Lori landed a small giggle to accompany the question. "Are you getting hungry? I can come down and fix dinner now that I'm all presentable."

Sandy spoke first. "Give us a few more minutes. We have a few more questions to get through. You can start fixing if you want. We should be done in ten or fifteen more minutes."

Lori did not respond. Sandy was pretty confident she was pouting. Before they resumed the conversation, there was a loud noise upstairs.

"What was that noise?" Paul said.

Sandy said, "It's just Lori moving around up there. There is no way to move around on that loft floor at night without waking the dead."

Paul gave Sandy a funny look but let it go.

"Well, Dad teased Mom and the one tease she like the most was the no marriage in heaven thing. He would say, 'Now, Ruthy, don't you forget that when we are in heaven we aren't married anymore. Matthew 22:30 reminds us that marriage ends once we leave this life, and after that, we'll be like the angels in heaven.'

"With no need for marriage in the earthly sense, you know?

"Then Mom would chide him, playful-like, 'Well, that's not very romantic, you old wet blanket!' Momma said she was sure he brought this up just to deliver what she called his "silly little punch line." Apparently, he'd say, "Now, you probably won't recognize me as an angel, but I'll recognize you—you won't change at all.'"

Lori made her way down the spiral staircase. She descended with wet hair and a man's large T-shirt as a night shirt. It kept her covered, but she was trying to get his attention for sure.

"As Lori came down the spiral staircase, Sandy glanced over. Paul had noticed but seemed to be uncomfortable.

"I hope this is okay. It was in the open closet next to the bathroom, and it was more comfy than putting all the clothes back on."

"Yeah, it's fine. I didn't bring extra clothes either. Maybe we can swing by a thrift store tomorrow, pick up a few things?"

Lori seemed disappointed and she plopped down between them on the couch and put her feet on the ottoman between them. Paul continued unphased. "After Dad died, Mom would get real quiet and I could tell she wasn't with us here much. Truth be told, she was longing for heaven. She'd pray out loud at night, and most times she ended her prayers the same way: 'Lord, if it's Your will, please take me tonight so I can be with You in paradise. And if it's okay with You, Lord, can You arrange for me to worship You somewhere where I can see John? I know it's different there, so it's Your will, not mine. If You were to grant that request, I would be very grateful.'"

Lori looked bored as she rose from the couch and scooched past Paul, making sure she dominated his view on the way out. Paul averted his eyes politely and spoke, "Excuse me."

"Anyway, when Momma talked like that, it upset me as child. I would say, 'If you go I am all alone. Why do you want to leave me? I still have questions and things I need to know.' The ever-practical Ruthy would reply, 'Child, you never alone wid the Lord. Das why you have to run to Him soon as you can. Dey hain't no guarantee in this life 'cept heaven or hell. Don't count on me or no one else. We will disappoint ya. The Lord. He is di only Rock!"

They talked for just a few more minutes or at least so it seemed. Lori called out, "Dinner's ready."

Dinner turned out to be breakfast. Eggs over easy with sausage links and thick-cut bacon. Homemade biscuits with strawberry jam and a jar of local honey she found in the pantry.

After dinner, they all cleared the kitchen and cleaned the dishes then settled onto the comfy couch. The glass front of the home allowed them to see the darkened world outside, just a sliver of moon left in the sky. Lori leaned into Paul's shoulder and laid her bare legs up on the overstuffed matching ottoman.

Sandy said nothing. She decided they needed to know whether Lori was really just a neighbor or perhaps she knew more. Either way they needed to know before Paul got hurt, either in the heart or worse.

Sandy spoke as she sipped some herbal tea. "So, here is the plan. We stay here tonight, and we bug out tomorrow. I can't tell you where we are going though."

Right on cue, Lori spoke up, her voice pitched for Paul. "Tonight, It's already tonight. I don't even know where we are now. It's stressful not knowing."

Sandy laid a few magazines on the coffee table at the end of the couch just before dinner. As Sandy expected, Lori scooped one from the top, rolled it up in her hand, and said, "Well, I am wiped out. I think I'm done for the night. This boring country living magazine looks like just the thing to put me to sleep." She made sure Paul was watching her get up. Nothing overt. Just making sure.

After Lori was on the stairs, Sandy spoke quietly to Paul. "You take the first shift in the bedroom. It has a Jack-and-Jill bathroom with the shared door in the kitchen just around from the stove. Knock softly before you enter the bathroom, just in case."

"Also, sleep in your clothes," she added. "You never know."

Sandy shut off the lights and moved by flashlight. She snapped her fingers and R2 dropped down from the beams. He saw the bags packed and came to the same conclusion.

It was 1:20 a.m. when she heard it. The phone lifting quietly from the cradle. Muffled sounds, as if the receiver were being held close to something. Then Lori's voice came through clearly.

"Yes, NF104197, we are at 5500 County Road 9, Mansfield, Ohio. We are supposed to leave in the morning. If you want them dead, you need to do it tonight. I am in the upstairs bedroom, so anyone on the ground floor is your target."

The phone returned gently to the cradle.

Sandy watched through the wall of windows. She had a front-row seat to it all.

She waited until it was quiet, then woke Paul. Sandy explained quietly what was happening. They sat in the living room and waited. Sandy asked Paul to go into the laundry room and disconnect the incoming phone line. No chance of any second phone call now. Nothing to do but wait. They could have snuck out and left Lori there, but that would lead to a chase they would most likely lose. Sandy and Paul were both curious about who might show up.

Within the hour, four black SUVs rolled into the driveway across the street with their lights off. Paul now could not deny that Lori was part of it all. He had still held on to some hope that Sandy was wrong. That hope vanished.

Sandy whispered, "Go get Lori. Let's see how long she tries to play the game."

Paul went up, gently woke Lori, covered her mouth, turning his accent back on he said, "Dey 'cross the street at the neighbor house, c'mon down." He handed her the jeans at the foot of the bed but stayed and did not offer to turn around. She pulled her pants on right in front of him, annoyance plain on her face. Paul was not going to give her the chance to bolt.

As she reached the bottom step, Sandy emerged from behind the center post of the spiral staircase completely obscured to Lori. Sandy grabbed both hands quickly and pulled the zip tie from her mouth and tightened it on Lori's wrists behind her back. She tossed Paul the duct tape, and before Lori knew what was happening, she was bound and taped to a wooden kitchen chair in the middle of the living room.

Tactical lights moved through the empty house across the street. A team of eight.

With Lori secured, R2 was ready to go. They headed for the back door where the Explorer was parked. On the way past the fridge, Sandy grabbed the Ziploc bags of leftover biscuits, sausage, and bacon, snagged the honey, and threw it all into a paper grocery bag in the laundry room.

They were out the door and into the Explorer.

The merry band went from three and a cat to two and a cat, just like that.

She started the Explorer and, lights completely off, eased down the driveway.

"Open the glove box and hand me one of the two paper bags," she told Paul. "Keep the other one."

He started to ask. She cut it off. "Wait for my order, then throw it over the Explorer into the road behind us."

Flashlights moved through the windows across the street. They had figured out nobody was home.

Within seconds, tactical weapon lights clearly mounted on assault rifles judging by the bouncing beams of light headed through the yard and toward the vehicles. Sandy's Explorer glided out onto the road into the moonlight ahead of the four black vehicles.

“Now!” Sandy said.

Paul chucked the first bag up and over. She gunned the accelerator when the bag of roofing nails scattered across the dark road behind them. Sandy waited another five seconds while accelerating and threw hers over the top of the Explorer as she drove forward.

The blacked-out Suburbans roared onto the road in close formation. Almost in unison the front two began to swerve as they appeared to coordinate running into opposite ditches. The next pair kept coming, but they did not make it very much further than the others. They of course found the second batch of nails that Sandy had thrown just a little bit later.

The final score. Four SUVs disabled and one intact Ford Explorer speeding away with no one chasing.

Paul let out a “Whoop.” R2 let out a “Yowl,” more from annoyance than exuberance.

Sandy flicked the headlights on, caught the chaos in her mirror, and turned at the next crossroad.

Free and clear for now.

32

The Impact of Laughter

Sandy and Paul drove all the way to Timberbrook on back roads. It was a tradeoff. Easier to stay hidden but it was a lot slower. Sandy asked Paul, "Faster and riskier or slower and safer for the way home?" Paul grinned and said, "Well, when you put it like that, slow and safe is the clear winner."

So, they avoided the freeways and Sandy took the time to wind through on a nostalgia tour of where she was happiest in life. Trying to run from that many pursuers on a freeway was just too dangerous anyway. Once you were spotted, you were in for a chase that boiled down to who had more gas in the tank.

It took far more time than jumping on I-71 would have. When there are three SUVs, each with a spotter and a driver, losing anyone in broad daylight on a busy highway would have been nearly impossible. Even stopping for gas was a difficult task against those odds.

Paul took over the driving while Sandy enjoyed some quality time with R2. They talked like they had known each other for years, both wanting to learn as much as possible about the other, knowing their time together was limited. Soon it would be back to business.

"So, where were we before Lori distracted us," Sandy said.

Paul spoke up rather abruptly. "First, I have to ask. How did you know Lori was in on it?"

"Well for starters, I am an outsider. In that situation it is easier to see the patterns. She was your long-time neighbor, right? That means she probably knew when you came and went. Valuable information to have if you are being surveilled. I mean with you talking to your Mom it would be in the best interest of these people to know what you know or at least know where you are. She had the opportunity to keep tabs on you for a long time. I didn't know it as a fact, but it was an easy conclusion to draw," Sandy said. "She was assigned to watch your behavior. Ruthy was a big part of what these people were doing. She was not aware of the details but she was too good a nurse to get rid of, oh Paul, I am sorry I said that."

Paul said, "Keep going, so far everything you have said is true."

"Lori had several tells. The biggest one was obvious from the beginning. She never asked to be let out of the danger and be left alone. Think about it this way. These guys were looking for you, not her. She was free and clear once you gave them the slip.

"Anytime from the relative safety of Buckeye Donuts, would you have been shocked if she had said, 'Hey, neighbor, you're nice and all, but I don't understand what you're into, and this is not my business'? Instead, she stayed and endangered other friends in the process like the friend from Gumby's Pizza. If the tables were turned, would you have risked a friend's life the way she presumably did hers?"

"I kind of did that to you, didn't I?" Paul said.

"No, we met on neutral ground. You showed me proof that you were Ruthy's son, and you didn't make me take you home. I did that. That was on me." Sandy started to lose control of her voice. "And do you want to know something else?"

"Yes, what is it?" Paul replied gently.

"I'm glad I did it. I can't pay Ruthy back for what I did to her."

Sandy turned to look out the window. R2 looked up, then lay back down.

"No, no," Paul said firmly. "That's not right, Sandy! My mama never let anyone tell her what to do. What she did or didn't do was her call. She cared about you, and she knew the stakes. My mom always made her own choices."

Sandy let his words sit. She knew if she responded she would fall apart again.

After a pause that felt longer than it was, she pivoted. "Paul, whose idea was it to reach out to me for a meet up?"

The look on Paul's face answered before he spoke. "Lori."

"Had she ever met Melanie or Greg?"

"No, I hardly knew her until that night."

"She was in charge of the whole thing!"

Those guys at the mall, How did they know we would be there. She set this whole thing up!"

Sandy nodded. "Shooting into your window was never intended to kill you. They could have done that anytime, anywhere. The gunshot supplied the pressure needed to bring Lori into the fold."

"I see it now. For someone who studies conspiracy theories I really blew this one. There is one more thing I am dying to know about. Do you always have bags of nails in your glove box? When did you put them there?"

"Of course, I keep bags of roofing nails in the glove box. Don't you?" Sandy said. "I grabbed them from the garage, over by the potting bench. I usually keep three or four handy"

"You mean," Paul asked, "you knew before we left?"

"Not knew. Suspected. But, hey, and this is a serious tip I have learned over the years. There is ALWAYS a good reason to keep paper bags of roofing nails in your glove box. And now you know why."

They both laughed.

"So, to close the loop on Lori," Sandy said, "I placed the magazines face up from the empty house and made sure they were in plain sight."

"That's right she grabbed one and curled it up like she was going to look at for bedtime reading!"

Sandy continued. "I heard her make the call around one in the morning, R2 and I were all ready to go anyway. Sorry I couldn't tell you sooner, but if she was any good, she knew your body language by now. I couldn't risk you hiding it from her and inadvertently tip her off."

"No, that's smart. I get it now." Paul shifted. "Since that part is done, let's talk about Mama. I spoke with her twice that week. Once the day you arrived, and again the day both of you went to the beach. That was the night before she was murdered."

"Did she talk about me?"

Paul grinned wide. "You're joking, right? You were all she talked about both times. I barely got a hello from her; she was focused on telling me about you. On the first call she mentioned a new client in Suite 18 and how easily she settled in. Said they had drugged you for the flight. She even went after the doctor from that flight. She was very angry about drugging you and the baby."

"Did she happen to say the doctor's name?"

"No, sorry," Paul said, then continued. "She kept going on about your cat. I assume that she was not talking about this Roger because he looks too young. Anyway, she was excited about you and your baby. She had another patient too, she never got around to her though she was too busy going on and on about you and that cat. You made her feel respected, welcomed. That doesn't happen often with Americans who come to the island. She also said she saw light in you."

"What does that mean?" Sandy asked.

"Mama just had good instincts. She could meet somebody and tell almost immediately if they were real or just playing a part. She never said it was some gift from God or anything like that. She'd just say, 'God gave me good sense, and I plan to use it.' As far as I know, she was never wrong about people. That's how I knew I could trust you. That's why I called you that night."

He paused, finding the memory. "The second time she called was after you went to the beach. She was excited, full of life. Not desperate, more like, I can't wait to see what God was going to do next. That's how she always was. Her glass was never just half full. It was overflowing. The only time I ever saw it close to empty was when Dad passed. But even then, she tried her best to shield me from that pain."

"What did she mean by 'can't wait to see what God does,' specifically, do you think?" Sandy asked.

"I think what she meant was that something good was coming. She called it 'beauty from pain.' When good things rise up from evil plans. She had funny ways of putting things together that a scholar or a child could both understand. She would joke that Satan makes Devils Food and God turns it into chocolate cake! She used to say that one all the time. And she had this way of using 'Joseph' like it was a verb. That night she said, 'Dem jet people trying to Joseph that sweet girl and that baby. Well, they going to see. Their cows going to bow down.' That part right there I remember clearly. The rest I might be paraphrasing, but that line stuck."

"Paul, your mom was the most amazing woman I have ever met."

"She was, for sure," Paul said warmly. "And she could spot a kindred spirit pretty easily."

Sandy took Paul through Caledonia, where she had lived as a young child before her parents passed. She showed him the house across the street, the one where three boys had grown up. She talked about how kind their parents were. The school building had been right behind their house, and she used to walk to school with her friends.

She was quick to clarify she was in foster care at ten, so this was the only version of childhood she remembered. She walked to and from school with the kids on her street, Tammy and her sister Lisa and Tracy and her sister Mindy. That was the most normal detail she could remember.

She cut through Marion and drove by the house she left on her eighteenth birthday also known to her as Freedom Day. Had she made a mistake bringing him here, opening up too quickly? No. If he was anything like Ruthy, he probably did not scare easily. It seemed that way already.

As Sandy's thoughts wandered, she wondered again what Ruthy had meant about the Joseph comment. She would look that up when she had time.

They took Route 4 out of Marion and headed toward a small donut shop on Main Street. Sandy was not sure it would still be there. Her mother and father used to take her when she was very young. When she saw the sign, she squealed. Still open.

The selection was small but she was just thrilled to see it was still in existence that she did not care. She talked the donuts up into legendary status remembering them as the best she had ever had. The shop was tiny, barely twelve feet from door to counter. The racks behind the counter were mostly empty, but the case still held donuts. The woman behind the counter looked older now, but Sandy knew it was her the moment she spoke.

She ordered half a dozen round chocolate-frosted vanilla cream-filled donuts, three round white-frosted vanilla creams, and three round white-frosted jelly-filled donuts. As the woman bagged them, Sandy smiled and repeated her father's old line. "And the jelly-filled, no white frosting, no sale."

The woman froze.

Sandy handed over a fifty-dollar bill and told her to keep the change. "These donuts and the memories they bring back are worth every penny."

Just before they reached the door, the woman spoke in the same broken English Sandy remembered from childhood.

"It was you," she said. "You come with your father. That was his joke."

"Yes," Sandy said. "It was."

"You stop coming. Why?"

"They both died. Mom and Dad."

The woman nodded. "So sad. Funny man. Same joke. Still make me laugh. I do not laugh much." She paused, then smiled. "I put extra jelly donut in bag. No white frosting."

She laughed, a full laugh this time.

Outside, Paul shook his head slow and happy. "You weren't kidding these donuts are amazing! They put way too much cream in these things. You can almost hear them pop when you bite them."

"That's what Dad used to say," Sandy replied.

They filled up the Explorer with gas and continued on to Timberbrook.

From the outside, the drive was uneventful. But in a few short hours they had learned more about each other than most people do in years. A bond formed between them, one that would serve them well heading into the future.

Like Ruthy said. Joseph. What man meant for evil, God will use for good.

33

An Uncomfortable Chair

JANUARY 3, 1992 – MANSFIELD, OH

Lori sat, or rather wriggled, in the wooden chair. She kept thinking about what she had said on the phone: *I am in the upstairs bedroom, so anyone on the ground floor is your target.* And she was as downstairs as it was possible to be. She was right smack dab in the middle of the entry room. She couldn't even speak, so she was at the mercy of whoever came in the door first. *How did they know? What gave me away?* Years of covert work down the drain.

She stopped twitching and rocking and watched as the four SUVs crept out of the road and slowly up the driveway to the house. *How were they doing that?* she wondered. The lights appeared to be dimming and brightening in a rhythm, though at a different pace, some on the left and some on the right. As the SUVs moved closer to the house, she could see they were all nursing at least one flat tire, and at least one of them, the front one of the group, appeared to have three flat tires.

After Sandy had thrown her bag of roofing nails, there were just too many to dodge. They couldn't really be seen in the low light of the moon, and it did not help that the SUVs had their lights off to avoid being seen. They had been trying to turn onto the road, which meant the roofing nails hit the tires at all kinds of angles, which made it easy to see how successful Sandy's plan had been.

The four SUVs lumbered up the driveway and converged on the house. All eight men poured out with pistols drawn and rail lights on. They avoided the front of the house because of all the windows and stormed in through the main side door where Lori had entered just the day before. They slowly opened the door after picking the lock. They all knew there was probably no one left, but they approached methodically. In this business, if you get sloppy or let your guard down, you end up dead.

When at least two agents had breached the room, they began swinging their pistols with the rail lights side to side around the main room. It did not take long for the lights to sweep across Lori's taped-up and panicked face. The white light across her ginger hair and pale complexion made for an unflattering scene. As the rest of the agents entered the room, the first agent, code-named Simeon, started stripping the tape from Lori's face. He tugged hard and managed to peel it off with difficulty. Lori screamed, but she was still tied with her hands behind her back. He told her to shut up, then moved on to sweep the rest of the house with the other members of the team.

"I know you're not Sandy, because I have met her before, and you are not even close. If I find out you betrayed us or set us up, I'll put a bullet between your eyes myself."

It was about 5:30 a.m., and in that part of the world, farmers would already be heading to the fields. The neighbor on the other side of the woods had a kitchen light on and was probably finishing his breakfast and coffee. The other agents had all the tires off the SUVs and had them propped up on jack stands and whatever else they could find in the large brown barn.

A tire truck from Bob's Mobile Tire Service came down the driveway and began putting on the new tires it had brought, already mounted on the correct rims. On the front of the box truck was a long magnetic bar that stretched the width of the vehicle. The driver lowered it to just inches off the pavement and within minutes had picked up the loose nails from the street before ruining his own tires pulling into the driveway.

Twenty minutes later, the house was back in order. The nails were removed from the magnet, bagged, and thrown into the back of one of the SUVs for safekeeping. Lori was escorted into the front SUV, and all the shredded old tires were loaded back onto Bob's truck. They pulled out of the driveway in succession and turned right to avoid the neighbor who was already up and moving around. At the next four-way intersection they split, then the remaining vehicles did the same at the next four way, returning to the freeway at different times and different ramps.

They were heading back to Columbus. Someone was going to have to brief Miss Veil.

Simeon and Benjamin shared the same vehicle on the way back. They had shuffled vehicle partners to keep the commiseration of failure to a minimum. Benjamin finally broke the silence.

"Back there you said to that other agent you had met Sandy before. You must know my new partner and instructor Issachar then?"

Simeon smiled. "Well, there's a name I have not heard in a long time. You and Issachar, huh? He is one of the best. Yes, we were together on her official record, but we were on two different teams. He was transportation and delivery that day. I was on the confirmation team. But I have known Issachar a long time. You have the best mentor you could have."

Simeon turned toward Benjamin so he could see his face. "Rumor has it he will replace General Strand, and he is the kid's favorite. That's the one you want to impress. Miss Veil is important, but that kid, he is the real deal. Don't screw it up and you are on the gravy train to the top."

"Oh, I won't," Benjamin said. "I know a good deal when I see it."

But he thought, *Everyone has a closet and something to hide in it. Why wait for him to get out of the way and lead you to the top when you can just push him off and climb right up?*

34

Opposition Strategy

JANUARY 4, 1992 – COLUMBUS, OHIO

Sandy and Paul finally arrived at her place on Timberbrook Lane. They had spent hours talking on the back roads, with Sandy filling the time by reminiscing. Both felt as if they knew each other better than anyone else in their lives, yet they were cautious. They had only met days earlier, and adrenaline has a way of confusing intimacy with certainty.

They knew each other now, but did they know the whole person or just the road trip version? And how did two loners get past that?

What they both knew was simple. They were in danger. They had been through a stressful few days, and neither knew what should come next.

Sandy asked, "What's your plan for tonight? Do you have a car back in Columbus we need to go and get?"

"No plan and no car. What a loser, huh," he said, half joking and half self-deprecating.

To his surprise and brief disappointment, Sandy said, "Yeah, what a loser. Picks a crazy girlfriend who tries to kill us, then turns out to be an articulate guy with plenty of options. What a loser."

She smiled. He laughed. If that did not break the tension, the faint yowl from the sleepy Siamese put an exclamation point on it.

Sandy said, "Look, Paul, we both know something bigger than us is going on right now, and we need to figure it out if we want a chance like Greg and Melanie. Why don't you stay the night, on the couch of course, and we can take the evening and tomorrow to figure out our next steps. It sounds like we need to find you a reliable, inconspicuous car for a start."

"I don't have any money," Paul said. "What I managed to save was in my apartment, and even if it's still there, I shouldn't risk going back."

"Don't worry about that," Sandy said. "I have money. Greg's people have paid for everything, so I've been putting my paychecks away. It will be deliciously ironic to buy you a car with their money."

Paul started to object, but Sandy cut him off. "Let's go get one now. There are a bunch of dealers up on West Broad Street. If we keep it in the five-to-eight-thousand-dollar range, it won't raise eyebrows. If things turn fast, you need transportation."

She was already grabbing her keys.

Back in the Explorer and heading toward Broad Street, Sandy said, "Remind me to pick up chicken before we head home if this doesn't take too long. What kind of car are we looking for?"

"I've never owned one," Paul said, sounding stressed. "Maybe a conversion van. That way I can stay mobile, use campgrounds and stuff."

"That's a good idea," Sandy said. "I might go that route someday if we don't get this figured out."

They stopped at Bobb Chevrolet and stepped out to look at vans. It took all of one minute for a salesman to stomp out his cigarette and walk over. "Looking at vans? I can show you the best deals on the lot."

Paul was about to send him away, but Sandy jumped in. "John, Mom sent us to get you a van today. She has the money, and if you take too long, she'll change her mind. Let's at least look."

She turned to the salesman. "What's your name, cutey?"

Clearly flustered, he said, "Bob. For real Bob, not the Bobb from the commercials. No relation. I just work here."

That enthusiasm made him easy to work with. He showed them three vans, and they both liked one. A 1974 Econoline conversion with a fold-down bench-bed combo, a mini fridge, and a recliner in back. Thick shag carpet sealed the deal.

The price started at sixty-five hundred. Sandy flirted it down to fifty-five. She put two thousand down in cash and left a check for the rest. By six-thirty, Paul was following his "sister's" Explorer toward Sisters Chicken and Biscuits.

Back at Timberbrook, Sandy and Paul ate their Spicy Chicken, but R2 preferred the original. The cat ate tuna instead and expressed his displeasure through tail flicks and pointed looks. Paul understood the message clearly.

With dinner finished, they talked about what came next.

Paul settled onto the couch. Sandy sat in the chair. Silence stretched between them before Paul finally spoke. They needed answers before they could act. Running without figuring the bigger picture out would only delay the inevitable. Sandy of course agreed and was not willing to stop until she had found her son.

They agreed to split up. To gather information. To communicate quietly.

By the time they said good night, exhaustion had settled in. Sandy went to her room with R2. Paul lay on the couch, one ear open.

Lights out.

"SVI to base"

"Go ahead for base"

"Lights out. All is quiet"

"Copy that SV1"

"SVI remains on alert"

35

Divide and Conquer

JANUARY 7, 1992 – COLUMBUS, OH

The next morning, Sandy woke to the smell of breakfast. It was only 6:00 a.m., and they had talked well past midnight.

Why was Paul cooking so early?

She got out of bed, freshened up, and slipped on jeans, a colorful striped sweater, socks, and shoes. She never felt dressed without them, especially around Paul. Feeling undressed made her nervous.

In the kitchen she saw biscuits, sausage, and bacon, leftovers from Lori's feast the day before. Had it only been a day? So much had happened. She stored the leftovers in the back of the Explorer, where the cold kept them fresh.

"Good morning," he said as he scrambled some eggs. "Sorry for the early breakfast. I was wide awake by 5:45. I remembered you grabbed Lori's leftovers, so here we are. Let's eat."

Sandy smiled warmly, then caught herself.

Don't give him that look. You are about to split up. Friendly, not flirty, Mister Right scolded.

She adjusted her expression to something more buddy-like and poured some coffee. The aroma alone would have drawn her out. The food was a bonus.

On the table sat four Dixie Cream Donuts.

"Wow, we ate eight of those yesterday?" Sandy asked.

"Maybe seven," Paul said. "I might have eaten one while sleepwalking at 5:50 this morning. Probably over the sink. But the even number makes them easier to split right."

"We agreed not to talk about that," Sandy cut in.

Paul's quirky grin returned. "I just meant it evens shared custody of the remaining donuts. What did you think?"

Sandy glared, making him laugh.

They ate the leftovers and eggs, leaving two donuts: a chocolate iced vanilla cream and a white frosted jelly.

"I'll flip a coin for our donut custody battle," Sandy said.

"I'll take jelly-filled, but no white frosting. No deal otherwise," Paul replied.

They put the donuts in separate lunch bags and cleaned up. Paul went to shower. His only clothes needed washing, so Sandy said she would try to get the smell out and toss them in the dryer.

She walked to the kitchen window on impulse. After all the time she spent eluding and running, she developed a sixth sense, what she sometimes called her sixteenth sense. No one was out there. All was quiet on Timberbrook but she knew things could get loud fast.

Paul took a long shower. Sandy washed his shirt by hand and hung it damp on the bathroom doorknob.

She called through the door, "Paul, your shirt is on the doorknob."

A few minutes later, Paul emerged, smelling better. As he entered the kitchen, he was already talking.

"Sorry, I used your deodorant, strong enough for a man, but made for a woman. I also found a toothbrush and toothpaste. I hope that was okay. My mouth was rough."

He rounded the corner and stopped. Confusion covered his face.

Sandy had retrieved a heavy lockbox from under a loose panel in her closet. She unpacked the contents onto the kitchen table and closed the curtains.

On the table lay twelve boxes of nine-millimeter hollow points, a Beretta 92, a Sig Sauer 9mm, and three extra loaded magazines. R2 saw the guns come out and ran under the coffee table, making a sound combining fear, dread, and confusion. The original Roger would have laid down on a pile of cash and laid his head on the pistol while taking a nap. R2 was not quite there yet.

Next to the guns was cash. Stacks of well-worn twenty-dollar bills in neat bundles, each with a bank strap indicating two thousand dollars. She divided the stacks into two equal piles. Paul guessed the total at well over one hundred fifty thousand dollars.

"What is all this?" he asked.

Sandy spoke slowly, her voice steady but weighted.

"This is my life savings. Seeded by the money earned that day back in 1979, by my decision to give up my son. The same decision that took me to Saint Croix. I have saved almost every cent I have earned since my return. I exchanged larger bills from the bank and cashed checks with smaller, older twenties from the cash room at work."

She paused.

"The irony was not lost on me. My life savings is now meant to save the life of my son, to buy his freedom from the bondage I put him in."

She swallowed.

"To this day, I cannot hear a bell without thinking of that moment. I wish I could take it back."

Paul said nothing.

"I want us to use this money against them. I never spent it on things. I had all I needed, thanks to Greg. I did not save in a 401(k) or pay for health insurance. I maximized every paycheck."

As she spoke, the doorbell rang.

The sound of the bell and the timing, as she thought of her son, hit Sandy hard. Paul saw it instantly. Her body wilted, then stiffened as the echo faded. The Sandy he knew returned.

It was only 8:30 a.m. Sandy rarely had visitors.

Paul checked the peephole and whispered, "It's a Girl Scout selling cookies. Do you know any kids around here?"

"No," Sandy said, but she opened the door.

A girl about eight stood back from the porch in a winter coat too big for her. Her sash crossed the coat. A canvas bag with the Girl Scout logo hung from her shoulder, heavy with boxes.

Sandy felt a flicker of normalcy.

"Hi there," she said. "What's in the bag?"

The girl stepped forward and opened it, revealing a brown clasp envelope marked Sandy Foster. A station wagon idled at the curb, likely her mother waiting.

Sandy bought two boxes, shortbread and peanut butter sandwich, slipping the envelope between them.

"Thanks for stopping by," she said. "Good luck."

Inside, Sandy locked the door and watched until the car pulled away. As she reached for the envelope, the phone rang. Paul handed it to her.

"Hello."

"Sandy, it's Greg. Did you get my envelope?"

"Just got it. Haven't opened it yet."

"No need. It's like before, minus the car keys. Listen carefully. Time is short. You did not call the store manager Alice at work yesterday, did you?"

"I forgot," Sandy admitted.

"My little firewall for you has apparently been compromised. I assume it has to do with the people surrounding Paul. When you didn't call, Alice called it in to someone else. I was not aware Alice was compromised or at least compensated. I am really sorry. Anyway, whoever she called has strings on my boss, General Strand, who runs Enclave. Alice came by your house and knocked yesterday afternoon. Earl called me to bring you in and take Paul out. Apparently, no one wants you and Paul to trade notes. You two need to split up now. The longer you stay together, the more danger you are both going to be in."

Greg gave instructions. New paperwork. A lease at the LeVeque Tower. New IDs. No banks. Melanie's address for Paul. A note to be left on the counter, make it out to your brother, exact words. Be gone in thirty minutes.

The line went dead.

Sandy relayed everything quickly. Then she turned back to the table.

"Paul, I don't have time to explain all of this with any more detail."

She went to the entry closet and pulled out two large travel bags. She tossed a black one to Paul.

"Take half the cash and the Beretta with its three loaded mags. Add six boxes of ammo. Grab food and anything else you think we need."

Paul started to object, then stopped.

They packed. Sandy coaxed R2 out. Paul loaded the bags into the vehicles. Sandy finished the note and left it on the table.

They stood facing each other in the garage. Fear and sadness held them both. They might never see each other again.

"I don't even know how we will find each other or communicate," Sandy said.

"I know what Mom would have said to us," Paul replied, smiling faintly. "Why you gwon ti worry when de Lord got you in His hand tight-tight? He ain't a gonna forget ya, no."

They both managed a smile. Neither could laugh.

Sandy kissed Paul's cheek. "Don't you dare get killed, Mister. I have plans for us."

There was no embrace. Neither could have let go.

Engines started. The garage door lifted. They left.

Five minutes later, Sandy was on I-70 toward downtown. Paul took I-270 to Dublin.

Twelve minutes later, a black SUV pulled into the empty garage. Greg, also called Issachar, and his trainee Benjamin stepped out with guns drawn.

The house was quiet in the way only a recently vacated place can be.

In the kitchen, Benjamin called out, "Sir, there's a note here for her brother."

Issachar read the note, unaware an almost imperceptible smile formed.

Word for word. That's my girl, he thought.

Benjamin watched him closely. Something felt off. Then he noticed the smile.

Issachar's answers were too quick, too rehearsed. As a propagated male, Benjamin leaned alpha. He wanted to rise fast. Finding a weakness in Issachar's armor would get him there sooner.

Maybe this woman was the weakness.

36

POV 2: The Black Snake

SEPTEMBER 1998 – COLUMBUS, OH

Two men in a black Suburban sat in the McDonald's lot across from Taco Bell, eyes locked on Sandy's Lexus.

"There she is."

The driver slid in three cars back, hiding behind a smoking Dodge Caravan. The passenger keyed the mic.

"Chariot 1 to Pharaoh, over."

"Pharaoh, Chariot 1. Go."

"Eastbound Broad. She made us the second we rolled. How hard do we push? Over."

"Maintain distance. Don't let her smell the trap. She's smart. If she bolts, we're done. Chariot 1 out."

The driver rolled his eyes. Issachar acted like this girl was Houdini.

"Third tail you've ever run, right?" the passenger smirked.

"Shut up."

Pretense dropped. Neither agent liked each other very much, so both agents were ready to end this.

Then brake lights. Traffic locked solid at the Broad Street Bridge.

"Chariot 1 to Pharaoh."

"Go."

"Full stop. Moving in on foot to eliminate."

"Negative. Stick to plan. Your face hits a traffic cam at six o'clock, you're dead before payday."

Greg knew the gamble. He couldn't warn Sandy. Nobody else on the five-man team knew this was staged.

He made a call.

A man answered immediately. "Yes."

"She's boxed in. Two trigger-happy rogues on her tail. Need her in the alley. No way to signal her it's staged. Ideas?"

"I'll send marked units to clear the jam. A couple uniforms on foot will rattle your boys. Mother will figure the rest out. She always does."

Click.

Across town, Gabriel's most trusted advisor, Harold, knocked while opening the door and walking in. The timing was poor. The door was fully opened as Greg's receiver had hit the cradle with a thud. Greg's face still twisted with strain. Harold frowned and left Greg in silence.

Back on Broad, the two rogues lost patience. Radios off. Out of the truck. Hands in jacket pockets on their sidearms, threading between cars.

Then an engine screamed. Cars jerked left and right. Metal scraped.

They pushed forward until her SUV crawled straight up the middle.

"Forget it," the radio man said. "Back to the truck before Issachar finds out."

"Only way he finds out is if you open your mouth."

They waited for the chaos to settle. They knew where she was headed. The LeVeque. She would never leave the cat.

"Pharaoh to Chariot 1."

"Where have you been?"

"Power cord came loose."

"Good cover," the driver whispered.

"Subject beats us to LeVeque. She'll be on foot. Need a blocker at Pearl to turn her into the alley."

"Copy."

Greg exhaled. His contact had delivered.

"Walker, reposition across Broad. Step into the crosswalk so she sees you. Turn her into the alley."

"Affirm."

At the LeVeque, the Suburban screeched to the curb, hazards flashing. The two rogues bolted inside just in time to see elevator doors closing on Sandy.

"Gun!"

The lobby erupted. Fingers pointed straight at them.

The agents piled into the other elevator car.

"Get off at five. Work the stairs down. No way she's still going for the cat."

They sprinted down the stairwell. On the final landing, the radio man tried to leap the last four steps. He landed on roofing nails.

He screamed as the short, thick nails punched through his shoes. His partner stepped around him.

"Move!"

One walked into the alley. One limped.

Just in time to see Sandy dive behind the dumpster.

Greg and Paul waited in the second SUV, watching her bury herself beneath garbage bags. Greg heard the faint prayer, pressed a finger to his lips, and let her finish.

Five men closed in.

Greg hauled her out, sold the rage for the audience, and fed her the coded lines only she would catch.

The needle slid home.

37

Fixing the Sink

JANUARY 8, 1992 – DELAWARE COUNTY, OHIO

Paul drove to the address Melanie and Greg had left for Sandy the night they visited. He liked his new used van. The ride was smooth, the heater worked great, but it still had temporary plates, and he had forgotten to ask Sandy about the magnetic plates she had reminded him were critical.

Pulling up to the gate, he double-checked the address. Satisfied he had come to the right place, he eased forward, looking for a call button. He noticed the red light of a camera mounted high in a tree. It blinked once, then the gate began to open. He drove through cautiously, still getting used to the high torque of the van's rear wheels.

The long driveway was flanked by tall trees. At the clearing's edge, the house came into view, an elegant structure of glass and steel set precisely within the wooded acreage. Before he could park, the attached garage door opened. A woman, presumably Melanie, wearing her white winter coat stood inside, waving him in urgently.

Paul pulled the van into the garage and shut off the engine. She greeted him politely but with more caution than he expected.

"Hello," she said. "I am Doctor Mills. Are you the plumber here to fix the sink?"

Paul blinked. Dr. Mills? Where was Melanie?

He stepped out of the van and immediately registered his mistake. No gun. He had never met Melanie in person, and he was standing in a stranger's garage unarmed. His hand went instinctively to his hip just under his coat and found nothing. *Brilliant, Paul*, he thought. *Next time, keep the piece on you*. He forced his expression into neutral and leaned into the only option he had.

"Yes, the sink. Your part-time secretary, Sally, I tink she call and set it up, but I didn't write it all down proper, eh. My partner Gary, he gone out for the parts already. He say you got a Kohler faucet installed, but we gon' have to switch you to a similar Moen model. Kohler don't make replacement parts for that style no more, you hear? Hope that sit all right with you, Doctor Mills. Gary should reach here shortly. That accurate?"

She studied him for another long second.

Then her posture softened. "Are you Paul?" she whispered.

He nodded.

"You'd feel better if I showed you my plumber license, eh?"

She almost smiled. "A single gal can never be too careful." Paul handed her a business card from his radio show. She glanced out and said with finality, "That license will suffice. Now get moving. That kitchen sink isn't going to fix itself."

They crossed into the house together. She turned on the television, raising the volume just enough for background noise.

"I'm going to watch *The Guiding Light* while you fix it," she said sharply, fully back in character. "Don't bother me."

Paul noticed the faucet had already been partially disassembled. Then she stepped out the back door.

At the pond, her voice changed completely.

"Thank you for playing along. Sorry. Greg and I aren't convinced the house isn't bugged. Let's go out back by the pond where we can talk. It won't take long. We don't live here together, of course. That's a conversation for another time."

"Why the garage?" Paul asked.

"Because of my position with LIFE, they keep close tabs on me. They're building a new headquarters along the river. EPS is providing site security. Nothing elite, but enough. Helicopters pass through often. They buzz my house regularly. Listen to me. I don't even really know who 'they' are anymore."

"Did you say construction site on the River Road? Outside Dublin?"

"Yes. Why?"

"We stopped there the other night while heading north. R2 needed a break from the road. I wonder if that put eyes on us."

Melanie considered it. "Possibly. Though it's more likely routine cameras protecting materials. Still." She paused. "I'll listen more closely going forward. That kind of coincidence is worth noting."

She shifted. "Greg wants you to look into several loose ends. You have a reputation for curiosity."

"That's fair," Paul said warmly.

"I'm a doctor, not a detective," she said. "But I'm learning."

Paul smiled. "Before we get into all that, lemme tell you what Sandy and I have worked out already, so we stay aligned. No sense doubling up the work."

He walked her through it. He was heading to Marion then Caledonia where she was born. He was going to work on her genealogy. Library records. Family deaths. Patterns.

Melanie listened carefully. "That matches our thinking," she said. "But there's one thing you left out."

"What's that?"

"Stay safe." She smiled faintly. "Your appearance may well stand out in a small village like Caledonia. You will need a solid cover story."

Already thought about that. Paul grinned. "I been workin' on that sweet-sweet, don't worry." He handed her his "Know-It-All Paul" business cards like the one he showed her earlier as his plumber's license back in the garage. "Look what it says down at the bottom."

"I'ma mystery chasin mad mon." People like my thicker accent and they tend to get cooperative and more friendly if they think they might end up on a radio show.

"I think you'll manage," she said. "Based on what I just witnessed in my garage, I think you'll manage just fine."

They sat quietly for a moment by the water, the kind of comfortable silence that only forms between people who understand each other without needing to fill the space.

Melanie looked at the pond. She said nothing for a moment.

They went back inside as the television announced a dramatic medical cliffhanger.

Melanie resumed Dr. Mills without hesitation. "Is that sink fixed yet?"

"Yes, ma'am. Gary should be here any minute with the new parts. Nice-nice Moen faucet, good as new."

She handed him a clasp envelope marked with his name, finger to her lips. "Do not scuff my floors."

In the garage, she retrieved a black zippered bag from a tool chest and handed it to him. "A gift for you and Sandy from Greg and me. We hope it helps."

Then she hugged him once and turned away.

A helicopter thundered overhead and began descending. Paul jumped into the van as Melanie hit the button for the garage door and the gate. He was gone before the skids touched down.

Minutes later, Miss Veil stepped out of the helicopter.

"You have a beautiful home," she said, scanning the space with eyes that missed nothing.

"Thank you," Dr. Mills replied evenly.

Miss Veil's gaze landed on the half-installed faucet. "Oh good, I'm so glad to see you're getting that sink fixed. How tedious. Tradesmen can be so unreliable. Always coming up with excuses to sell you a new brand when the old parts would do perfectly well."

"Yes," Melanie said carefully. "What else can we do? I don't recall telling you my sink was broken?"

"Well," Miss Veil said, smiling thinly, "Hmm really? Lucky guess I suppose. Oh, did I tell you the wonderful news, darling? I'll be living just down the road once the new headquarters is finished. We'll be practically next-door neighbors. Well at least when you consider how quickly the helicopter can get here from there. So, if you ever need a cup of sugar or anything just give me a ring."

Melanie said nothing.

Miss Veil smiled wider. "Isn't that fantastic? Well, I must be going. Lovely to see you, darling. So glad you got that sink fixed. Tah." Smiling as she headed back out the glass door to the waiting helicopter and within seconds of the door closing on the black copter they were in the air and gone.

Melanie stood stunned for a minute. *Well at least we know for sure this house is bugged*, she thought as she closed the back door that Susan had left wide open.

38

Moving on Up

JANUARY 8, 1992 – COLUMBUS, OH

Sandy did not take long to reach the LeVeque Tower. Stepping into the lobby, she stopped cold. The marble floors, brass fixtures, and vaulted ceiling looked back at her without apology.

Greg, is this a joke? This is far too fancy for me.

She approached the counter with only her envelope and a cranky R2. He had slept through most of the day's excitement and was displeased about being hastily placed in his carrier. He shot Sandy a look that seemed to say, there is always time for manners. He yowled and complained during the entire ride, but upon reaching the lobby he adopted a cool, sophisticated demeanor, as if he had always belonged here.

Sandy pulled her new driver's license, checkbook, and pen from the envelope. "Good afternoon," she said. "I am Sandra. My lawyer told me he arranged an apartment here for me."

The young man behind the counter was immediately attentive. "Oh yes, Miss Simmons. I have the lease right here. You will not need your checkbook. The rent is paid in full for the year. Your attorney took care of it. I just need your signature, a copy of your license, and the make, model, and license plate of your car for the parking lot. Your assigned parking spot is 25A on the twenty fifth floor, left when you exit the elevator."

Sandy signed the lease, carefully writing Sandy Simmons. She had not had the time or the inclination to change her name again. She handed over her driver's license. After he finished copying it, she asked for a rolling cart to carry her few belongings upstairs.

"Oh no, ma'am," the young man said. "My name is James, and I will take your stuff up for you."

"Thanks, James, but we do not know each other well enough. You might drop my suitcase and see my unmentionables, and then I would have to ask your boss to fire you to avoid the daily embarrassment that would cause me."

James blushed deeply and, struggling to respond, handed her the key cards while mumbling a reminder about the twenty fifth floor.

Sandy went up with R2 first to check out the apartment and let him out of his carrier. They entered the ornate brass door elevator across from the check in desk, and she pressed the button for the twenty fifth floor. While riding up she decided to store her new credentials and stick with the old ones. She was checked in as Sandy Simmons, but she would not change her last name again. She would remain Sandy Simmons and keep the other name and ID hidden for an emergency.

The elevator's bell dinged as the doors closed.

Within a split-second Sandy was back in the exam room, listening to Melanie explain her options before the timer went off. What would life have been like if she had simply said no thank you? Would she have been allowed to walk away alive? Where was her baby boy? Some of those people were now her friends. Others she would never see again. Ruthy's words returned quietly. What man meant for evil, God uses for good.

The elevator's second bell rang, snapping her back to the present.

Carrying R2's carrier, Sandy turned left from the elevator and quickly reached the door marked 25A. She unlocked it and stepped inside. The apartment was the nicest place she had ever been, surpassed only by Suite 18 on the island. A long foyer with a coat closet on the right opened into a spacious furnished living room with floor to ceiling glass windows and a deep metal ledge, perfect for plants or the occasional cat nap.

Sandy set the carrier down, and before she could unlatch it, R2 yowled loudly.

"Come on, buddy, let us check out the view together," she said, opening the door.

R2 leapt softly from the floor to the ledge in one fluid motion. The view was breathtaking. The Scioto River and its bridges spread out below. Sandy scratched his head as he purred, watching him settle from sitting to lying down, gazing at the world below. He looked like an Egyptian cat surveying the city from a palace.

"Make yourself at home," she said. "I will go get our stuff."

Sandy rode the elegant elevator down to the parking garage, moved her Explorer to her assigned spot, and grabbed a porter cart from the lobby. She loaded it with her few belongings, making sure her lockbox with cash, Sig, and ammo was covered. Back on the twenty fifth floor she unloaded everything into the master bedroom, set up R2's litter box in a discreet corner of the living room, and returned the empty cart to the lobby.

James spotted her from across the room and waved.

Sandy approached him. "Hey, Jimmy, right?" she said with a slight lilt. "Do me a favor, please."

"Sure," Jimmy replied, a bit too eagerly.

"My ex-boyfriend is a bit of a stalker. He is handsome, not as handsome as you, of course. But he might come looking for my apartment number. Can you let me know if anyone like that stops by? Sometimes he has a creepy pal with him to intimidate me." She flashed a warm smile.

Jimmy perked up. "Sure thing, Miss Simmons. Anytime you need ol' Jimmy, just let me know."

"Thanks, sweetie, oh, I mean Jimmy," she said playfully.

As she crossed the lobby to the elevator, Jimmy watched her like a smitten puppy.

First layer of the alarm system: set.

Back on the twenty fifth floor, she found R2 fast asleep on the ledge. She set out his tuna and fresh water. He kept sleeping, so she grabbed some beef jerky and her last Dixie Cream, the vanilla cream filled one from the morning's lottery. Her thoughts drifted to Paul, wondering how he was doing.

A strange chirping sound came from the master bedroom. Investigating, Sandy found a telephone receiver in a bag inside the nightstand drawer, ringing with an unusual electronic tone. Disguising her voice, she answered.

"Hello?"

"Sandy, it is Paul!"

Sandy, unfamiliar with cellular phones, pulled the bag out and set the phone on the metal ledge by the bedroom's glass wall. She dragged a chair over, sat down, and gazed out the window. They talked for nearly an hour, catching up on Paul's visit with Melanie and Sandy's new apartment. She wished he could see the view.

As the battery light blinked, Paul said, "Man, this is better than coded messages in the newspaper. This way I can hear your voice and stay safely connected. Still, let us keep that option open just in case something happens with the phones. Truth is, I do not even know how to pay the bill on this thing."

"I am pretty sure Greg has it covered, but I will ask," Sandy replied. "I wish we did not have to cut this off, but my battery is blinking."

"Mine too," Paul said warmly. "I am up in Marion, staying at the Harding Motor Lodge. I am going to order something to eat and call it a night. I will keep in touch, but if you need anything just call."

"Paul?"

"Yeah?"

"I miss you," she said softly.

"I miss you too, Sandy. Sweet dreams."

They hung up, each plugging their phone in to charge.

Paul used the motel's house phone to order a burger, fries, a piece of apple pie, and a Coke Classic. A kid dressed in jeans, a T shirt, and an ugly dark brown Harding Motor Lodge blazer delivered the food. Paul tipped him three dollars, closed the door, and ate while flipping through the phone book.

He located the library, spread his maps across the bed, and studied the route to Caledonia.

After looking at the maps, Paul decided to gather his thoughts and make a list of questions that needed to be answered and any answers he already had that needed the right question applied.

He grabbed the desk stationery provided with the room and a pen. The first pen would not write. Paul tossed it in the trash. The second pen worked, so Paul began his notes. Who exactly is chasing them? There are plenty of people on the island who know about the plane visits and babies. Why is that allowed to continue? The most compelling question was a compound question. Where does the money come from for the purchase of the babies and the considerable medical and travel expenses? How do you raise them, educate them, and provide food and shelter for all those kids over the years without blowing your cover? Answer, you either have to have large facilities hidden in remote areas with large groups of caretakers, or you could break them into smaller groups and place them into almost family like units in places where no one would notice or care to investigate. Places like small towns. Maybe there is more than one answer to these questions. Maybe they use the power of and instead of the limitations of or.

Paul set his list and maps in the drawer of the nightstand and fell quickly asleep.

39

Origins: Grains of Sand

1945 TO PRESENT – SUSAN VEIL'S PLAN

Caledonia, Ohio, never drew a crowd. It sat quiet along State Route 309, a village of seven hundred souls who farmed the land or drove to Marion or Mansfield to punch a clock in the factories. A high school that graduated "Donians," a single-pump gas station, and a green grocer who knew everyone's business. Nothing flashy. Nothing loud. Exactly the kind of place the Foundation liked to disappear into.

By April of 1950, the Addison-Foster Foundation had already marked Caledonia, specifically the pockets of rural Marion County, as one of its first settlement zones. Not the village proper (too many eyes, too much gossip) but the edges: Mud Pike, Rural Route 746, and all the back roads named for the family farms that dominated the maps. The farm lots no one paid attention to. The places where a new house could go up and no one would ask who lived there or why.

Sandy would never know any of this growing up. To her, Caledonia was simply home, the only home she had ever known. She didn't realize that many of the kids she saw at the grocery store or at the annual Farmers Festival could have been Unwanteds, children folded quietly into the Foundation's care long before she was born. She didn't know she had been orbiting them her entire life.

It started in 1940, when the first Unwanteds were placed just outside town. Quiet transfers from hospitals and orphanages. Babies no one claimed. Babies no one missed. By 1941, out-of-wedlock births were rising across the country, and the Foundation saw opportunity in the chaos of wartime America. By the time the war ended, the system was already humming.

Then came the projections. The Baby Boom. Ten years of explosive growth. Ten years of children the world wasn't prepared to raise. The Foundation took advantage of all of them.

By 1955, the plan was in full swing. Newborns and toddlers arrived through discreet channels: hospital back doors, orphanage ledgers, sympathetic nurses who knew how to look the other way. Older Unwanteds, now teenagers, were paired according to the A-FF rules and given the smaller ones to raise. It wasn't charity. It was structure. It was the beginning of the family-cell model.

When abortion became legal, the Foundation's reach accelerated. Nearly 1.7 million Unwanteds were already embedded across America, hidden in plain sight in rural Montana and Wyoming, tucked into cul-de-sacs in Indiana and Kansas, living in small towns and farming communities from the Appalachians to the plains. Not whole towns (that would be too difficult). Just pockets. Sections. Neighborhoods. Dead-end roads all across the country. Enough to blend. Enough to grow.

Miss Veil's original formula was simple and ruthless. Children from birth to age three were raised by older children, with a handful of sympathetic adults overseeing the process. Once the older kids were old enough to raise the younger ones, the system became self-sustaining. The adult supporters were quietly retired. Where they went, no one ever said.

Caledonia was just one node in a vast network. But for Sandy, it was the center of the universe. The place where the lie was built.

The Foundation provided the education materials for the small private schools and the homeschool clusters that sprouted around Caledonia. Nothing flashy, just binders, lesson plans, and workbooks that looked like any other mid-century curriculum. But the message threaded through every page was unmistakable:

"You were unwanted by your parents. But we, the Foundation, love you. We saved you from their indifference. And we will raise you to help us build a new world from the inside out."

Most of the kids never questioned it. Why would they? It was all they had ever known. And for the ones who did wonder, the Foundation had an answer ready before the question even formed. This was the purpose of LIFE and Enclave. They unknowingly hid what lay beneath.

40

Mister Didn't

JANUARY 9, 1992 – MARION, OH

Paul woke to pounding on the thick metal door of his room at the Harding Motor Lodge.

"Sir, open up! Marion County Sheriff's Office. We need to ask you a few questions."

Before Paul could respond, the officer pounded again.

"Okay, okay!" Paul called; voice groggy. "You wake me up, mon. Gimme a sec to grab a shirt."

He snatched his shirt from the bathroom curtain rod and crossed the motel room to the door. Leaving the chain lock in place, he peered through the gap, confirming two sheriff's deputies outside. Paul slid the chain off and opened the door.

Paul, a tall, dark-skinned man in his early thirties, wasn't an athlete, but his natural good looks and healthy lifestyle gave him an athletic air. Leaning against the door frame, one arm propped at the top, he watched the closer deputy step back, betraying unease. The officers expected a meek, frightened man roused in a strange town. Their early-morning pounding hadn't intimidated him.

"Mornin', Sheriff. Mornin', Deputy," Paul said brightly, nodding at each like a cowboy in the Old West. "I'd say, 'What warrants the pleasure of this welcome?' but I ain't too fond of the word *warrant* when it comes to officers of the law, eh. Either way, that Mike Tyson punch you threw at my door say this is urgent-urgent. So, how can I help you fellas out?"

Paul steadied himself. Chasing fringe news stories as a grassroots journalist required confidence, tenacity, and a knack for bluffing. Lori's betrayal as a planted agent had thrown him, but Sandy's strength had grounded him. She had been in this mess longer, her control forcing Paul to find his footing right here in this doorway.

"Mister, what did you say your name was?" the sheriff asked.

"I didn't," Paul replied coolly.

"Well, Mister Didn't," the sheriff said with a smirk, "there were car break-ins last night. Your van's back door makes me think you should be more helpful."

The deputy chuckled.

Paul lowered his arms and stepped toward the van. The deputy flinched, mistaking it for aggression. Paul ignored him, inspecting the open back doors. No damage, nothing missing. He had taken the valuables inside last night, including the cash.

"No damage. Nothin' gone," Paul said, leaning close to the latch. "How they get in, eh?"

"That's why we're here," the sheriff said. "Twelve break-ins, eight of them right here in the Lodge parking lot. Yours was the only one not jimmied or smashed. Why's that?"

Paul leaned back against the van, easy and unhurried, filling the space without crowding it.

"So lemme get this straight, mon. You sayin' I leave the back of my van wide open all night, break into every car right next to mine, then go sleep in my room for maybe an hour waitin' for you to come poundin' on my door, then act all confused when you wake me up? That's the ting you workin' with?" He shook his head slow, almost smiling. "This is why people call small-town cops local yokels, eh. If I was breakin' in, I woulda jimmied my own lock to keep tings quiet. The suspicion you throwin' on me don't make a lick of sense, nice-nice officers."

"We considered that," the sheriff said. "This local yokel has questions that could help us both if you'd let me ask without the attitude."

Paul paused. He preferred a flies-with-honey approach, and the rude awakening had thrown his rhythm. Time to dial it back.

"Fair enough, fair enough," Paul said warmly. "What'd you say your name was, Sheriff? I guess I missed it somehow."

"I didn't," the sheriff shot back, grinning.

Paul laughed, full and genuine. "Eh-eh. Guess I earned that one, Sheriff Didn't."

They chuckled, and the tension eased.

"Your van's got paper tags, just purchased," the sheriff said. "Anyone else have a second key?"

"Good question, mon," Paul said. "I asked the dealer where my sister got it, and the sales manager told me they only had the one set."

"That's odd," the sheriff remarked.

"Didn't think much of it then," Paul said, thinking aloud. "But ain't a dealership supposed to have a key cutter? Why they ain't make another set, eh? Why give me one key and leave it at that?"

"My thoughts exactly," the sheriff said. "Could they have lied about the keys?"

Paul tilted his head, working it through slow-slow. "Why you ain't just give me two sets, make it look normal, avoid all this suspicion? And why break into other cars just to mask targeting my van? They could've been in and out clean-clean. So, the question ain't what they took. The question is why they came at all."

"Maybe they left something in the van," the sheriff said. "Or put something in."

The deputy scribbled notes, less nervous now.

Maybe I misjudged these yokels, Paul thought. *But their story's too neat. Those Slim Jim marks were too clean, like they staged the break-ins.*

"How they know to look here, though?" Paul said, more to himself than the officers. "I ain't tell nobody where I was goin'."

He popped the van's hood. Paul unlocked the driver's door and tossed the keys to the sheriff, who unlocked the passenger side. The deputy snapped photos. Paul checked under the driver's dash. The sheriff did the same on the passenger side.

"Look at this," the sheriff said.

Paul leaned over. A black box, chalkboard-eraser-sized, was screwed under the passenger dash, its red light glowing steady.

"That a tracker?" Paul asked.

"Like trucking companies use," the sheriff confirmed.

Paul straightened up, calm as anything. "Leave it be for now, mon. They might come back again. I need to understand why somebody trackin' me before I go pullin' tings out from under my own dash, you hear?"

"So do I," the sheriff said, a hint of suspicion threading back into his voice.

Paul wasn't fazed. A sharp cop would sense he was hiding something. This sheriff was sharp — maybe too sharp. Sharp enough to be playing a deeper game. Maybe for Enclave.

"So how we playin' this?" Paul asked easily. "You want me leavin' today or stayin'?"

"Let's start fresh," the sheriff said.

"Works for me, mon," Paul said. "Name's Paul Matthews. What about you?"

"Sheriff Bryan Clavell," he replied, shaking Paul's hand. "This is Deputy Scotty Froman, one of my best."

Paul shook Scotty's hand with a warm grip.

"I'm stayin' in Marion, but I was headin' to Caledonia today," Paul said. "It close-close, maybe thirty minutes. I'd be back by dinner easy. But I don't want no tail, eh. Any way to keep that tracker quiet for a bit so I can move free?"

He paused, then added, "Or, I could check the library right here in Marion today, since it's on my list anyway. We keep eyes on the van tonight, then I head to Caledonia tomorrow. No shadow this time around."

"That works," Bryan said. "Scotty'll watch from an unmarked car in the lot. But why all this trouble, Paul? What are you after in Marion?"

The sheriff's too sharp to bluff, but I can't spill everything. If he's with Enclave, like that dealership, I'm already in a bad spot.

"I'm a reporter out of Columbus," Paul said, easy and open. "Got a late-night radio show, Know-It-All Paul, AM 610. I dig into odd stories before I air 'em, makin' sure the source ain't full of smoke, y'know. Can't go on air with somethin' that ain't real-real solid."

Scotty's eyes went wide. "I knew your voice! I listen but don't call in. You cut your New Year's show short and haven't been back on."

Paul grinned wide. "Good to meet a listener, mon. I'm doin' some diggin' before I get back on the air. Plenty-plenty to look into."

"Not saying I'm a fan," Scotty said quickly. "But the show's real. Sheriff, I think he's okay. For now."

"Alright," Bryan said. "See you tonight. Have a good day."

"Will do, Sheriff Didn't," Paul said, pointing at him with a grin. "Real-real pleasure."

The deputies drove off. Paul got a new key from the front desk, where the delivery kid Danny smirked behind the counter. Inside his room, Paul checked his belongings and stepped into the shower.

Bryan teased Scotty as they headed toward the Marion County Jail.

"Wow. 'I'm a fan,'" he mocked. "Smart, nephew. He'll figure out we staged those break-ins to rattle him. We were supposed to spook him, learn what he knows, where he's going. Hard to stay hidden as a fanboy. Next time, keep quiet or you'll end up in a dumpster." He paused. "I'm not threatening. I'm saving your life. My sister would kill me if anything happened to you."

Fresh from the shower, Paul stood very still.

The sheriff and deputy staged those break-ins. Slim Jim marks too clean, too consistent. They're likely Enclave. Tracking me for a reason. If they have me, Sandy might be next.

He called Sandy on the bag phone. She answered on the first ring.

"Good morning," she said.

"Morning. It's already been a day, and it's not even nine yet. I'll explain everything later. For now, check under the Explorer's passenger-side dash for a black box with a light on it."

"Got it," Sandy said calmly. "Sounds like a tracker. If I find one, I'll have Greg stick it on another car. Do the same with yours."

Paul chuckled. "This happened to you before?"

"Once or twice," she said coolly.

"Heading to the library," Paul said. "I'll call tonight so we can line up notes."

"Sounds good," Sandy replied.

"I love you, Sandy. Stay safe," and ended the call.

Sandy set the phone down slowly.

"Roger," she said quietly, "that's the first time in ages someone said that and I believed it."

She grabbed her keys. "Be right back, buddy. Gotta check the Explorer."

41

Marion Public Library

Paul was out of clean clothes. As soon as he hung up the phone, he grabbed his keys and headed to a nearby thrift store.

He picked up a few pairs of jeans and some T-shirts, then drove back to the Harding Motor Lodge. At the first red light he glanced in his mirror and sighed.

This guy Scotty is lousy as a tail. The white Honda Accord was close enough that Paul could see Scotty's full face reflected back at him.

He thought it through carefully on the drive.

Someone, likely the sheriff, has a key to my van. If I take the cash, the pistol, and the notes with me, they could search the van while I'm gone. If I leave them in the motel room, a master key gets them in just as easily. I need to think this through very carefully.

Paul drove toward the mall and turned into the lot on a right turn near McDonald's, with the Honda following at a not-so-discreet distance. Paul swung around the mall and crossed Barks Road into a car wash booth, then got out of his van. This forced Scotty's hand. He couldn't park at the gas station. Scotty decided to loop around the mall just once, and that was all it took. Barks Road to the back side of Chateau Ridge, past Route 95, and on to the Public Storage facility. Paul rented a small unit and unloaded into it, being careful to keep his back to the camera.

He went straight from there to the Marion Public Library, where he knew Scotty would pick up the tail again. As he approached, about three stoplights from the library, there was Scotty just a few cars back. "Way to go, Scotty."

Paul arrived at the library just a few minutes later. He walked from the attached parking lot adjacent and behind the entrance drive. He walked to the front of the building toward a glass-doored entry vestibule at a brisk pace. The cold air justified his hurried walk.

At the vestibule doors he glanced back. The parking lot was no longer visible around the building's corner.

Scotty was just pulling into the lot from the opposite side, the Honda nosing into a space not far from Paul's van.

Paul made his move.

Instead of entering the glass doors leading to the restroom lobby. Paul kept moving forward off the sidewalk and continued walking along the shrubbery beds, staying carefully in the mulch. Once around the corner of the building where he was no longer visible from the glass lobby door, he broke into a sprint, and ran all the way back to the parking lot, making a full circle around the library. By then Scotty had entered the glass door and passed through the second set of glass doors into library, looking around for Paul while trying not to be obvious.

Back in the parking lot Paul spotted the Honda just a few spaces away from his van.

"Real sorry about this, Scotty. This isn't personal." He said out loud to himself.

Paul slammed the flat of his strong right hand against the Honda's gas cap cover. It popped open on the second try. He removed the cap, crossed quickly to the nearest shrubbery bed, and grabbed two generous fistfuls of rotting mulch and arborvitae leaf pieces. He shoved it all down into the fuel fill pipe. The goal was to clog the fuel line filter with debris and hopefully foul the fuel pump in the process. He replaced the cap, closed the flap, and ran back the way he had come.

He arrived back at the glass front doors on the other side of the building, went into the vestibule bathroom to wash his hands, and then entered the main library. He could see Scotty heading down the stairs toward the children's section, head darting left and right, clearly worried.

Paul waved enthusiastically to Scotty from the main lobby near the record players, where people sat with headphones listening to music.

"Scotty, meh man!"

A stern look from the hawkish librarian at the circulation desk landed on him like a gavel. Her expression said she dared him to continue. Paul lowered his voice and moved closer to Scotty.

"Whatcha doin' here, Mister Scotty, eh? Research day?"

Scotty tried to play it cool. "Looking into some new surveillance methods. Cop magazines."

"Oh, that sound nice-nice, mon. Lemme roll with you. We check dem out together, eh?"

"Oh, I, I was just heading out actually," Scotty said, trying and failing to appear disinterested. He asked, "I completely forgot you said you were coming here. Find anything important?"

"Nope, not really," Paul said easily. "Well, I headin' back to the Motor Lodge. I catch up with you and Sheriff Didn't tomorrow, eh?"

"Sure, sure, sounds good," Scotty replied.

They walked out together. Paul said, "Gonna hit the restroom one more time. Went too hard on the water last night, you hear?"

Scotty was more than accommodating. He wanted to reach his car before Paul could see how close he had parked. He jogged ahead, slid into the Honda, and sank low in the seat.

Paul took his time in the restroom, then walked out to his van. He swept the parking lot with his eyes. Scotty would expect that. Of course, spotting the Honda sitting suspiciously still, he pretended not to notice, hopped in, and started his van. Pulling out slowly, he watched his mirror as Scotty eased out of his space and began to follow.

The Honda made it as far as the exit lane.

Then it started bucking slightly. Just barely at first, then more noticeably, like when someone is driving a stick-shift car for the first time. Then it stopped completely.

Real sorry, Scotty. I hope the Sheriff doesn't take it out on you.

Paul turned right and headed toward Caledonia.

He stopped at a car wash on the edge of Marion and used the cover and lights of the washing bay to dismantle the tracker from the van. *Man, I wish I had fresh plates on this thing*, he thought. *I'll need to figure that out soon.* He pulled out of the car wash, turned right, and stopped very shortly at the Meijer.

42

Meijer's and Tires

Paul went into the store and purchased the smallest car battery they had in stock, a soft-sided lunch cooler, and two rolls of Gorilla tape. He wrapped the tracker wire around the battery terminals and taped them down. The lights came alive again. He placed the battery and tracker into the cooler and zipped it closed. This was where he needed a miracle.

Paul had been quiet about his faith. The truth is he was not sure if his faith was really his. When you grow up with Christian parents, it is easy to assume that you are also a Christian. However, in Paul's case, after meeting Sandy, after losing his mom and never really stopping to mourn her passing, he was not sure anymore. Did he miss a step? Was salvation passed down or personal?

Shaking the thought off, he needed to find a semi heading further north. The entrance to Route 23 North was right off the parking lot. Paul wondered if any of the delivery semis heading to and from the Meijer loading docks were heading north. He chose this Meijer over Walmart for that reason. They were a Michigan retailer, meaning maybe more northbound trucks.

He drove to the back, pretending to be lost, just turning around and leaving. There were cameras on the back wall; this would never work. A tractor-trailer emerged from around the back corner and headed toward him. The truck pulled alongside the store, and then Paul heard the air brakes. The driver hopped out and headed into a small employees-only side door. He wasn't sure if this truck was arriving or leaving or where it was heading, but this was his only chance. The tracker had been back on for about fifteen minutes. He could not stay long now that the tracker was active.

Hopping out of the van, he ran to the side of the truck. He began feeling under the passenger side of the trailer closest to the cab. He needed to find somewhere to attach the cooler. Finding a horizontal piece of steel running behind the tire, Paul grabbed the cooler and crawled under the truck. As he did, he prayed, *Lord, don't let this truck move yet, and when it does, please send it north.* It sounded glib in his head. He immediately thought, *Lord, I'm sorry if I treat You like a vending machine. Your will be done. But if You could, I'd rather not get run over or snatched.* Paul wrapped Gorilla tape around and around the cooler and the steel part of the trailer. He didn't bother to cut the roll; he had wrapped more than half the roll around and around. He just left the rest hanging underneath.

When he finished, he rolled out. He barely cleared the truck's tires at the same time the air release sound could be heard right before the truck began to move. About six seconds slower and he would have been flattened. The driver didn't see him roll out. Paul hurried back to the van and watched the truck loop out of the back side of the lot. He stayed behind it as it came down the service road and to the light for Route 95. When the signal turned green, the truck went wide left and a quick right, up the ramp to State Route 23 North. *Looks like this one is Michigan bound.* Paul finally exhaled.

Immediately, Paul turned right on 95 and headed toward Caledonia. *Lord, I know I am not supposed to put You to the test. Too many things there to even begin to understand how to thank You. Thank You for Your mercy. Thank You for saving my life and thank You for Your patience with me as I try to understand this on my own. I know Mom and Dad believed, and I think I do as well, but my doubt is crippling sometimes—and today was no exception. Yet You love me anyway. Amen.*

Ten minutes later he visited Caledonia and talked with a few older longtime residents. He wandered around town playing up the "Know-It-All Paul" happy Islander conspiracy chaser. Eventually people became suspicious, mostly the farmers. The townspeople were a lot easier to get along with than the farmers outside of town. Next stop was the Food Connection restaurant right on Route 98. He ordered a quick cheeseburger, fries, and a Coke to-go. While he waited, he had sufficient time to pry out a few more interesting tidbits from conversations. His to-go order was called out, which pretty much killed his ability to chew the fat with the remaining waitresses and the busboy Frank.

He drove toward Marion for a few minutes and then took a right onto Ulsh Road for the night. Finding a small barn in the middle of a field appeared to be his best option. Turning off his lights and pulling inside, Paul got out and shut the barn doors facing the sparsely traveled road. After making sure the van was locked, he turned off all the exterior lights and pulled the inside curtain across to block any light from the back of the van. He ate his meal, turned off his small flashlight, and fell asleep in the surprisingly comfortable recliner chair bolted in the van. Not once thinking of the improbability of such a safe place ready for him to rest and who might have been the one to provide such comfort.

The next morning, he woke up early, feeling surprisingly refreshed. Leaving his comfortable barn behind, he drove straight back to the Public Storage facility and cleaned out his space back into its hiding places inside the van.

From there he headed south on Route 23 to find a hotel farther from Marion. He needed to check in with Sandy and compare notes. Paul had one conversation at the restaurant with the busboy Frank that he thought Sandy ought to know sooner rather than later.

What Paul did not know was that there were men out all night looking for him. Sheriff Clavell had men patrolling Marion and Caledonia, checking all the known hotels and motels to find him. Two of these patrols passed right by that old barn like they had many times before. The ground was frozen, so no tracks in or out were seen from the van. The rickety door still shut tightly and he slept with a full meal in his stomach and peacefully in the silent protection of that old barn. As he slept the enemy prowled past him within thirty feet twice that night and were rendered blind to his presence. He was granted peaceful and restorative rest.

This was, as many are, unnoticed God's provision. Not flashy or big. They are in-the-moment and quietly perfect. Paul didn't acknowledge the intervention. Why would he? His mother Ruthy would have seen it for what it was. She focused on not only what did happen in life but also what did not. Things many call lucky or coincidence she called protection and provision. She was aware that good and evil coexisted for now. She was tuned in to see that every good thing came from the Giver. Paul didn't recognize it. He didn't know it happened. Such are the ways of the Lord. It's the Red Sea moments we look for, the big miracles. Those are exciting, but God's greatest miracles are often in the mundane.

43

Recon 1

JANUARY 18, 1992 – DUBLIN, OHIO

A vehicle approached the intersection of Home Road outside Dublin, Ohio. Just past the intersection, the SUV slowed to thirty miles an hour, heading north. At the large construction site on the right-hand side of the road, it doused its lights and pulled into an empty field on the left. Under a waxing gibbous moon, there was just enough light to see without drawing attention to the slim figure dressed all in black who emerged from the SUV.

The figure darted across the road into the tree line next to the newly paved driveway. A sign at the road's edge, with red letters on a reflective white background, blazed under a flashlight's beam:

WARNING: THIS IS AN ACTIVE CONSTRUCTION SITE. DO NOT ENTER UNLESS AUTHORIZED. VIOLATORS WILL BE PROSECUTED, AND VEHICLES WILL BE TOWED.

Sandy had to stifle a laugh as Mister Right broke the silence in her head. He read the sign just a little differently:

Warning: Violators will be shot, dragged into a hole, buried, and never seen again. Oh, and your car will be towed!

There were too many odd questions surrounding this place. Sandy assumed it was Enclave that was building something, but Melanie now believed it was some other power structure with Susan at the center. She believed Enclave was merely providing security for the construction site.

Her inner crazy was active tonight, most likely due to the stress.

Getting real dark in these trees. Why are we doing this? We are going to get caught! Paul will have to bail us out of jail!

Sandy needed them to stop.

Man, you guys must think I'm stupid sometimes.

To which they all replied in unison:

You're the one talking to yourself!

Then they fell silent.

She switched off the flashlight and tucked it into a pocket on her Patagonia crossbody hiking pack. She covered her left eye with her left hand. She'd read this trick in a war book in high school, and to her surprise, it worked.

After hiding in the shadows for about ten minutes Sandy could now see better in the dark out of her right eye while her left eye was covered. She moved through the wooded area toward the construction site's interior, a roughly twelve-acre lot.

With her left eye remaining covered, and navigating the dimly lit woods slowly, she approached the clearing in the center of the lot. Lights glowed from a construction trailer showing two silhouetted guards. There upper bodies visible through the large trailer window.

Sandy ducked down, panicked. *If you can see them, they can see you. Focus.*

She edged back into the trees. *At least they don't have dogs*, she thought.

As she took in the whole scene, she spotted a large dog at the river's edge. Then just a few seconds later a second dog emerged from the darkness.

Great. There are two dogs.

So far there was no sign of above grade construction. However, Sandy could see a massive hole in the ground with container-like structures placed inside. The containers were connected by vent pipes and what looked like utility cables and pipes. Sandy was no construction expert, but this didn't look normal to her. It seemed out of place or at least odd enough to risk taking a photo. After all, once they build on top of it who knows what the below ground will be used for later.

The dim light prevented a clear photo, and a flash would draw the dogs instantly.

She pulled out her Canon Photura, an odd, tube-shaped camera she'd practiced using one-handed. Double-checking the flash settings, she avoided the shutter button near her thumb.

She was only going to get one chance at this, so she prepared to run immediately afterward.

Sandy confirmed her truck keys were secure in her pocket for a quick escape and mentally mapped the fastest route back through the trees to avoid tripping.

She aimed the camera using her right eye and hand at the excavation, containers still visible, counted down silently, and pressed the shutter button.

A piercing flash shattered the night.

The dogs bolted straight for the location of the flash, barking.

Sandy kept the left hand in place and navigated with her right eye. This proved to be more difficult after the flash of the camera, but she held it in place long enough to get a head start through the tricky parts of her exit route. She sprinted toward her truck in the field across the road, sticking to her initial path. She did not see the two men with guns join the chase.

Breathing, barking, and the sound of her heartbeat were all she could hear.

Sandy approached the roadway, running as hard as she could. Still holding the camera in her right hand, she pumped both of her arms and sprinted toward her now visible truck.

Clearing the wooded edge and entering the road, the men stopped their pursuit and drew their sidearms. Sandy was unaware they had guns.

The dogs covered ground and closed in fast.

Sandy was gasping for air now and starting to lose steam. Adrenaline fueled the last leg of her dash.

As Sandy neared the Explorer, she was certain she felt the hot breath of the pursuing K 9s and could feel their paws landing just steps behind. Swinging her right arm just a little further backwards then normal to aim the flash of the camera closer to the pursuing dogs estimated eye level. Then without hesitation she pressed the picture button again and the flash activated with the shutter button. The dogs were just seconds from leaping and bringing her to the ground when the flash pulsed. The dogs yelped, disoriented, and then collided and fell tripping over one another.

Sandy's moment of triumph turned out to last only seconds. Sandy reached the Explorer, fumbled the key into the lock, hands trembling, chest heaving from exertion. Just as she jumped into the seat, a gunshot rang out, then another.

She screamed and ducked lower than she thought possible, slamming the door shut. The glass from the back hatch exploded into glass pebbles, spraying forward into the rear seats.

The dogs jumped up and snarled at her side window as she fired the engine.

Shifting into drive and keeping her head as low as she could while still seeing, the Explorer bounced over the uneven field.

Two more shots, no apparent hits.

She sped away.

Within a minute she was back on the road, head lights on to avoid crashing. Glancing at the side mirror she watched the dogs growing smaller in the distance.

"Bad dogs!" she said.

Her back window was completely gone.

That'll be easy to spot. I'd better get that fixed right away.

What in the world are you doing, Sandy? You could have been killed, and right now I don't think you'd go where Ruthy went! scolded Mr. Right.

Back at the construction site, the agents radioed Enclave to report the intrusion, chase, and weapons discharge. By 4:45 a.m., not long before sunrise, the original two agents' bodies were loaded into a black SUV, and two new agents were assigned. The cleaners finished and drove away before sunrise.

As Sandy drove, she was rattled, about her close call with the dogs and that men were shooting at her with the goal of killing her. No one knew where she was. If she would have been killed tonight no one, including Paul, would have known what happened to her. And Mister Right was in fact, well, right. *And if I die before I wake, I pray my Lord my soul to take.*

She was confused, but she knew more was at stake than dying. That really would not matter at that point.

"Ruthy, I wish you were still here with me."

"God, what am I doing?"

So Enclave is building a new place. To actually shoot at someone for taking a picture seems over-the-top. I mean, they actually tried to kill me! I knew it was dangerous, but not get-shot dangerous!

She drove back home thinking about prayer. She was certain she wasn't approaching it correctly.

"My prayers feel more like the questions I would have asked the Magic 8-Ball."

"Ask again later."

"Very doubtful."

Ruthy relied on prayer. To Ruthy, prayer was not intended to secure a specific outcome but rather to trust the certainty of the best outcome.

That is what I need to figure out.

I have relied on my inner crazy too long.

Her mind shifted to Paul.

She looked down and realized her hands were still trembling as she loosened her grip on the steering wheel.

Just then, her bag phone rang on the passenger seat.

And there are answers to prayers I haven't even thought to make.

She smiled in spite of herself.

As she picked up the phone to answer, Lefty, Mister Right, and Campus Hippie could be heard in her mind, teasing, *Sandy and Paul sittin' in a tree . . .*

That was as far as they got before Sandy shut them down.

"Hey, stranger," she said. "I was just thinking about you."

"I was just thinking about you and wanted to hear your voice. I know we talk tomorrow but I just wanted to make sure you are alright?"

"I am now," she said. "I'll give you the details tomorrow but right now I have an odd question. Don't panic, just help me answer the question. I promise I am fine.

"Where would you take an Explorer to get a rear window replaced that was shattered by a gunshot without getting a bunch of questions."

"What?! Sandy, why am I not surprised. Easy question though. Any automotive repair shop near campus. No one asks anything around there—cash is king on campus."

"Paul, thanks for the answer without the lecture. Tomorrow is Sunday. I am looking forward to it. Right now, though, I gotta go and pay attention to my driving. I don't want to get pulled over and have to explain this."

"Good night, Sandy, talk to you tomorrow. Please stay safe."

As soon as the call ended Paul began to cough a deep and painful cough. After about forty-five seconds he managed to reel the cough back in. He took a drink from his water glass next to his chair and then he slumped back into his chair to rest.

44

Sunday Phone Call

JANUARY 19, 1992 – PHONE CONVERSATION

Sandy watched as R2 sat up, reacting to a bird that flew past the long glass windows that made up the entire wall. His tail curled and flicked as he perched in front of the skyline of downtown Columbus. Sandy was just starting to drift off to sleep as she watched the colors of the sky deepen. However, not tonight, never on Sundays. She was waiting, waiting to hear from Paul. Sunday nights were their phone call nights, not just to compare mission notes, but to hear the other's voice.

The bag phone rang. She grabbed it quickly, not caring if she appeared excited about his call. After all, he was an important field agent.

Somebody misses Paul, Mister Right mocked.

"Knock it off," Sandy said out loud and gruffly, just as the line connected.

Paul started his call with, "Uh, okay then. Wait, what did I do? I haven't even had a chance to cause trouble yet."

That was when Sandy realized she had said it out loud, and through the phone. She sheepishly admitted, "My Inner Crazy was just teasing me again."

"Ha," Paul laughed. "Alright, thanks for being honest. Maybe you should lie down a bit, yeah?" he joked.

"Okay, okay, enough about my Inner Crazy for now. Let me give my outer crazy a little time in the sun," she said with a mocking tone.

"Serious now, how are you doing for real?" Paul asked. "You didn't get your Explorer window shot out again, did you? Please tell me that didn't happen a second time."

“No, I did not. Thank you very much. Your tip for repair was perfect. All fixed and no questions were asked.”

Paul turned his head and coughed.

“Are you sick?” she asked.

He got the cough under control and said, “Just a little too much rolling around in the snow. And yeah, the bath house shower is freezing, then I have to run back to the van. But the shore power is solid. That little space heater has the van nice and cozy.”

“I’m sorry you picked up a cold. Are you taking care of yourself?” Sandy asked, sounding concerned.

“Yeah, about as good as you can be when you’re living in a van down by the river, y’know?” Paul said the last part in his best Chris Farley voice.

Sandy laughed loudly.

R2 turned his head with annoyance toward Sandy. The bird on the outside of the wall window ledge that he had been stalking flew away, startled from the laugh.

R2 had demonstrated great patience as he put in the necessary time to set the birds at ease so he could scare them off the ledge. “Thanks a lot!” seemed to be the expression he shared. Not to be deterred, he put his head back down to face the window and began the long wait for another victim.

Paul chuckled and continued his report. They always reported first and chatted later, just in case they lost connection. The chats were important, but the report carried higher consequences if information wasn’t passed between them.

“The van and camper setup work pretty well for staying mobile. Campgrounds are completely empty this time of year. I’m at Delaware State Park off Route 23, so I can hit Marion or Caledonia and get back out easily. I picked up this beat-up Geo Metro for fifteen hundred from some old guy, then gave him another five hundred to leave the plates on. I pulled the plates and glued magnets on the back, same way you did, then realized the whole car is plastic. Magnets don’t stick to it at all. So, I mounted a little metal piece through the bumper cover, and that is holding really well. Now I drive the Geo into Marion or Caledonia and leave the van at the site. And I can take the van other places without worrying about the plate showing up on the sheriff’s radar.

"I hit a thrift store in Delaware and picked up some clothes, different sunglasses, caps, hats, coats, all sorts of things. I've gotten pretty good at switching up my look and blending in. My biggest issue isn't in the small town, though. It's outside of town, and that issue seems to be my skin color. Folks in town are friendly enough, but man, some of those farmers and young families on the outskirts are just downright prejudiced. I mean it doesn't bother me they keep to themselves. But the looks they give me make me think they have never seen anyone who looks like me. Of course, I know that can't be true, but that is the vibe I pick up. The village only has about eight hundred people, and everyone knows everyone. So, Caledonia is a little harder to move through, but I have a few assets there to help me out."

Sandy asked a few clarifying questions and jotted some notes in her notebook. Her report back to Paul was not as varied.

"I've been spending most of my operational efforts trying to figure out three things. Who is building along the river here? What will that large building be? And the most important one, where is my baby?

"As for what LIFE or ENCLAVE or maybe someone else is building on the river, it appears to be an underground compound masquerading as an opulent luxury estate. This place is massive. It's not completed yet, but if I were to guess, the below-ground areas are going to be larger than the above-ground home. I don't know why Dublin, Ohio, yet, and I don't know the purpose, but the way it's being guarded, coupled with the covert nature of the site prep, it must be important to their long-term plans, whatever they are."

Paul was quiet. Sandy thought maybe the line went dead.

"Paul?"

He started to speak and then coughed once, cleared his throat, composed himself, and spoke.

"Sandy, it sounds like you have been plenty busy. Digging for answers and getting shot at and chased by dogs of course. But I do have one last thing to report myself, and I'm not exactly looking forward to it."

Sandy stayed silent, so he pushed forward.

"I will get this hard copy to you, but I want to read it to you word for word."

"Ready," Sandy said.

"This comes from the April 10, 1960, front page of the *Marion Star* newspaper.

"A young woman was found dead in Hospital Park this morning at approximately 6 a.m. The preliminary cause of death is listed as suicide. Authorities believe this same unidentified woman, estimated to be in her early twenties, gave birth to a baby girl at Marion General Hospital on April 7, 1960, at around 4 p.m.

"The infant was left with the mother for only a few minutes for initial bonding. When the nurse returned to take the newborn back to the nursery, both the mother and the baby were gone.

"The search for the missing infant is ongoing.

"Law enforcement is seeking two individuals for questioning: a man and woman known only as Gunther and Abigail Glut. Both reportedly speak with a heavy German accent.

"Anyone with information regarding the baby or the individuals known as the Gluts is asked to contact the Marion County Sheriff's Department and request Senior Deputy Bryan Clavell."

Paul continued, knowing he might need to walk Sandy through the implications.

"The date on the newspaper article was April 8, 1960. That is the day after you were born, of course. Now, that by itself could be coincidence, but the deputy listed as the contact, Bryan Clavell, he is the sheriff now. And he is the one who showed up banging on my motel room door my first morning here. His nephew Scotty is the one who tried to follow me. These two, Sheriff Clavell and Deputy Scotty, they most likely know something. If only based on how fast they picked up on me. Their interest probably started at the dealership when we bought the van."

Paul paused. "Are you with me so far? I still need to fill you in on the rest I learned from the conversations."

Sandy said, almost in a whisper, "Keep going."

Paul didn't like the way she sounded, but he knew she wanted all the information, and he knew she would work through it when she was ready.

"I talked with a few people in Caledonia before they circled the wagons and clammed up, and one thing kept coming up in all the stories. The Vanovers were well known in town. They owned one of the two grocery stores and were very involved in community events, sponsoring baseball uniforms for kids' teams and doing all sorts of things. Mrs. Vanover worked the store every day, and when she had a baby, nobody, and I mean nobody, knew she was pregnant. She ran the cash register several times a week, and nobody could say they ever saw her look pregnant at all. Then one day, she suddenly had a baby girl.

"You know how people are, though. Everybody just assumed she adopted and was saving face. People in Caledonia speculated back then that maybe they couldn't have kids and were too embarrassed, so they tried to pretend and relied on everybody else minding their own business."

Paul continued. He knew she was actively listening; he could hear her breathing. He wanted to stop, but he knew that wasn't best. Better to get all the ugly out before trying to console her.

"Mrs. Vanover had only two living relatives, her sister and her niece. The rumor among those around at the time is that her sister called her. She asked directly where she got the baby from and then accused her of finding and keeping the baby from the dead woman in Marion. They got into a fight over the phone, and later the next day, the sister and niece were both killed in a car accident.

"The only reason anyone knows about the fight is part of it was overheard by the next-door neighbor Donna. Does that name sound familiar to you?"

"Donna? I think . . . Well maybe? I am not sure. I kind of remember the name?"

Paul spoke softly, almost apologetically.

"There is one more odd thing. Do you remember what the doctor looked like, the one who came and comforted you the day your mom, I mean Mrs. Vanover, passed? Well, anyway, do you remember what she looked like?"

Sandy said, "Yes, mostly. I guess she made an impression on a very traumatic day. Why do you ask?"

He replied, "As I left town when we started these investigations, my first stop that you wanted me to make was Melanie's. She gave me an envelope that Greg had left for me. Just some loose ends he wanted me to look into as well. In that envelope was a picture of a woman. He gave me two, actually, one older one from 1955, making some kind of public speech, the other taken in 1983 at some press event."

Sandy said, "I'm not following where you're going."

“Greg wanted my opinion on the two photos. The woman looks similar, maybe plastic surgery, but the pictures from 1955 and 1983 show a woman in her thirties.”

“Wait,” Sandy said. “So, the pictures are taken twenty-eight years apart and the woman looks the same? Now I’m tracking with you. Is it some kind of turn-back-the-clock beauty treatment stuff? Perhaps surgery? Or is it a different woman?”

“She looks almost the same, so much so that it appears to be the same woman, but that’s impossible, so something weird is going on. Anyway, I don’t know for sure, and I haven’t been able to get this info back to Greg. If you have a chance, would you relay it?”

“Sure, but what does that have to do with the doctor that came and visited me after, for now I’ll still call my mom’s death?”

“There were pictures in the *Marion Star* of your mom’s death and your tragically popular news story. Someone captured a picture of you in the background talking to the doctor, or rather, psychiatrist, while they were removing Mrs. Vanover’s body. The woman in that picture with you is the same woman in those photos. I’m certain of it.

“But before you speak, Greg and Melanie’s note on the photo they gave me, well, it gets even stranger. Greg believed that she was also Doctor Appleton. She was wearing a mask, but even Melanie thinks it probably was her. They didn’t want to go on record yet without proof.”

Sandy began to cry, first quietly, then more freely. She set the phone down, not to hang it up, but to wipe her eyes and gain composure. R2 came over and curled into her lap, locking her gaze with his azure blue eyes, just as Roger used to do when she was upset. It worked.

She wiped her eyes and picked up the phone again.

Paul hadn’t spoken. He could hear her cry and knew there was nothing to say. He felt bad that he caused it, but he had too much Ruthy in him. He knew the truth was the best thing, no matter how painful it might land. A thought ran through his mind like a flash, *That’s not Ruthy, that is the Holy Spirit.* It took Paul a second to regain his internal composure, just in time to listen to Sandy speak.

“As much as I want you back here, there is still work to be done. Can you find out anything you can on Donna, Jane Doe, and the Gluts, or whatever their real name was back then? This convergence of stuff in the small town and its nearby county seat is both puzzling and hopeful. Maybe we can get more answers. I will work with Greg on this weird ageless woman in the meantime. I also have some other recon work I need to do."

"You got it. Can I ask you a favor as well?" Paul asked, turning very serious.

"Whatever you need, Paul."

"Well, whatever you're working on and the other recon you mentioned, please keep someone like Greg or Melanie, even Enoch, anyone on that end in the loop so you are not flying without a net."

"Will do," she said quietly.

"One more thing, I want to learn more about this Donna neighbor. I think it is odd you remember so many small details. Even the joke your dad told the donut lady but you have no real memory of Donna. The house where she and her husband raised their children right next to the Vanover's old home is currently for sale. I talked to the bank manager Wayne about payments, etc. I think I am going to buy it. I can always sell it later. By buying it I get to become less of a threat and will learn more that way. I think I can learn more here than in the library at this point. What do you think?"

"Paul, I think you are a very smart mon, ya."

From that point, the conversation turned personal, warm, and familiar.

As Sandy placed the phone back into the cradle, she said out loud, "Lord, thank You for Paul. Please keep him safe. I know I don't have a right to ask anything from You. I am a slow learner and even slower to believe. We both know I know You are there. Help me overcome my unbelief, and help Paul in his as well."

She prepared for bed, and she and R2 went to sleep with Roger literally lying on her chest. She could feel his purr, and he could feel the gentle rise and fall of her breathing and the beat of her heart. In this state, they both drifted off to sleep.

Paul did the same, but alone in the back of his van. He also prayed for about ten minutes, and with renewed peace, he fell asleep sitting in his recliner.

45

Paul's Tower

JUNE 2, 1992 – CALEDONIA, OHIO

Paul's task in the agreed-upon division of investigation was to find out why Sandy was the object of so much attention. Why her? Why Roger? And now, Why Caledonia? What was her baby's purpose in all of this? So, Paul purchased a home at the heart of it all. It was not just any home. He bought the former home of the neighbor, Donna. Even though Paul enjoyed van life, it was easier to blend into a small town when you put down roots.

Paul explored the house from top to bottom. The attic was still full of stuff accumulated from everyone who had lived in this home. Originally built by a prominent early family and had welcomed relatively few people in its long life. Yet there were sewing mannequins, an old mirror, wooden crates, a few now-broken glass lamp covers, and boxes and boxes of old newspapers, wrapped in plastic.

The bedrooms were all empty, and some of the wallpaper looked to be from the early 1900s. The master bedroom consisted of three rooms: the main room and what looked like a ladies' dressing room with a very large walk-in closet. The next bedroom in the hall was also large, about twenty-four feet square, with a walk-in closet that went under the stairs to the attic. All the bedrooms were connected by interior doors from room to room, with the exception of the master bedroom.

Bedroom three was connected to number two and was slightly smaller, at about eighteen feet square, with a smaller framed-in closet. This room was at the end of the hall and connected to the small bedroom that made up the corner of the house. This was the room Paul had chosen to sleep in due to its easy access to the TV antenna tower outside.

The only other room upstairs was a bathroom with a pedestal and on that pedestal rested a cast iron claw foot tub. The house was listed by the county as being built in the early 1900s, but according to a newspaper article, the Victorian Italianate was completed for a wealthy family in 1882.

There was much more to the home, but the most interesting thing Paul discovered was in the crawl space under the stairs of the hand-dug basement. The crawl space was long, deep, and dark, with a single light bulb at the very beginning. Paul pulled a flashlight out of the van and went in.

Lots of spiders and old liquor bottles littered the space closest to the opening. But hidden around a blind corner, created most likely for this purpose, was a large handmade wooden box. Paul pulled it out into the larger room and opened its lid. When Paul realized what the contents were, he quickly shut the lid and shoved it back into the crawl space.

One mystery at a time, Paul thought. He would tell the team about it later. After this current business was behind them.

After only a few full nights in the house, he woke up abruptly. Around three in the morning, he heard it: The front porch screen door's rusty metal spring gave a moderate creak. It was the sound the door made when someone closed it more slowly than the spring was designed to allow, preventing it from slapping shut.

The first priority for safety when Paul moved in was to change the locks. You never really know who has keys to an older home.

The creaky spring was installed by Paul himself. He had put several other "early warning" precautions in the house the day he moved in. He loosened a few steps on the main staircase heading up from the ground floor to the bedrooms upstairs. Not just random steps, though. He was logical. He had done enough snooping in his day to know the pitfalls of being in a house and trying to stay quiet. That experience drove his logic. He loosened the boards on both edges of one stair and the middle of the next. So no matter how you came up the stairs (unless you leaped loudly up two stairs at a time), a noise was, for all practical purposes, unavoidable.

Based on what he heard, Paul was certain that someone was now in the house, specifically in the kitchen. This was confirmed by the soft squeak that followed as the intruder stepped from the kitchen into the living room.

Most of the other larger homes in town were brick. Even the town council building, the original firehouse, and the old jail were constructed of red brick. Paul was not surprised to find a brick plant operating on the outskirts of town. Brick was plentiful and inexpensive compared to other regions. However, the doctor had wanted wood, so the house was built of timber with hardened lath-and-plaster-lined walls. This made it difficult to run wires. Paul used the next best thing: the old furnace ducts. He had run a living room light switch into his bedroom so he could turn the living room light on from upstairs. The surprised exposure of an intruder by lights was usually effective at setting an average intruder into a panic. The living room was close enough to the front door that it would most likely encourage them to turn around and leave. However, Paul had been waiting for this. His goal tonight was recon.

To the right of the kitchen entryway stood the staircase leading to the bedrooms. The first flight rose to a small landing, then turned back on itself. There were four steps that Paul had loosened to make sure the old tread plates squeaked. He loosened the middle part on one and both edges on the next. He did this at the bottom of the first flight and close to the top of the second flight coming off the landing, so that no matter how you tried to walk them, one of them would make a sound. These steps led to the main upstairs hallway for all of the bedrooms and the upstairs bathroom. Otherwise, the steps were wide and sturdy, and equipped with an easy-to-grip handrail on both sides.

It was a warm evening, and the upstairs rooms grew too hot to sleep in with the windows closed. The old wooden counter-weight balanced window beside the built-in single bed was already open. Still wearing a T shirt and shorts, Paul slipped into his slippers as quietly as he could the moment he heard the first squeak from the front door spring. By the time the intruder reached the top of the stairs, Paul was already descending the antenna and moving around toward the front porch.

At the porch, he had options. He could go to the neighbors or hide along the hedgerow that covered the backyard. Paul needed to follow the intruder back to their home or car or wherever they came from originally.

He made his way quietly to the front porch the intruder had occupied only minutes before. Instead of going back inside and catching the intruder, he crouched down on the porch edge that led to the backyard. He pushed himself into the hedgerow as far under it as he could and waited.

The intruder was not being quiet going room to room upstairs. Based on the footsteps, it sounded like he was approaching the final bedroom where Paul had just been sleeping not long ago.

Paul heard the stairs, and then he heard the door begin to open. The intruder stood on the porch and pulled the door closed as quietly as he could manage. He slid a pistol back into his holster and looked around nervously. Paul was not surprised at who the intruder was when the light from the street lamp hit his face as he turned.

There stood Deputy Scotty in his uniform.

How stupid are you? Wearing your uniform to break into my house to kill me? Intimidate me? Sheriff Clavell must be desperate. At least I don't have to follow him in slippers since I already know who he is. As Paul watched the nervous young man start walking down the street toward the park, he felt sorry for him. He was clearly going to take the heat for any trouble Paul caused. And Paul was planning a whole bunch of trouble.

Paul waited for Scotty to walk far enough down the road that he stopped looking back. It appeared he was more interested in getting to his car. Paul went back inside and watched out of the living room window. It was not long before Scotty came gliding by the dark home in his Marion County deputy's car. Now Paul knew they were setting Scotty up for failure. He needed to meet with Scotty and turn him. This meant having leverage, and Paul knew just how to get it.

Paul called Greg the next morning and discussed his plan. Then he called Sandy and left her a message. She didn't answer. Paul wasn't worried. She was capable of taking care of herself. Honestly, he was more concerned for the person in her sights than for her safety.

46

Watching Scotty Grow

JUNE 3, 1992 CALEDONIA, OHIO

Creak.

The rusty spring on the screen door groaned again. Paul's eyes snapped open in the darkness. He was already dressed, already waiting. The sound came from the foot of the stairs, exactly where he expected it.

It was time to turn Scotty from a pest into a partner.

He slipped silently down the television tower. The cool night breeze brushed his face. Plastic trash-can lids scraped across the blacktop as the wind knocked them loose, the only other sound in the sleeping village. Paul moved like a shadow across the yard and onto the front porch the intruder had occupied only minutes earlier.

He eased the screen door open, catching the spring with his hand before it could betray him. Using the large rock under the porch swing, he propped the door open without a sound.

Inside, he crossed the brown-and gold linoleum on bare feet, barely breathing. He slipped into the mudroom that shared a wall with the stove and sink, then crouched in the blind corner, the perfect spot. From the last cubby, he removed the false back and pulled out the Beretta Sandy had given him. He checked it once, the motion practiced and silent. Loaded. Ready.

He waited.

Footsteps creaked down the stairs again, then padded across the kitchen floor on the other side of the thin wall. Paul's pulse thudded in his ears. He tightened his grip on the pistol.

The intruder stepped directly in front of the mudroom doorway.

Paul raised the Beretta.

"Hey there, Scotty."

Deputy Scotty froze mid-step.

"Put your weapon on the floor," Paul said quietly, "and turn 'round slow."

Scotty's breathing hitched. He looked terrified, pale, wide-eyed, on the verge of tears. The snub-nosed .38 Special trembled in his hand before he carefully set it on the linoleum.

Paul kept the Beretta steady, voice low and calm but edged with steel. "Look, Scotty, I don't want to be standin' here holdin' dis gun on you any more than you want it pointin' at you. But you came for me, so I figured it was only fair I set the trap. Now go 'head and come in. Have a seat, Deputy."

Scotty looked terrified. This was not his style, and he clearly did not want to be there, but orders were orders. When he turned to face Paul, he was pale and seemed close to tears. The pistol he had placed on the floor was a snub-nosed .38 Special.

Paul slipped back into his Crucian accent with ease. After all, Scotty also knew him from the radio, and it was too early to tip his hand. "Look, Scotty, I don't want to be standin' here holdin' dis gun on you any more than you want it pointin' at you. But you come here for me, so I feel like it only fair I set the trap for you. You would say dat fair, Scotty?"

Scotty replied, barely able to stop from hyperventilating. "Well, uh, yes, I guess it is. I mean, I really could do without the gun pointed at me. Could you put it down, please? I'm not going to run. I'm pretty sure I'd be wheezing before you even break a sweat. I'm just here because my uncle made me. Check my gun. It's not loaded."

"Go 'head and come in, have a seat, Deputy."

Once Scotty was seated, Paul checked his gun. Sure enough, it wasn't loaded. Paul put Scotty out of his figurative misery.

"Well, Scotty, there's more to you than meets the eye. I should probably tell you mine is loaded, but the first two rounds are just dummies."

Paul dropped the magazine and cleared the chamber. He handed Scotty the round from the chamber as well as the one he peeled off the top of the magazine. Paul set his now-disarmed sidearm on the couch next to him and tossed Scotty back his empty gun.

"Well," Scotty said, "now what?"

Paul answered, "Well, Scotty, not really sure."

Scotty said, "You know back at the library? I knew you messed with my car. I saw you head around the back of the building from the high windows in the stacks under the stairs. If I stand on the bottom bookshelf edge, I can see out. I didn't want to chase you. My uncle Bryan made me. So I figured when I saw you messing with my car, that was my golden ticket. Worked like a champ too. Uncle didn't beat on me, and you got to go do whatever it was you were heading out to do. Of course, I may have exaggerated the effectiveness of the junk in my gas tank. But I got to spend the evening catching the latest episode of *NYPD Blue* that I had taped on the timer. Even had me some Jiffy Pop. I still love that stuff."

Paul sat speechless. Then the corners of his mouth began to curl like the edge of a clown's smile. Then he laughed so hard that Scotty thought he might pass out.

Regaining his breath, he finally said, "Well, Scotty, seem like I the fool today. You more than you look, boy."

With the ice broken, it was down to business. Paul and Scotty talked for several hours. Scotty was deeply worried about what his uncle, Sheriff Bryan, would say if he came back empty-handed. Paul learned that the goal that night had not been to hurt him but to scare him into backing off. He also learned that the people the sheriff reported to were very angry about the house purchase and might soon take stronger measures.

Over the course of the conversation, Paul formed a plan.

"Scotty, here's what we gonna do."

"I'm all ears," Scotty said.

Paul chuckled, because Scotty did, in fact, have large ears. Scotty gave him a look that said, *Do you think you're the first one?* Paul stopped laughing. "Sorry 'bout that. Might not be funny to you no more, but it sure hit my funny bone hard.

"Okay, so what about this. You go back to your uncle and tell him I freaked out. Say you got the jump on me, locked the bedroom door for hours. You didn't talk, you just made noises outside the door. You pretended to call some local hoods or gang guys or whatever kind of bad men you have around this little village. Like you had me trapped and were deciding whether to kill me. Play it like you were tough. Make it look like you scared me."

Scotty interrupted. "I am 100 percent certain my uncle is not that stupid. I put the fear into you? I think you need a plan B."

Now it was Paul's turn to interrupt. "Now, Scotty, hold on. I ain't finish yet. I'll call the sheriff, complain, tell the same story from my side. It make you look good to your people. They think I scared. Then I ask for protection. Sheriff see it as a positive. Your guys watch me out in the open. That give me a chance to learn without hidin'. But it only work if you sell it. I'll do my part. You could count on that. What you think?"

"Well, now's my chance to be impressed. That's pretty good. You really are Know-It-All Paul. I actually did listen to your show. That's how I know I can trust you. But what exactly are you looking for here anyway?"

"I have a good friend grow up here who now thinks her parents wasn't her real ones. She just tryin' to get answers, that's all. For some reason people don't want tell her the truth, so I'm helpin'."

"Well, count me in. I hate my uncle. He's mean to my aunt, and he's lazy and corrupt. The only reason I'm a deputy is so he can keep his claws in me. Well, that and I'm scared to death of confrontation and violence, but you may have figured that out. That's why I love *NYPD Blue*. I pretend I'm Detective Andy Sipowicz, and that seems to make him happy enough to leave me alone when I start yelling at people. Course I only do that when they're in the holding cell. I'd be too intimidated otherwise. Anyway, keep me in the loop. I'll help where I can, as long as Bryan doesn't find out."

"Hey, one ting. You could look at a picture for me?" Paul asked.

"Sure," Scotty said. "Not sure if I know them, but I'll look."

Paul pulled out the 1983 picture that Greg had given him and handed it to Scotty.

Scotty's face went blank as he stared at the photo.

Paul broke the silence. "Hey, Scotty, does that mean you know her?"

"No. I don't know her personally, but I know of her. She lives in New York City. She comes to see my uncle sometimes. Not often. Maybe twice that I know of. But no one ever says her name. Heck, I assumed she didn't have one. Just 'yes ma'am' or 'miss' all the way around with her. She is scary. But then again, I think most everyone is scary."

"So you don't know her name?"

"No," Scotty replied, "but I do have a street address in New York."

"What? Are you kidding me?" Paul said excitedly. "Why?"

"Uncle Bryan sends packages sometimes. Well, I mean, he makes me send her packages. He's too lazy to go to the post office."

Scotty pulled out his wallet and unfolded a piece of paper that had been folded so many times the creases were nearly cuts.

"I can't give you this. Uncle is crazy about this address staying a secret. But you can write it down."

"Man, Scotty, this a real help. I glad we ain't shoot each other today. Well, I coulda get a shot off on you, but you couldn't really shoot me. No bullets."

Scotty pulled out a large folding knife from his waistband. The blade flipped out of the handle.

"Nope, but this is an eight-inch out-the-front blade custom-made by a guy in Amish country. This bad boy could hurt. But I would only have used it if I was sure you were going to kill me," he said, smiling.

"Well as long as we being nice and honest. I don't really have an island accent anymore. I just use it as a tool when I am investigating something. People like a smiling guy with a cool accent." Paul finished with a grin.

Paul shook Scotty's hand firmly. "It was a real pleasure meeting you, Scotty."

"Right back at you, Know-It-All Paul. And I have to tel ya dat I do have dee Island accent and am fakin the regular, true-true," Scotty said with a grin on his face.

Scotty left through the garage at the back of the house and cut down the alley toward the ballpark where his car was parked. He could not leave through the front door because it was so late in the morning that kids were already sitting on the porch waiting for the school bus. Donna had insisted on it during the winter to give the students shelter, and the tradition had remained.

Paul went upstairs and called the sheriff's department. He spoke to Sheriff Bryan as though they were old friends and as though Paul were frightened and needed help. Now he had to trust that Scotty would do the same.

After he hung up Paul sat down in the chair in the corner of his bedroom. There were so many things that were starting to take shape and a great many other questions

Paul thought about Sandy. He knelt beside his bed and prayed simply.

"God, I don't understand this, but Mom and Dad relied on You for everything. I'm trying to do the same. Forgive my unbelief. Help me grow. Thank You for the squeaky front door and for my new friend Scotty. Be with Sandy. Keep her safe. Amen."

47

Reflections of Roger

JUNE 10, 1992 – NEW YORK CITY

Roger stood before the full-length mirror in his Manhattan high rise apartment, inherited from his poor departed mother. Roger loved nice things. He learned early how good looks, charm, and his clinical lack of empathy, diagnosed in his early teens as narcissistic personality disorder, were the perfect recipe for acquiring them.

He observed the privileges of appearance firsthand through his three times divorced mother, a onetime widow after the mysterious death of her wealthiest husband. She manipulated four husbands to the altar, each wealthier than the last, and the fourth to the grave, amassing tens of millions in the process. Nice things followed her everywhere.

But Mother made it clear Roger would have to earn his own fortune. As the good little sociopath she raised, he vowed to murder "Mommy Dearest" and claim her wealth. She taught him well. Despite being the prime suspect, he escaped charges by committing what was, in all likelihood, the perfect crime.

She would be proud, Roger mused, smiling inwardly as he recalled that night.

He played the long game, gaslighting Mother whenever and however he could. The plan took months but the payoff was a vast estate, no consequences, and guilt that could not be traced.

He began by creating an uncontrollable source of anxiety. He rearranged her keys, credit cards, cordless phone, prescription drugs, and alcohol. He emptied toothpaste tubes. He shook new light bulbs before placing them in their fixtures. When the light switch was turned on, the compromised bulbs popped, sparked, and burned out immediately. When Mother became concerned, Roger suggested faulty wiring and urged her to watch for electrical hazards. He even fired the maid to prove she was not the source of the problem.

After the maid's dismissal, he escalated. He moved furniture, unlocked locks, relocated her car, and slightly rearranged rooms, just enough to sow confusion. He ordered pizza deliveries, knowing she never ate pizza. He opened her incoming mail and erased answering machine messages.

As the dutiful son, Roger made sure friends and hangers on found stashed alcohol and pills in obvious places: kitchen drawers, a basket under the glass coffee table, or the guest bathroom vanity. Everyone checks the medicine cabinet, he thought. Three months of this created a deepening paranoia witnessed by others. The stage was set.

Roger obsessed over weather forecasts until he heard what he had been waiting for. On Good Morning America, Spencer Christian announced a winter storm warning for New York City. Freezing rain. Heavy winds. Snow beginning at six.

Perfect.

Roger's mirror smile spread as adrenaline surged. "Mother will be so proud of me," he said aloud. She would be, even in her eternal punishment, he reflected. He would be alone soon.

Theirs was not love. It was mutually assured destruction. Her dependence on alcohol and pills gave him the edge.

He secured a parking space on the fifth floor of the garage directly across from her building, offering an unobstructed view of her balcony. Earlier that day, he placed two construction cones at the front of the space and shattered a wine bottle on the ground, handling the glass with gloved hands. He knew no one would bother cleaning it up. He also knew his car could straddle the shards without damaging the tires, while others would park elsewhere to avoid the risk.

The storm arrived on schedule. Snow swirled against the glass and steel wall at the front of her balcony. She rarely stepped out in winter and Roger made sure bourbon and pills were always within reach.

She called, as she always did when she was drinking.

Roger answered with the urgent, practiced relieved tone. "Oh, Mother, I am so glad you are all right. I was just about to call you. A man contacted me. He would not give his name. He said he was going to kill you tonight. Something about avenging Walter."

He paused, letting the alcohol slow her thinking, then continued. "Do not worry. As soon as I hang up, I will call the police."

"No cops," she slurred. "I can't have them asking questions."

"Okay, Mother," Roger said calmly. "Let me think." He waited just long enough to hear her breathing quicken. "Put on a warm coat and shoes. Turn on every light in the penthouse. Shut all the doors. Once you are dressed, go hide on the balcony. Leave the balcony light on, but keep the curtain drawn."

He softened his voice. "If the killer arrives, he will search room by room. With the lights on, he will move slowly. He would never expect to find you outside during a snowstorm. Once you are on the balcony, crouch by the glass edge wall and stay low. Watch the sliding door like it is an alarm. Stay quiet. Listen."

"Do you understand, Mother? It is important to me I know you are safe. I will come deal with the intruder personally."

A sober woman would have questioned this. She did not.

She followed his instructions: lights on, doors shut, fur coat, hat, boots. She crouched unsteadily beside the glass wall.

Within ten minutes, Roger drove to the garage. Traffic lights flashed through streets abandoned to the storm. He removed the cones and parked. Checking his mirrors, he saw no one. His maniacal grin reappeared.

Across the street, her balcony light glowed. Her silhouette settled into place. Roger rolled down his window and latched the car door quietly. He placed his gloved hand on the horn and paused, savoring her fear.

Then he pressed it.

The blast cut through the storm as he shouted, "Mother, don't do it!"

She spun toward his voice in panic, believing her hiding place had been revealed. Bourbon, pills, stiff joints, and icy footing betrayed her. She toppled over the railing.

Twenty floors. No signs of a struggle. Dressed to be outside. Dead before impact. Roger never touched her.

Witnesses heard the horn and his scream. The apartment told the story of a paranoid alcoholic's despair. Roger told authorities she was suicidal on the phone. He lamented publicly, "If only I had not been delayed by the ice and snow, my dear mother would still be alive."

And that was how Roger afforded his nice things.

He adjusted his tie, shaking off the memory. "Perfect," he said, admiring his reflection as he practiced his mirror smile. Twenty muscles moved with learned precision to a predetermined shape. The smile formed but the involuntary muscles around his eyes betrayed him.

For the first time, Roger noticed it. He had known for a while the pursuit of nice things and beautiful women was no longer satisfying. Now he sat in the quiet and lonely luxury penthouse he inherited from his deceased mother. He could almost sense her drunken fear from that night. She was no prize for sure but to die betrayed by your own son?

Roger had not changed his public persona. He was still arrogant, rude, and self-centered. That was what the world expected from Roger Snow. The Snowman with ice in his veins. Lately, regrets were outpacing cravings. His ironic humor gave way first to the sardonic and by now it was self-deprecating sarcasm. Most people have someone to walk them through that and pull them out. Roger had pushed away anyone who might have been able to help him shake off the depression.

He thought about Sandy. He was glad she would never pursue him after what he did. Now he lay awake at night wondering what his life would look like if she had. She was the one, the only one, who was ever able to gain power over him with her rules. Rules, if he followed, might have yielded him a much happier life. Too late now. He would never see her again and he was happy for her but he wished things could be different. What he used to consider the spoils of war now felt more like spoiling the war.

His favorite phrase used to be, "I do not recall an exquisite wine's brand or name," he would say with a grin if asked, "but I never forget the joy of drinking it." It turned out that with Sandy she was the exception. He could not forget her name and he regretted it so much there was never joy.

48

The Undercover Undertaker

JUNE 11, 1993 – NEW YORK CITY

Enoch sat in the coffee shop, occupying a high stool at a long table facing the street. Through Greg, he had become part of what felt like a small but growing group. Greg knew him from Enclave and trusted him. Enoch had been placed into a life of service dealing with the dead through his funeral home, both those who died naturally and those who met a more traditional Addison-Foster Foundation demise.

He was a forced cleaner operating an otherwise legitimate funeral home the A-FF owned. He longed to be free, but he also knew what happened to funeral directors who turned. They became his customers. Even being in New York instead of Columbus was a risk.

He was here on a mission. Greg needed more information on a man named Roger. All he had was a first name, a composite sketch from Sandy's memory, and the location of a newsstand. The goal was to track Roger down, identify other leaders, and begin to understand the scope of this unknown group.

Greg also asked for a photo and something with DNA if possible. A used coffee cup, a cigarette butt, or a few hairs from a coat would do. Anything Enoch could get without putting himself in danger.

The newsstand sat directly in front of the coffee shop window where Enoch waited.

He had been at it for two weeks, and his cover was wearing thin. As a new face ordering coffee every morning and sitting in the same place, he had already made the regular barista uneasy. Maybe it was his undertaker vibe leaking out. Whatever the reason, he could feel her uncertainty every time he ordered. Something about the way she scanned the room.

He pulled a small notepad from his shirt pocket and took cryptic notes he would translate later. If he was unsuccessful today, he would have to return another time. Tonight, he had plans back in Columbus he could not miss.

Wait. Was that him? A man passed directly in front of the window. After glancing at the sketch, Enoch saw a very probable match.

He pressed his Nikon AF 600 close to the glass and blocked it from view with his newspaper. He pressed the shutter three times.

He grabbed his coffee and headed out the door, walking straight to the newsstand. As he approached, he noticed two people watching him from just past the corner. Maybe he imagined it, but he stayed alert. If there was a larger contingent of Main-Landed operatives, New York City was where they would be.

At the newsstand, Enoch got a good look at Roger. He took two more pictures as quickly as he could. He could not aim, so he hoped he had captured something useful.

The man working the stand greeted the customer by name, and Enoch was close enough to hear.

"Ah, it is my best customer. How are you doing today, Roger? I have not seen you in a little while."

Roger replied, "I have been out of town on business, but that business is concluded, and you know what they say?"

"What is that, Mr. Snow?"

"All work and no play make Roger a dull boy."

They both chuckled politely.

Roger refused his change, tucked his purchase under the arm of his expensive coat, and began walking directly toward Enoch.

Enoch reached for a magazine to provide cover. His hand landed on a Mad magazine. For most people, it would have been a poor choice to blend in, but for Enoch it was perfect.

Roger gave him a disdainful look but focused only on the magazine, not Enoch's face. Straight-backed, he passed directly in front of him. Enoch "tripped," and his tall, lanky frame fell toward Roger Snow. He used the stumble to grab Roger's shoulder on the way down.

Roger let out a small pained noise as he lost three hairs from the back of his head during the brief contact. He shot Enoch a glance, but when Enoch stood back to full height, Roger must have remembered he was a lover, not a fighter. He spoke harshly and continued on, walking the short distance to his apartment building.

Enoch purchased the Mad magazine from the clerk and decided to try a question.

"That guy sure gave me a dirty look."

"Oh, Mr. Snow? He would give that look to his own mother if he had not already killed her."

"What!" Enoch feigned shock. "For real?"

The newsstand man was already heading toward another customer, but over his shoulder he said, "All I know is I am going to be nice to him. I do not want to take a twenty-floor nosedive."

Enoch used his long legs to follow in the direction Roger had come from and caught a glimpse of him in the lobby of a nearby high rise. Mr. Snow stood waiting for the elevator.

As Enoch studied him for the brief moment available, he put pieces together. According to the newsstand guy, this handsome and wealthy man had gotten away with murder. Honestly, that made sense. Good looking people seemed able to break the rules in all areas of life. Pretty privilege. So why not murder.

He looked up and took a picture of the address above the door, then hailed a cab to his hotel.

Once in his room, he pulled out the phone book and found the New York Public Library branch most likely to have old newspaper articles stored on microfiche. He asked the concierge to help him book his flight home late enough to allow time for a library visit.

The concierge took charge of his luggage after he checked out and put him in a cab to the Stephen A. Schwarzman branch of the NYPL. Enoch dove into his research. He was anxious to go home, but he wanted to help. After printing several newspaper articles about the murder investigation of his mother, whom he now knew was named Virginia, he was ready to leave.

He arrived in time to catch his flight. The concierge found a one-way flight to Columbus, purchased a ticket under his false assigned identity, and Enoch headed home.

On the plane, he needed to write mission notes. The problem was prying eyes. Normally, on a full flight, this would be an issue.

However, if you dressed like an undertaker and held a Mad magazine, people preferred to find another seat. It also helped if you spoke softly.

The clincher went like this: "Hello, my name is Enoch. Friends call me the Undead. You know, because Enoch in the Bible went to heaven without dying. So, what do you do for a living? I am a funeral director." Then he would offer the double hand over hand greeting used to console grieving families, whispering, "Sorry about my hands. I had to pick up a fresh body for a funeral next week. I have washed them several times but they still feel a little sticky. Oh, do not worry, it is only embalming fluid; it leaves a residue, it is not something gross."

So Enoch had his own row of seats for the duration of the flight, and by the time he landed, he had a ready-to-deliver report. He smiled at the thought of delivering it tonight. This would be fun.

The facts were clear. He knew the man's name was Roger Snow. He knew the building address where he lived. He knew the tip about the newsstand was solid. He had photographs and three hairs plucked with the follicles still intact. The major reveal was the suspected murder of his mother. It was also helpful to know that local police believed Roger had gotten away with it.

It should be easy to find news reports, police records, or some trail to gain more insight. All in all, not a bad trip.

The jet lagged funeral director got off the plane, picked up his car, and headed toward the Continent Shopping Center. He grabbed a bite to eat at the French Market and then greeted the manager.

The sign inside the door read, back by popular demand from his latest cross-country exploits.

The advertising piece read, Tonight and tomorrow only: The American Tourister. Clean comedy for the whole family. He was not as famous as the Unknown Comic, but he had his own regional following.

This was what Enoch really loved to do. After years as a funeral director, he was tired of watching families cry together. Not that there was anything wrong with helping families through the loss of a loved one. His work was important. However, making families laugh together was more enjoyable and just as important.

49

The American Tourister

JUNE 12, 1993 – COLUMBUS, OHIO

The comedy club at the Continent was packed. It usually was whenever The Tourister performed. Enoch sat in the green room. Tonight was family night and the room was filled with parents and their children.

When Enoch performed his comedy set, he played a character called The American Tourister, a fun-loving yokel who wore Bermuda shorts, a Hawaiian flowered shirt, white tube socks, and open-toed leather sandals. His knobby knees were attached to long, lean legs. Enoch was athletically built, though not in an obvious way. This allowed his character to do a lot of physical comedy; his tall, lean body made the exaggerated movements even more hilarious.

The most iconic part of the outfit was the hat. He wore a traditional white beach bucket hat, just like the one Gilligan wore. Enoch pulled it down all the way to his nose so only his chin and mouth were visible. He cut eye holes in the hat and glued a pair of mirrored aviator sunglasses over them. The earpieces rested on a pair of Mr. Potato Head ears glued to the sides of the hat. To finish the look, he added a Mr. Potato Head nose and mustache.

On his chin, he glued a single-strip soul patch in the center of his large lower jaw. His mouth was wide and flexible, allowing for the "mouther-isms" used to intensify the physical humor. To keep it all intact while he bounced and flipped onstage, Enoch added a chin strap. Its only purpose was to protect his identity from being recognized by any member or asset of his full-time employer meant the Undertaker Enoch could become some other colleague's cadaver.

"Ladies and gentlemen, boys and girls! Hold on to your hats! Load up the minivan, because you are about to travel with—THE AMERICAN TOURISTER!"

A round of applause erupted, followed by a wave of laughter as the absurd spectacle loped onto the stage.

"Folks, it is so good to be here. I just flew in from New York City and boy are my arms tired," he said, flapping his long arms and moving his neck in and out like a great blue heron in flight.

His trombone-and-drum guy let out a big "Wah-wah-wah-wahhhh," and the crowd roared. The Tourister shot him a look of hurt betrayal.

"Like I said, I was in New York City, and you know what? It's a real crazy place. They got people everywhere! They got so many people they had to put their trains underground! You can't trust what they tell you neither. They use words all pushed together, you know, like 'forgettabowtit' or 'knowwhutImean.'

"I was asking a man, 'Excuse me, my good man,' letting him know I'm an adjudicated mad who knows proffer English. 'Where do I go to get to meet that famous movie star guy that always wears a hat?' He told me, 'Take this subway and get off at the stop for the Manhattan movie star guy.' So I grabbed his sandwich bag that said Subway and got on the subway.

"I still don't get why New Yorkers push everything together. Maybe it's because the city is big and they need a lot of signs. That would make it cheaper. Instead of 'Man and hat on,' they pushed it all together into one word: Manhattan. They can't even spell! Everyone knows hat only has one T. I settled into my seat, opened the bag he gave me, and there was a big sandwich. The lady next to me said it was a footlong. I said, 'Nah, it ain't that big.' I put the sandwich on the floor and stepped on it, and when I lifted my foot she was right. It was as big as my foot, just much flatter. I ate the sandwich fast just like a real New Yorker. Everybody there talks about 'taking the Subway.' Well, gosh, that could get real expensive giving those away to everyone.

"Now I'm at a coffee shop when I see this guy walk past me. In real life! I mean, here I am hanging out with Moody Stars and News Rankers. You know, the guys in suits that read the news to you on the television."

The Tourister switched to a deep, resonant television voice. “A man was charged with the death of his mother, who appeared to have fallen from her twentieth-floor balcony at the Highwise Hen Houses. A witness at this newsstand nearby was unable to comment on any suspected foul play for fear of restitution.”

In the audience, Greg sat at a two-top table along the wall, very close to the stage. He purchased two tickets and made overt gestures of annoyance while waiting on a date who never arrived. He leaned forward to grab a mozzarella stick and glanced into his pocket, reassured by the blinking red light on the recorder.

“Anyway, so I run outside and snap a few pictures, like one of them Poppa Rocksy fellas. Then I got scared, because I’ve seen those Moody Stars punch them Poppa Rocksy fellas in the face.

“But I digest! Just then I heard the newsstand owner say, ‘Hey there, Mister Snow, I haven’t seen you in a while.’ Hearing his name, well, that is when I worked myself up into a full bladder and threw coffins to the wind. This guy was a full-blown, world-flamous male module!

“When I saw him, I pancaked. I needed to play it real cruel. I bought the most intellectual magazine ever produced—Mad Magazine. What a perfect thing to get autographed.

“‘You’re him! You’re the guy! I’d know that jawline anywhere! Your wife and kids are picture perfect too! Your family’s photo is the official photo of the Walmart eight-by-ten and five-by-seven picture frame section since 1984!

“‘I have the whole collection! I got the 1986 Family in the Meadow frame. I got the 1990 Sunset at the Beach wallet-size. I’ve got them all labeled in cosmological order on my wall at home. Prince dean condition! Still in the Jello-frame wrap with original price stickers!

“‘But your best work is your solo work. Who can deny your genius in the classic inside-wallet photo? You’re in every new Walmart wallet sold in the past ten years! The face of American currency storage. Can I get your Alfred Hitchcok? Like those Four Fathers who signed the Declaration of Index Pendents!’

“Before this guy could react, I had already pulled out my camera, wrapped my arm around his shoulders, and snapped a picture of us together. I think he wanted some more pictures, because he tried to grab the camera. That winder must have got caught in his hair. I went to advance it again, but it didn't click. When I looked, there were two long black hairs caught in it. He said, 'Ouch!' and took off.

"I dropped a twenty on the counter to pay for the Mad Magazine and then started running after the male module guy all the way back to his building, hollering and waving my Mad Magazine the whole way. 'Hey, Mister Snow! Can you autograph Mad? I mean my Mad? I mean, I'm not mad, I want your Mad. Wait, mister, I didn't mean to get you mad. I meant the magazine is Mad. No wait, wait, mister, wait! Oh, don't be mad!'

"I arrived in front of his highwise penthouse building just as he was pointing out the window at me to his friend, the security guard. Can you believe it? He was as excited to meet me as I was to meet him! He was waving his arms and pointing at me through the glass. What a swell guy! The security man, however, looked less excited. So, I left. Flickery spit!"

Greg left at intermission; he had what he needed.

After the show, Enoch stayed and signed every autograph request. Tomorrow he would be embalming a grandmother and preparing a young man from a car accident for his funeral.

The last autographs he signed were for a fourteen-year-old girl named Roxie. She displayed the common traits of Down syndrome. Her parents were beaming as this magnificent young lady vibrated with excitement to meet The American Tourister. She giggled as he signed her purchased video and as he began signing the poster, he paused.

Roxie was quoting his malapropisms: "Poppa Rocksy's," "Male Modules," "Moody Stars," "News Rankers," and she kept going until she repeated all of them from his entire set. She caught every one.

Her mother explained it was Roxie's favorite part. She liked to mess with people by doing them herself. People were afraid to laugh, thinking maybe she didn't know they were incorrect. She let that sit just long enough, and then, her comedic timing always perfect, she giggled to let them off the hook with a "Gotcha" or "Fooled ya."

Roxie said to Enoch, "You know how to make me laugh."

He wrote on the poster for Roxie something he never did before. It was risky and it remained to be seen if it would ever come back to haunt him.

To my biggest fan and my future comedic partner. With love and affliction, Enoch "The American Tourister"

He gave it to Roxie and spoke briefly to her parents.

"Roxie, and you good folks—"

"Oh, excuse us. I'm Stanley Neds, Roxie's dad and this is my wife, Sally."

"It's a real pleasure to meet you both," Enoch said. "Very few people know my real name. I have kept it secret because it could cost me my full-time career and maybe come at a higher-than-expected personal cost. My costume protects me and allows me to carry on with this dream of making people laugh."

Then he addressed Roxie directly. He looked right into her smiling eyes and said, "I have given you my biggest secret. Can you keep it for me?"

Stan and Sally were quiet, averting their eyes as if holding back tears. Roxie smiled and met his gaze. She paused, leaned in toward Enoch, and in a quiet but resolute voice said, "You can count on me. My lips are peeled," and then she giggled and they all laughed.

Roxie's timing and delivery were perfect and she broke the tension Enoch was sure she could feel building. Hugs and handshakes were exchanged and Stan and Sally promised to keep the poster where no one else could see it. This would be their secret. Enoch asked for a phone number so he could arrange Roxie's tickets for his next show.

Enoch paused when he climbed behind the wheel of his Nissan Sentra, the car he only drove as The Tourister. He laughed out loud when he caught his face in the rearview mirror and drove back to the empty funeral home—empty of the living, anyway.

Enoch drove back home. Walking upstairs, he removed his costume, and slipped into sweatpants. While the washing machine churned, he sat in his study and bowed his head.

"Father in heaven, may You help me show You proper honor and strive to glorify Your name. While others reject You, let me be found in Your presence. Let me be strong in heaven according to Your strength and help me remain strong on earth. And Lord, if it is Your will, help me choose Your joy over sorrow. Help me live from day to day, counting only on today's provisions and knowing tomorrow's will surely come from Your hand.

"Forgive me, Lord, for my sarcasm and timidity. Forgive me for my doubt and fear. Help me provide the same forgiveness to even those like Roger, who feel like a lost cause to me, yet whom You love and care for as well. Lord, let me not be tempted by pride or fear. Help me focus on You, Lord, and protect Roxie from the growing darkness that seems to be hidden in plain sight. Deliver us from the schemes of the evil one and those who serve him here on earth.

"And Lord, thank You for the beautiful fruits You have provided through the gift of laughter. Help me see and give proper respect and dignity to every soul I lay to rest within these walls. Lord, if Your plan for me ever includes a wife and a child, I would be grateful, but Your will, not mine. I can be content with this one connection and this one moment You provided tonight. In Your great name I pray, amen."

50

Origins: Old Woman, Young Mother

LATE 1944 – NEW YORK CITY

At twenty-four, Susan had already become an exceptional leader. Under her direction, Mister Foster turned the Great Depression into a financial windfall for the Foundation. She formalized its internal expenditure policies and eliminated outside vendors entirely. If the Foundation needed a service, they bought or created the company to provide it. Not once but repeatedly, multiplying the same businesses across states and regions. Strangers did not enter Foundation facilities. Ownership at every level was safety.

By the end of the war, the system took on a life of its own.

That afternoon, Susan softened her voice. "Let's go see a movie."

With Gustav, she never commanded. She charmed. He was the only person she felt connected to deeply enough to call it love. Romantic, perhaps but a line she would never cross for the sake of the Foundation.

If Susan was a victim of Addison Foster's cruelty, Gustav was the proof. They loved one another from the beginning. First a protective, brotherly love, but as she matured, they both realized it too late. They were inseparable and trapped in a life not allowing more. A quiet tragedy. A waste of two lives.

"A movie sounds like a perfect diversion, Madam," Gustav replied.

He brought around the car they chose together, a two-toned blue 1941 Packard 180 limousine.

Susan slid into the front seat beside him, as she always did when they were alone. Improper, but theirs. Their one sliver of normal. Gustav cherished it.

The Roxy Theater was too close for a long ride but the movie and the drive home would have to be enough.

Susan chose *The Will of the People*, starring silver-screen icon Lauren Baxter and a handsome but out-of-his-depth actor named Harry Stanford. Susan was uncharacteristically giddy. They bought popcorn and sat close to the screen, far from familiar faces.

The war reels held her attention. She watched closely, calculating how the outcome might affect the Foundation. She despised the Nazi approach, crude and wasteful, yet she remained committed to Mister Foster's objective: collect, improve, breed, refine, and finally remove the unfit.

During the film, Susan threaded her arm through Gustav's. He did not move. This was not the Susan the world knew. Gustav loved her anyway.

When the lights rose, she turned to him. "That is it. Lauren Baxter's mystique combined with that optical illusion. The one where, depending on where you look first, it is either an old woman with a scarf or a young woman with a choker."

"I do not follow," Gustav said, "but I recognize that look. Let us talk in the car."

They talked for an hour in the Packard.

It began with a giddy Susan, sounding like the ten-year-old girl he picked up years ago. She would never have let her guard down with anyone else. But this was Gustav. He was safe.

"Do you remember the drawing? The old-and-young-woman illusion?"

"Of course. It is German," he laughed. "So, your plan as you age is to distract the world from the old woman in the scarf with the young woman in the necklace."

"Exactly." Susan leaned in. "I have been wrestling with a concern. How do I remain in control as I age? And what if I do not live long enough to see the end? To see whether my improved version of Addison Foster's dream actually worked. The solution is Hollywood magic."

Gustav opened his mouth to speak but she was on a roll, and he let her continue.

"It is just like Louanne Ringel. Ordinary woman. Ordinary life. Until someone taught her how to emerge from her cocoon. Louanne Ringel became Lauren Baxter through training and patience. And her voice. Everyone hears the power in that husky voice."

She slapped his arm playfully. "Gustav, you cannot argue that when Lauren Baxter is on screen, everyone else diminishes. They stay that way until she leaves the scene and lets them have their moment."

Susan would do the same. Remake her outward shell into a Lauren Baxter persona.

Power would never leave her hands. She would remain unseen, directing from the shadows.

Appearance alone was insufficient. Voice, gesture, cadence. Those were the deception. Susan would master the character modeled on Lauren Baxter, then teach her future iterations using the same materials: movie reels, interviews, anything publicly available. Baxter was easy to emulate and even easier to teach.

"What if I choose a replacement now," she said. "One of the Unwanted's around fifteen. After ten years of training, learning every line Baxter ever uttered, by the time I am thirty-six our young fifteen-year-old will be twenty-five. We slip her into a picture here, a magazine article there, and suddenly she is the new me. She charms the world, and I keep the plan moving. Seamless."

"You will always be young to me," Gustav said.

"Stay focused," Susan replied. "You are the only one I trust."

She outlined the process. Films as manuals. Repetition. Memorization. Behavioral imprinting. Baxter's catalog as doctrine.

"You are creating iterations of yourself," Gustav said. "No one will expect an impostor if continuity is perfect."

"In the public eye," Susan said, "I become immortal."

"And Baxter?"

"Imitation flatters. We take only what is necessary."

Gustav hesitated. "Promise me when we are alone, you will still be my Susan."

She faltered, then nodded. "You have my word."

A moment later she recovered, slipping back into her controlled self. "Now be my love and find a real movie projector. I will call the studio and purchase private screening copies of this film and all others. I need to find the next Susan soon."

"Can you control them," Gustav asked.

"Who controls me," she replied. "Not even Mister Foster was able."

"You cannot number them publicly. You will need a way to name them."

She smiled. "We alter the spelling. Veil. Vale. Vail. Vael."

"And if you must issue orders."

"I am always Susan Veil. If I must appear, I send a successor."

"And if age or one of them betrays you."

"I will solve that too."

"Then it is agreed. You will help me. I will need help molding these successors, and having a big, muscled man at my side will discourage betrayal as we move into the next phase."

51

The Letter

JUNE 23, 1993 – NEW YORK CITY

A woman in her mid-forties sat alone at her desk, using a silver letter opener to open the day's mail. She opened the personal letter first. It was addressed correctly but instead of a proper name where the recipient would be listed it simply said in quotes "Dear Weird Lady Stalking My Life." The letter had been posted from a P.O. box in Cincinnati, Ohio, just a few days ago. She dropped the letter opener and ignored the rest of the mail. She went to her boss's office and quietly knocked on the door, hoping not to be answered.

"Come in," was the clipped, frustrated-sounding reply in the husky lower voice that not only was she used to but sounded much like her own. She heard the click of the electronic door lock unlatch and pulled the pocket doors apart. She closed the doors behind her, turned, and immediately began to speak, extending the letter toward the older version of herself behind the desk.

Not one for idle chatter, her boss grabbed the envelope and pulled out the letter Sandy had sent to the office, marked to whoever this is.

The letter was short and concise:

Hello.

We need to meet face to face. You might remember me from the classic moments of my life. Like when I was ten years old, the day the woman I thought was my mother died in front of me. Or maybe you remember me from when my son was born in Saint

> Croix and you were able to start his breathing? By the way you look as good now as you did in 1955 and 1983. I can't wait to learn your beauty care secrets.
>
> Yes, I know my baby is a boy, and no, no one from your secret little team betrayed you. I just outsmarted Dreadful Debbie which really was not that difficult. You really need better help.
>
> I have a lot of questions that you will answer either voluntarily or, if you prefer, under duress. Oh, and I have questions about my real mother and father as well. See you soon.
>
> Hugs and kisses, Sandy

Miss Veil's reaction was calm, her voice sharp and controlled.

"Leave my office at once. Never speak of this letter. Do you understand?

Before the woman could leave her office, she said "Wait!"

"Susan, it is imperative that you stay calm. As the third and current face of this Foundation you must not panic. You are Susan Vail the Third deception. You are me. You will act with dignity. When I looked up from my desk, I did not see the visage of strong and defiant characters of Lauren Baxter. Oh, sure you looked and sounded like her but the eyes showed fear and your hands trembled. Do I need to retire you early and bring up Miss Vael?"

As the younger woman stood in front of Susan, the first and still preeminent architect of the deception, she drew her strength back in.

"That is better. Now send a message to my son he is to come home from college for the weekend. He and I must talk privately, face to face. Stop wasting my time staring. Go!"

The younger woman gladly left the office and did as she was told. After she had gone and the door shut behind her, Miss Veil remained still.

Why force a confrontation now? Unless for some reason she believes she can win it? If that is true then that meant one of two things: She either knows something I do not, or she has flipped or compromised someone close to me.

Susan Veil reached into the top-right drawer of her antique desk and began writing her own letter. She copied the P.O. box from the envelope and sealed her reply for outgoing mail.

A wry smile touched her lips.

Like mother, like daughter.

She may still have a use after all.

52

Ageless

AUGUST 4, 1994 7:45 A.M. – NEW YORK CITY

If someone had just stumbled in from the street, it would have felt like a trap. It still felt like a trap for Sandy and Paul; they were just expecting it. The information that Enoch had gathered had been put to good use.

After all, when is a trap not a trap? Answer: when you walk in knowing it is.

The only normal feature visible in the lobby was a single elevator, its doors open. The interior lights were on, and the opening stood ready to receive. Now, while that might have seemed odd after all the building's exterior gave the appearance of being empty, this would not by itself make most people turn and exit.

It would be the two sets of double doors flanking the elevator that would make you feel immediately uneasy.

The office doors on both sides of the centered elevator would give pause even to the bravest. After all, the building appeared empty. Your thoughts would start simple and then build into palpable fear, pushing you toward the perceived safety of the public sidewalk.

Each double set of doors boasted strong, pounded steel plates cut into smaller, more manageable weighted pieces. The total weight of just one of each of the four panels making up both sides of each door had to be over 350 pounds. Each door appeared to be thirty inches wide and eighty inches tall, making the total entrance opening around sixty inches, or five feet.

Both sets had latches that met in the middle but extended so they overlapped, both arms crossing each other in front of a reinforced strike plate. When drawn together to secure the doors, each set boasted two modern hardened steel padlocks securing the arms to each other. The locks' curved shackles appeared to have a diameter of one inch.

These doors resembled something you might find protecting an industrial incinerator or a dangerous hardened criminal. In the lobby environment, they were disturbingly out of place.

This offered only one choice for the person entering the lobby: Either board the elevator flanked by doors that looked like they came out of a Stephen King novel, or turn back and exit to the relative safety of the streets of New York City.

Paul and Sandy entered the elevator without hesitation.

The woman from the photo sat alone in her now-empty office in New York. The entire building was deserted except for this one room. She had originally been scheduled to be the first to leave New York and settle into the new offices, but she had dragged her feet. Not out of nostalgia; she simply had one loose end to tie up and thought neutral ground was the best place for it.

No security remained in the old four-story brick mercantile-style building. The massive vault on the fourth floor stood open and empty. Both sets of pocket doors, hers and the ones that normally concealed the vault across from her desk, were pushed back.

They had far too much to discuss to wait.

She knew Sandy would come. She did not know when, but it seemed the wait was over as she heard the familiar whine of the elevator rising to the fourth floor. *That must be her now.*

The elevator stopped with a soft *ding*. The doors slid open slowly.

Before she saw anyone, she heard singing. A beautiful, clear voice drifted out of the elevator, sweet, smooth and effortless.

"I'm just a poor wayfaring stranger, Traveling through this world below . . . There is no sickness, no toil, no danger, In that bright land to which I go I'm going there to see my Father, And all my loved ones who've gone on . . ."

Sandy stopped singing when the woman spoke. Her voice was calm but measured.

"Hello, dear. I see you brought a friend. I can't say I'm surprised. I kept this office open for exactly this occasion. After all, I knew you had the address, didn't I?"

Sandy stepped out of the back right corner of the elevator, Paul right behind her.

"Where's my dad? I know that you know where he is."

That landed the first visible crack.

Paul hadn't spoken yet; he was scanning corners, watching for movement. Even he saw it: the tiniest dip in the old woman's shoulders.

Sandy's breath caught.

Is she having a stroke?

"Hey, are you okay?"

The words slipped out before Sandy could stop them. She crossed the room in three quick strides and caught the older woman's arm just as she swayed. Sandy lowered her gently back into the chair. She was older, but she wasn't frail, not physically, but something inside her had just folded.

"Look, I didn't come here to kill you or let you die of a stroke. Do I need to call 911? And if I did, what name would I give for the person in distress?"

Sandy almost finished the question with a full smile on her face. This was not going as she had planned. She did not expect the woman to respond; she had gone to great lengths not to give her name away already.

"Susan. My name is Susan. And yes, I was there with you when Mrs. Vanover died. But I was not there, as your letter suggested, when your son was born. I have had no part in your life since that day. I am glad to know you are doing well. I have thought about you often."

Silently Sandy prayed. *Lord, I am so confused. Please give me patience. Don't let me be tricked. My heart wants to believe her, but it is wicked and deceitful.*

Paul finally stepped fully into the room, satisfied they were alone.

As Susan regained her strength, she asked Sandy, "Why were you singing that song when you exited the elevator?"

"Are you kidding me?" Sandy replied. "You just admitted to me that my mom and dad were not the Vanover's. You didn't say it but you said "when Mrs. Vanover died. Not mom or mother just Mrs. Vanover. You are obviously well educated and a psychiatrist, and you can't figure out why I would feel like a wayfaring stranger as an adult?"

Sandy softened her tone enough to regain control of herself. Why was she so angry at this woman? If she was telling the truth, she had only met her once, and that meeting had been helpful. Sandy understood her tachypsychia better because of her.

There was a longer-than-normal pause as Paul moved in closer.

"You asked about your dad," Susan continued. "I know him. He is alive and well. Would you like to meet him? I know where you can find him."

"What's his name?" Sandy asked.

"Gustav," Susan replied. "That's all I know. I don't even know his last name. He is just Gustav."

She wrote down an address on a piece of paper from her phone stationery and handed it to Sandy.

"It's in rural New Jersey. Less than two hours from here, even with traffic."

Sandy tucked the paper into her pocket, then moved forward with her agenda. She began to ask more questions, and Susan shut her down.

"Some things are better left unsaid and discovered, dear," she said with a condescending lilt to her voice. "Go visit your father. See what he has to say. You may find it enlightening."

She glanced away, dismissing them.

"Now, if you'll excuse me, I have an important errand to run, and the timing is precise. I prefer to be punctual, and for me, on time is late."

Paul stepped forward before the opportunity was gone. He made the momentary decision to stay with the Island accent. Why? He wasn't sure. Maybe just to hold something back for effect later on. He thought, *Why give her information about me for free? She certainly isn't giving up too much for Sandy. It may not mean anything either way but I can't put the accent back once I give it away. The less this mystery woman knows about me the better. Something wasn't right.*

"I have a few questions before we go. First one is this: Why you gettin' so uptight? Sandy travels a long way to see you, and if you tellin' the truth, which in my mind is a big if, then why you gettin' so rude and so eager to push us out just now? There a whole lot of unanswered questions 'round you, and we want some answers."

Susan interjected sharply. "What are you babbling about?"

Paul regained control; his words deliberate now.

"How you could have two pictures of yourself 'bout thirty years apart, and you look near identical in both? I could see now you age some, but the two pictures I have make you look timeless."

He stepped closer; his voice unwavering.

"You pop into her life when she ten. You don't look any different than you did in 1955. You know who her real father is, but you let her rot in foster care. Somethin' not makin' sense."

"What's your point?"

"No point. Just a promise. If this a wild goose chase, we gonna find you again."

Susan's voice calmed. "I understand now why you are so frustrated. You are under some false notions. I am not part of either of your lives. I am a psychiatrist who spoke with you, Sandy, during your childhood trauma. I have no other connection. The reason I know who your father is because he sought me out years later after seeing my picture with you in the newspaper."

She paused.

Susan glanced at her watch. "I really need to go now. This errand will not wait. Come see me after you meet your dad, and we can talk more then. I'm not going anywhere. Just come back here when you're done."

Once they were settled in the Explorer in the parking garage, Paul broke the silence.

"You okay?" Paul asked.

"Yes. I think that helped me a bit." Sandy exhaled slowly. "I noticed you threw the patois at her. I think that was a smart call. I held back on confirming any version of my real name also."

Paul chuckled. "We are just two paranoid peas in a pod, aren't we?" Then with a more serious tone he asked, "Well, one visit down, two left. Who's next on the visit list? Roger? Or Gustav?"

"For some reason, it feels more urgent to go see Roger than Dad next," Sandy said, staring out the window. "I'd rather end on a possible happy note than in the key of Roger minor."

"Next stop: Roger," Paul said as he backed out of the parking spot.

Sandy navigated, and within fifteen minutes, they were parking in the garage across from the building that Enoch had seen him enter.

Paul broke the silence with a slight laugh. “The Highwise Hen house, it is, my lady.”

They both laughed.

53

Roger Down

AUGUST 4, 1994 11:30 A.M. – NEW YORK CITY

They waited, occasionally starting the Explorer to cool down the interior. They each had a pair of binoculars. Paul kept watch on the newsstand down the block while Sandy watched the front of his building, right at the exit doors.

Sandy saw him first. "I don't believe it. Enoch was dead-on. That's my buddy Roger, all right."

Paul swung his binoculars over to look and said, "The man in the pompous suit, that looks far to too heavy and hot to be wearing it in this heat?"

"Pale green tie," she said. "Wow, your taste in men really improves." Paul quipped.

He kept it lighthearted, attempting to ease whatever was happening in her mind.

Paul swung further right to see what else was nearby in case they needed a closer vantage point. That's when he saw it: a black Suburban waiting in the curb lane, facing toward Roger's building.

Sandy spoke. "Looks like he is heading toward the crosswalk to the garage. He must have a car here."

"We've got company. Black SUV sitting in the curb lane right by the building, Paul pointed and said "See, just there. I mean, New York's full of them, sure, but this one appears to be waiting for someone. Maybe just picking up a rider?"

He had barely gotten the words out before he raised his voice in an alarmed tone, "It's on the move in the curb lane, moving way too fast."

Sandy figured it out first. "Roger is stepping into the crosswalk now. They are here to kill him."

Sandy reached over and hit the horn as loud as she could, but it made things worse. She yelled, "Don't. Wait, Roger, look out."

Her actions had a negative impact. He stopped right in the lane and looked up toward the sound of the horn with a deeply puzzled expression on his face. The SUV hit him on a glancing blow to avoid running up on the curb. Instead of running over him, it knocked him backward onto the sidewalk, but it hit him hard.

Paul swiveled his binocs and read the license plate number, quickly writing it in his notebook. He jumped out of the Explorer, Sandy was already on the stairwell, running down. She reached him before anyone else, not because she was that fast, but because no one else wanted to get involved. They stood there stunned. As she came closer, she could hear a woman on the phone with 911. With that already being handled. She just needed to try to keep him conscious if he was bleeding. When Paul arrived down on the sidewalk a few steps behind Sandy, she was holding his head secure while he laid flat on his back, Sandy was attempting to keep his neck from moving, using the concrete like a backboard. The goal was avoiding any further injure to his spine, but it did not look good. The ambulance arrived almost fifteen minutes later. Sandy kept talking to him.

"Roger, it's Sandy. If you die, I'll kill you."

Roger was not lucid, but he moved a single eye toward her face. Both eyes were not tracking, and she knew that was bad, but one did. He did not laugh, but she could tell he caught the humor.

"I wish . . ." Then he passed out.

"Hang in there, Roger. Don't you dare go anywhere."

Lord, help me. He is dying. If he dies, he is doomed. Please, Lord, please spare him. I don't know why I am begging, but I am. I don't know why it matters so much to me, but it does. I do not have standing with You, God. I continue to drag my feet toward You when I know I should run. I am not asking for me, Lord. You and I both know I have wished this and worse on Roger since 1980. But either I have changed my mind or You are changing my heart. I do not want revenge. Please let him live.

Paul saw she was praying, but he also saw Roger fading. The paramedics were now heading toward her with a backboard and stretcher. As she moved away to let them treat him, it happened again.

Paul was already on the phone with Greg. He quickly explained why he was calling and said, "Plenty more going on, but I need a favor. Any way you could check license plates on Enclave vehicles without putting yourself at risk?"

"Yes, I can just check maintenance records with a close license plate match. The database will show me all the ones close to that number for planned service dates like oil changes."

"Great." Paul read him the license plate number and waited, not so patiently, for the results. He knew he was right, but he hoped he was wrong. After a brief pause, Greg came back on the line and said, "That one is tasked currently in Manhattan at the old office. All the maintenance records are near Manhattan, including a car wash and a service request just about three minutes ago at the downtown Chevy dealer. I did not know anyone was still in the Manhattan office. Whoever it is it must be someone important."

"That SUV just ran down Roger right in front of us, and I'm almost sure Susan was inside when it happened."

"What?"

"Greg, I have to go with Sandy to the hospital. I'll check in later."

Paul hung up and turned to look for Sandy.

Sandy looked down and noticed Roger's breathing had slowed. Then she noticed Paul was slowing, and as she looked around, everyone else was slow. It was happening again. Her tachypsychia was ramping up for a full swing.

Sirens dropped from urgent to a low thrum, almost like helicopter blades cycling between their respective pitches. She could see people moving, but they were blurred and indistinct. She looked down at her own hands. They were covered in red. She looked up to see a jet plane appear to be standing still in the distant sky.

There were people mixed into the crowds who appeared almost faceless, like large groups of people wearing fencing masks. They were not wearing masks, of course, but they were everywhere. She looked left and saw two near the newsstand. One appeared to be an older woman by the looks of her body and clothing, she appeared fit and trim but gray-haired and no face. The one next to her could not have been more than nineteen or twenty years old. She began turning her head in different directions to see if there were more. They were everywhere. All kinds of ages and sizes. There were no children, only young adults through seniors. They were still in slow motion like everyone else, but they were in sharper view than the people around them with faces.

Their fencing-mask-like faces were turned toward her. Maybe at Roger, since he lay on the sidewalk in front of her, but either way, they were the object of attention. Then there was a rushing sound in her ears as the world began speeding back up. The entire episode lasted six to eight seconds in real time, but in her experience, it felt like five minutes, though she always struggled to pin the physical duration time down after these tachypsychia events ended.

Paul was helping her off the pavement. “Come on, Sandy. We have to get to the hospital. The police have agreed to meet us there to take our statements. That means you can be with Roger. He doesn’t have a next of kin listed, so this could get really awkward. You sure you’re up to it?”

“Yes.”

Paul went to retrieve the Explorer to pick her up. As he headed across the street, the ambulance driver called out to him. “Got to go. Doing an exaggerated two-hand point at Sandy the paramedic said, she doesn’t look good either, and she’s begging to ride with us. I’m not supposed to, but I will if you’re okay with it?”

“Yes, yes, please. Which hospital?” Paul yelled as the distance grew.

“Bellevue.” Then the door of the ambulance shut with Roger and Sandy inside, heading toward Bellevue Hospital.

Paul made it to the SUV and prayed. “Lord, what’s my purpose in this situation? What do You want me to do? And what should I do now about Susan?”

54

Meeting Dad

AUGUST 4, 1994, 11:54 A.M. – BELLEVUE HOSPITAL, NEW YORK CITY

When the ambulance rolled up to the drop-off, the back doors flung open. Sandy and the paramedic closest to the door jumped out. Before Sandy could even move out of the way, the trauma team was all over Roger. Within seconds, the unconscious Roger was being wheeled toward another set of double doors. Sandy started to follow but knew she could not, so she stopped.

"Ma'am? Ma'am, hello, can I get some information from you?"

Sandy turned to see one of the ER intake clerks standing behind a small section of the long counter. She walked back and sat in front of the clerk.

"Are you his wife?" asked the clerk.

Sandy responded, "No, more of an acquaintance. You know, just happened to be there at the time."

"Oh, then I guess we don't really need to go through all this. Do you at least know his name so we can identify him?"

"His name is Roger Snow?"

"Thank you," said the clerk.

Sandy thought, *What am I doing here?*

Her Inner Crazy began to interject. She had been relying on her long-time companions less and less as her understanding grew. She suppressed them again, sat in a lobby chair, and fell asleep.

Paul stayed with her but began to pace around the waiting area to avoid falling asleep to allow Sandy to catch rest first.

"Sir, we need to ask you and the lady a few questions about the incident with Mister Snow. We need to know more about the car horn. Do you know who pressed it? Was it you? Or her?"

"Why is that important if you don't mind me asking?"

"Roger's mother was killed years ago and the last thing she heard was a car horn coming out of the parking garage. So, we figure it could be a revenge thing. You gotta admit its an awful big coincidence."

Paul responded politely, "Sure, I can see why you would want to find out more. But like I said. She is sleeping right now. This has been a traumatic morning. Could you please come back when she is more alert? I can wake her up but it may not really help her focus with such a short nap."

The officers looked at each other and one glanced at his watch. "Sure, we will be back later. But if you are leaving for any reason, let the desk clerk know. Bathroom, whatever?

Paul realized he had not asked for a badge number, name or rank but as he turned, he could see the detectives disappearing into the crowd,

Sandy awoke about 45 minutes later to the general sounds of the hospital and as she opened her eyes, she saw Paul sitting upright and alert, keeping vigil.

"He is in his first surgery right now. The detectives will be back; they let you sleep."

"What did they want to know that hasn't already been told? I don't really remember much."

"They believe that the horn was a signal for the SUV to run him down. They are looking at this as possible attempted murder, not a traffic accident."

"Why is that the biggest question mark? Black SUV, middle of the day, running him down from a complete stop. Why is the horn so important? I mean, enough to think it triggered the whole thing. We are in New York City; horn honking is almost its own language," Sandy whispered back.

"Apparently a loud car horn was the last thing Roger's mother heard from the parking garage just before falling to her death. Roger was the prime suspect, just as Enoch reported. You have to admit that it is quite an odd similarity. If I were the detective on this case, that is where I would start.

"How are you feeling?"

"I am okay. I had one of my tachypsychia events on the sidewalk. I really don't understand this one at all."

Before Paul was able to respond, a different set of men approached, producing a badge confirmed the impression as they arrived. "Hello, folks, sorry to keep you waiting, I'm Detective Davis and this is my partner Detective Haun. I've been meaning to ask you both to provide a witness statement and answer a few questions. However, we have so many eye witnesses to this incident. That may no longer be necessary."

Paul spoke first. "I am confused the other two said detectives already took my witness statement earlier. Sandy was sleeping, they said they would let her rest and come back later."

Both detectives looked at each other, puzzled. "Did you get their names or badge info?"

Paul simply said "No it happened while I was still on the initial adrenaline rush and just beginning to crash. I remembered almost as soon as they walked away but when I turned, they were already blended in to the crowd and moving away pretty fast. Sorry I know that would have been helpful,"

"Can you describe them?"

Paul responded professionally. "Sure. One was tall about six foot and was wearing a really nice suit. He was dirty blond and spoke with a slight Southern accent. The other only spoke once and that was 'thank you for your time we will be back.' He was shorter about 5' 7" and had several tattoos on his forearm. He was wearing a short-sleeved shirt so that made them easy to spot. No distinguishing accent or anything funny about the way they walked before you ask."

"Well thank you for the information. Let's exchange contact info and if you have any other conversation with these other officers, will you let me know, please?" He handed Paul a card with his badge number and contact info while detective Hahn got the information from their I.D.s and then handed them back with quiet professional courtesy. "Don't leave town please just in case." "Actually, we were heading to New Jersey to meet her father for the first time." Said Paul with frustration in his voice. "That's fine just make sure you come back." "We will" replied Paul.

Once released from the officers, Paul and Sandy were eager to hit the road to meet Gustav. They went to the cafeteria and bought some not-too-appetizing deli sandwiches in those triangle shaped boxes and a bag of chips. They waited for Roger to be stabilized from the first surgery. They were still not allowed to visit with him. The shift nurse politely kept repeating. "Mister Snow needs his rest more than anything else right now." To Sandy it seemed like a polite way to say, "You are not family and are not going in to that room."

Sandy left her name and info with the desk clerk who was just coming on duty and then she and Paul headed for the Explorer to go try to meet her father for the first time. Or at least as far as she knew it would be her first time.

AUGUST 4, 1994, 6:12 P.M. – BELLEVUE HOSPITAL TO RURAL NEW JERSEY

Paul pulled the GPS from the glove box and set it up. He entered the address and stuck it on the stand by the steering wheel. He turned off the sounds and drove.

After about an hour-and-twenty-minute drive, where Sandy gave in to sleep and Paul fought it, Paul realized where they were going.

"That's odd, Sandy. We're getting closer."

Sandy began straightening up in her seat and stretching.

"Where are we?" Sandy asked.

"I don't really know. We are in rural New Jersey but the GPS says we will arrive at the "New Jersey Bible Church" in another hour. It looks like we will get there around 8 o'clock."

"Is your father a religious man?" Paul asked.

"Your guess is as good as mine. I've never met him."

As she spoke, they turned right, and up ahead they saw a beautiful old stone church. The sun was starting to go down and the sky was mesmerizing. People were piling out of cars and heading in for what appeared to be an evening service.

"Maybe he's a country pastor these days," she said.

Paul did not respond. She looked over; he just appeared weary from the day and the drive.

He pulled into a parking spot and said, "Looks like it's starting. Let's head on in and see what's going on. We can ask someone there if they know your father. I know I usually turn on the island accent when we are in fact-finding mode, but tonight at church, I think I will just be me."

Sandy chided, "Sounds good, I'll do the same." "Tonight, I am Sandy Ruth Vanover-Simmons-Placeholder" Paul laughed, "How about just Sandy."

So, they strolled, arm in arm, through the parking lot. Families and seniors eagerly went toward the wide-open double doors. They picked up a bulletin on the way in and took a seat near the back. Several people acknowledged them with a smile that read, "Visitors! We don't see those very often out here."

The service was enjoyable and quaint, consisting mostly of a few hymns. Sung with wholehearted fervor by a church that believed every word. The rest of the service was the message from the pastor. No classroom or announcements, just a single verse of the Bible. The man teaching was large and might be intimidating if he chose to be. Instead, he was friendly, warm, and very pleasant to listen as he delivered his urgent message. He taught from his King James Bible on Matthew 5:5: "Blessed are the meek, for they shall inherit the earth." Paul and Sandy were surprised to learn the Greek word "*praus*," translated as "meek," but in the Greek it actually refers to someone who possesses the strength needed but keeps it under restraint. He evoked the image of a strong plow horse restraining its power in obedience to the plow man. So, they learned that meekness did not equal weakness and in fact took more strength.

Sandy and Paul were pleased at learning something new and they thoroughly enjoyed the service. The time was an unexpected blessing they were not aware they needed: a forced slowdown to focus on the Lord they both still seemed to be wrestling with hour by hour.

After the service an elder gave the benediction while the pastor moved to the back of the church. When he finished the benediction, the service ended with a simple "God bless you, you are dismissed." Lifting their heads from the benediction, the pastor was close to their seats, ready to bid farewell to his flock.

Paul and Sandy waited until they could take the last position. People continued to acknowledge them with warm smiles. They appeared eager to speak with them. However, they showed restraint like perhaps this was not the time. All around, it was a very real and emotional service as they grappled inside themselves with their lack of commitment to the Lord. They knew Him; that is, they knew He was real and present. They had even seen Him work.

They stood and walked toward the door. The pastor gave them a warm smile. Sandy became excited. This must be her father.

The pastor smiled and extended a hand: a kindly gray-haired gentleman with broad shoulders and an even broader smile.

"Hello there," he said. "What brings you to our little country church on this outstanding evening?"

Sandy spoke excitedly, "I'm here to meet my father for the first time. Maybe you know him. All I have is a first name. Does the name Gustav mean anything to you?"

The pastor looked stunned. He started his sentence with "Oh my child," but finished with, "he was my older brother, and he died here with me just a few weeks ago. You just missed him. His grave is out back. You must be Sandy!"

Her heart broke. Then rage filled it. *Why would Susan do this? How could she be that ruthless? I don't understand.* Without saying another word, Sandy walked outside alone. Paul came out a few minutes later and said, "Mattias said we are welcome back anytime."

They started strolling toward the Explorer, which now sat by itself farther back in the old church lot than either of them remembered.

Sandy broke the silence hovering between them, heavy like the hot August night's thick, humid air.

"Paul, I want to go back to New York to check on Roger. I also want to talk to Susan again before she leaves New York. She will be impossible to get to after she moves."

Paul said, "I'm good with that but my only suggestion would be to start with Roger first."

Sandy spoke with resolution and kindness. "Paul, I am okay. I just want answers. How about this." She slipped her arm inside his and used her other hand to hold on tight as they walked. Sandy was not trying to manipulate Paul; she was drawing strength and comfort from him.

She continued, "We take a drive. Maybe find an all-night diner, grab some food, catch at least a few hours of sleep in the Explorer, and then head back into Manhattan. First we catch up with Sadistic Susan in the early morning, then off to Bellevue Hospital to see if Roger is awake and able to take visitors. I really would like him to hear what I have to say before we head back to Columbus. Either way, we need gas. I'll drive; I'm wide awake anyway."

"That sounds reasonable but if you change your mind about driving, just let me know," Paul said while already walking to the passenger side of the Explorer to hop in.

After finding food and gas and a little sleep, Sandy woke before dawn. The moon was visible but only just: a waning crescent. Since a waning crescent shows only a tiny sliver, and because of its position on the horizon, it was only visible pre-dawn. Sandy was about to start the Explorer; Paul was still asleep. They were parked just off the side of the road in what appeared to be a police pull-off behind a billboard.

Instead of starting the car, she paused and remained still while she stared at the sliver of moon in the pre-dawn sky. Sandy thought about many things that evening during the drive but at that exact moment she was thinking about R2, wondering how he was doing, thankful Melanie was cat-sitting. She missed him. Was he missing her as much as she missed him? She thought about R2 and Roger the cat, his predecessor. She thought about the night she had to let Roger go and about the kindness of Greg and Melanie bringing R2 and placing him in the Timberbrook house the next morning.

She said out loud, barely a whisper, "I'm okay, Rog. I'll be home soon."

Then, shaking the moment off, she started the Explorer and turned the GPS back on to head toward Manhattan.

Less than fifteen minutes later in Sandy's apartment at the LVQ, Melanie was sound asleep. R2 woke up and stood and stretched. His azure eyes now wide open as he rubbed them gently with his paws.

The now fully-awake Siamese jumped back up onto the metal window frame, his favorite place, his version of the catbird seat. Normally he would sprawl out and enjoy the heat absorbed through the glass and metal window frame.

At this moment, though, R2 stopped and struck a pose like a statue: completely still. No tail movement, no darting head or ears.

He stood like a regal cat in an Egyptian glyph. His blue eyes pierced like the Bat-Signal in the comic books, cutting through the clear nighttime sky. His gaze was now fixed on the waning crescent moon, now fully visible in the pre-dawn sky.

Somehow, the pose R2 struck while staring at the moon gave the appearance the moon was staring at him, not the other way around. He made no sounds.

The only sounds heard were the hum of the streets through the glass and the air movement from the apartment's air conditioner in the dark room.

Then R2's posture relaxed, he laid down on the warm metal sill, and went back to sleep.

55

Susan Fractures

AUGUST 5, 1994, 7:20 A.M. – SUSAN'S OFFICE, NEW YORK CITY

Susan was pressing a pot of coffee when she heard the old elevator move toward the top floor. She had left the front door unlocked, expecting their return, and sent the elevator back to the ground floor to wait. She was not sure when they would return and was surprised they were back so soon.

Susan had purchased a moment alone with Roger from one of the nurses the day before, hoping there might be memory loss and she could call the mission a success. This was her unfinished business before moving to the new home in Ohio. Unfortunately for Roger, even barely conscious he recognized her right away. At least she assumed that from the rising heart rate and the crash team flooding the room just seconds after she appeared in the doorframe. He could not have possibly spoken yet, and she had to make sure he never did. Roger was still connected to a roomful of machines and was still mostly unconscious, according to the nurse who was short on her car payment that month. So she was safe for a little while. Susan left the possibility open: either his reaction was a complete coincidence, or he knew she was there and did the only thing his body unconsciously could do to preserve itself.

The elevator door opened and rather than a sweet voice singing, she heard rage.

"Are you proud of yourself?" Sandy said.

Paul joined in, furious, so frustrated he forgot to put his accent back in. "You are sicker than we thought. Why would you do something so cruel? Is this a game to you?"

Susan looked genuinely confused.

"What are you talking about?"

"Why did you send me to see Gustav at his brother's church when you knew?" Sandy's voice cut like steel. "What is the goal of your sick game? Paul and I are here for answers, and we will get them before we leave."

"Knew what?" she screamed. "What did your father tell you?"

With that last sentence, Paul and Sandy figured it out. They glanced at each other in recognition and let silence fall, everyone bringing it down a notch or two.

Sandy broke the silence.

"Susan, I think we have made an error here and assumed too much."

"When was the last time you saw Gustav?" Sandy asked.

"I'm not sure exactly," Susan replied, her voice hollow. "Almost three weeks ago, I think."

She paused, gathering the pieces.

"Gustav said he was going to visit his brother's church to get some clarity and would be back when we could talk more. I admit I thought meeting you would bring him back. I take it he isn't with you."

"Susan," Sandy said, pausing. "I did not meet Dad. He is gone."

"What?" Susan's voice wavered. "Maybe his brother knows where he went? Or maybe he is coming back here and you passed him on the way?"

"No. He is buried behind his brother's church. He died two weeks ago from natural causes. No foul play, no one hurt him. He died in his sleep. I did not get to meet him. He was gone before we arrived. I thought you knew and sent me there to be cruel. I am sorry I assumed that."

Susan stared at nothing.

"Gustav was the one thing in my life that was not a joke. Something real and satisfying and good. I will never see him again. You are lying! Now who is sick!" She caught herself. "No, it's true, isn't it?"

Her voice cracked.

"I have lost the only person who ever actually cared about me."

Paul came over, moved by her words and what he knew was coming next. He helped her sit. He did not ask; he just lowered her to her desk chair, and she did not even think to protest. For the first time in her life, she was lost.

"I don't think I even told him I loved him when he left. We had a fight. He wanted to go see his brother for a while and get some advice and perspective. He promised he would come back."

Sandy spoke softly. "You two were a couple? I didn't know."

With that realization spoken aloud, Susan sobbed.

She was inconsolable for hours. They had no choice but to stay with her, even though they wanted to check on Roger. They took turns sitting with the now frail and broken woman. She had showers and a kitchen, and Sandy and Paul were running on empty.

They took turns showering. Paul put on a suit from one of the closets. It looked brand new, and there were perhaps fifty more just like it. Paul made a note of it for a later conversation. Sandy took a tasteful dress from Susan's closet with her nodded permission.

It marked the first time Sandy saw Paul in a suit and the first time Paul saw Sandy in a dress. They struggled not to notice each other, but the effect would have been obvious to anyone who was not grieving.

As for Paul and Sandy, they were not married; they were in a relationship, but neither would have classified it as boyfriend and girlfriend. That did not begin to cover the depth of what they had been through together.

Sandy thought about this while Paul showered.

This is what could happen to her and Paul. Closer than most married couples through shared trauma. Sharing the same mother in a spiritual sense but never once feeling like brother and sister. And now bereft of the chance to ever fix some of these mistakes here on earth.

Is this a consequence for trying to undermine the Lord? A consequence of sin, she finally concluded. Something she had a lot of in her past and, as she was beginning to understand, plenty more to come in her future. Now she understood Greg's conflict. Lying, stealing, all for what feels like the right reasons. But is that how God views it?

The Lord is never surprised, which she still struggled to understand. He knows what is done in secret and what will be done. Christ Himself warned that His standards were higher than the law. If you are angry with a man in your heart, you are a murderer. Yet He had to die on the cross to cover those sins, past, present, and future. It wasn't that she did not understand the concept of grace. She didn't seem to have the capacity to execute it on any level higher than forgiving a harsh word. Maybe turning the other cheek when someone eats the last slice of pizza without asking.

God could wipe these people and their plans out in an instant, yet He chooses to work through train wrecks like me?

I need to think. I also need to keep Susan safe while staying safe from Susan. We don't really know her. She felt obligated to her because of her father, but how far does that obligation go? Does honor thy father and mother include parents who did not raise you? It's the only commandment with a promise, but does that apply to her situation? How? How do I do that?

What Sandy did not know was that Paul went through an almost identical version of this thought process while she was getting cleaned up.

So two people came in angry and hurt to meet someone they assumed was feeling strong and in control. Three broken and confused people left.

Once in the SUV, Sandy took the first leg of the drive and Paul would take the return. Susan stayed back and said she wanted to turn off the gas and lights since it was an old building and she was not sure when they would be back. Once alone, Susan left a note on her desk for security. It was cryptic on purpose, to keep from being followed. The note simply read:

I have some important personal business to take care of. I will be gone for a few days. Don't try to find or follow me. I will be in touch in two days. If you have not heard from me by then, you may begin the search, but if you start before then, you will not like the consequences when you find me.

56

The New Jersey Bible Church

AUGUST 5, 1994, 11:47 A.M. –
NEW YORK CITY – RURAL NEW JERSEY

On the road trip back to Mattias', Susan did not speak. She just stared out the window like the world had ended. And in her heart it felt like it had. The grief rolling off her was thick enough to choke on. It shocked Sandy. It shocked Paul. Neither of them knew how to console her.

The drive was almost an hour and a half of dead silence.

Sandy sat in the back and stared at the back of Susan's head. She felt sorry for her. The knot between them had been tied long before Sandy even knew Susan existed.

Susan was the kind doctor who had sat with little Sandy and explained tachypsychia like it was no big deal.

Now she was crying over a dead man.

And Paul. Sandy kept pushing him away. Later, she always thought. Maybe when this is over. Gustav just proved there might not be a later.

Paul was thinking the same thing up front. He missed his mom's voice. *Quit lookin' out there for answers, boy. Open the Bible sittin' two feet from your hand.*

Sandy and Paul kept catching each other's eyes in the rearview mirror. They had so much to say and no way to say it with Susan right there. The air felt heavy, like the car was shrinking.

They still did not know how to stop any of this. They only knew how big it was.

Sandy made herself a promise, quiet and fierce. She always kept her promises if it was in her power. She hated the ones she could not keep.

She remembered kissing Paul on the cheek once and whispering, "Don't you dare get killed, Mister. I have plans for us."

Plans. What plans? Keep him in danger? Disappear for years? Almost get him killed a dozen times? Real great plans.

If. If. If.

The church turnoff came up. She shoved it all down again.

Time to see Mattias. She just hoped he was home.

57

Mattias Gottlieb

They pulled into the country church parking lot a little after 1 p.m. The church appeared locked, as you would expect but there was a pastor's cottage just to the left of the parking lot. Paul and Sandy were certain Pastor Mattias lived there, which was confirmed when they saw him sitting on the porch swing as they arrived.

Paul parked, hopped out, and went over to greet Mattias, who was pleased to see them back so soon. He did not appear put off or even surprised. Paul was about to give him a rundown of what happened that morning and a quick overview of who Susan was but when he realized she was with them, Mattias stood and began walking toward the Explorer to open the passenger door for her.

He did not make it that far. As soon as Susan saw him approaching, she jumped out of the car and moved surprisingly fast for her age toward the tall old pastor.

Sandy was now out of the back seat and moving around the front of the car. She misread Susan's sudden burst of movement as aggression or anger. By the time Sandy was fully clear of the car, Susan was already wrapped in an embrace, both weeping and laughing, holding each other like long-lost family.

That is exactly what was happening.

Mattias bore a strong resemblance to his brother Gustav, and during Gustav's visits he constantly told his little brother stories about Susan. So much so the pastor already knew who was coming forward to embrace him. Through Gustav, they had already met, though not in person.

This was not at all what Paul and Sandy expected.

Mattias spoke first, his long arms still wrapped around Susan. "You are all welcome to come into my home but it is very small. We would probably be more comfortable in the church."

The idea of cramming into the small cabin was not appealing after the long drive, so he pulled out his keys and they walked quietly over to the church.

There, stories were shared. Laughter and tears flowed, and Susan seemed to heal a little.

Oh, Gustav, if only you were still here to see this.

Sandy could see Susan was acting differently here, in this place, with these people. She wondered if this was what Susan was like with her father, and if so, her father must have been remarkable. The bigger question in Sandy's mind was what Susan would look like tomorrow and beyond. Susan had not earned her trust and even though the circumstances were tragic, Sandy would not extend it until she had more real information about where Susan intersected with her life. Not just in the places she was aware but also where she was not.

Then there was Paul.

He was acting strangely too. Sandy kept catching him staring at her and he looked either unhappy or intensely focused. It was hard to tell the difference. She would need to talk to him later. Maybe it was the dress. She felt self-conscious in it, like a girl going to prom.

"Would anyone like something to drink? I have some fresh lemonade in the house," Mattias offered.

Paul spoke first. "I do. I'll help you bring it out." Without another word he stood and followed Mattias into the house.

I hope Paul is okay, Sandy thought. *He sure is acting odd.*

Paul waited until they were safely inside the cottage. Then it all came out in a rush.

"Do you recall saying you could officiate a wedding for Sandy and me when we were ready?"

"Yes, of course I do."

"Why did you say that? You don't know us at all. Why would you suggest marriage?"

Mattias paused. Seeing the distress resting on Paul, he said, "You are right. I should not have been so bold. I marry couples all the time but you both just seemed so right together. The way you talked about her and defended her after she walked away in anger, well, you impressed me. It was obvious she meant more to you than just a friend. Please forgive my error. It was wrong of me. Will you accept my apology?"

Paul spoke with urgency. "No. I won't accept your apology but I would accept your help. You were right. After what happened with Gustav today and seeing Susan's despair, I am gearing up the courage to ask if you could help me marry her today. Is that possible?"

Mattias smiled. "So that is why we are getting lemonade together. May I ask what you are thinking?"

"I have my mother's ring with me. I have carried it since she died. There was no safe place to leave it, so I kept it with me, hoping to someday use it for this very reason. After seeing the grief on Susan's face today and hearing her say, 'I made him wait too long, for reasons that do not matter,' I do not want Sandy to ever feel that kind of pain."

Paul smiled sheepishly and continued. "Sandy and I need to avoid those regrets. Would you marry us here if I propose today?"

"Short answer, yes. It would be an honor. The more complicated answer involves New Jersey law. There is a three-day waiting period and you must both sign in front of a judge. Let me think. Today is Friday. You must propose in the next thirty minutes if you want a chance today."

"You just said the waiting period was mandatory."

"It is for normal authority. Today I am appealing to an earthly authority and a heavenly one. Take the lemonade back while I make a call and pray. You had better hurry."

Paul returned with the lemonade and explained Mattias would be out shortly. Susan sat in the front pew facing forward. Sandy remained in the back where they sat before.

Paul handed Sandy a lemonade and carried one up to Susan. She was deep in thought, so he set it down beside her and waited for her eyes to acknowledge it. When they did, he walked back toward Sandy.

He realized then she was out of his league. The dress, her quiet presence, the way she carried herself. It took his breath away. Literally. He approached her and began coughing.

"Gonna grab a cough drop. Be right back."

He went to the Explorer and opened his go-bag. He found the small hidden zipper compartment and pulled out the engagement ring. It was his mother's, and he knew she would have wanted it to be Sandy's.

Back inside, Mattias was still absent. Susan remained bowed in the front pew.

Paul walked up to Sandy. She sat with her skirt falling to her ankles, green eyes fixed on him.

"Paul, are you okay? You seem out of sorts."

Paul met her gaze, something he rarely dared to do.

"Sandy, you talk about being a window. About surviving unseen. But you were never invisible to me. Not ever. Not to my mother either."

She began to cry silently.

Paul lowered to one knee and pulled the ring from behind his back.

"Sandy, I can't wait another day. After what I saw today, I know this is right. Will you do me the honor of becoming my wife?"

She looked at the ring, then at him, pausing to gather her voice.

"I bet you're really nervous right now," she said. "Do you remember what I said to you when we bugged out of Timberbrook?"

"I remember the kiss on the cheek," he said with a grin.

She smiled. "I said, 'Don't you dare get killed, Mister. I have plans for us.' Well, here we go. Of course I will marry you."

She wrapped her arms around his neck. "I love you, Paul. I have since the day I met you."

"That ring was Momma Ruthy's," he whispered. "She would be happy."

"That ring. Now don't be tryin' to sell me no six for nine," she teased.

They laughed and held each other.

When they pulled apart, Pastor Mattias and another man were standing nearby, smiling. The unknown man stepped toward Paul and spoke with a kind but authoritative voice.

"Paul and Sandy, I am Superior Court Judge Timothy Alberts. You have been advised by your pastor that New Jersey law is clear on a mandatory seventy-two-hour cooling-off period between application and granting of a marriage license. However, as a Superior Court Judge I have the authority to waive that requirement at my sole discretion. I have known Pastor Mattias for over thirty years and trust his judgment implicitly. He has asked me to waive the seventy-two hours and serve as witness on your certificate. After seeing you together, and being intentionally bribed with the pastor's famous lemonade, I will do just that. By the authority of the Superior Court of the State of New Jersey, please fill out this license application and I will both approve and witness it here and now. That is, of course, if I am given the honor of attending your ceremony."

Paul and Sandy agreed and thanked the judge and pastor but Mattias was already in ceremony mode.

"You heard the judge. We have a wedding right now, folks." He glanced at his watch. "Ceremony starts in thirty minutes."

People began pouring into the church. It looked as if Mattias managed to mobilize the entire congregation. Familiar faces from their visit the night before. Flowers appeared. A piano player arrived. Within thirty minutes the wedding was ready. *This must be what belonging feels like,* Sandy thought as she watched it unfold.

Sandy ran to the Explorer for her camera and handed it to a volunteer. "Can you get some pictures?"

"Lady, you picked the right guy."

Music played. Vows were exchanged. Hope was preached.

Later, Paul backed the Explorer out and saw "Just Married" written on the rear window. Everyone honked.

Sandy laughed and turned to Susan. "Are you okay?"

Susan smiled. "I've had an introspective day too. I just don't know what comes next."

Then she changed the subject.

The honking followed them all the way back to Manhattan.

58

Back in Manhattan

AUGUST 5, 1994, EARLY EVENING – NEW YORK CITY

As they arrived in the city, it became harder to tell the friendly honks from the regular traffic. Paul and Sandy held hands quietly as he drove. Sandy occasionally glanced at the sparkling ring on her finger. She thought of Ruthy and how unbelievable it was that she had made such an impact on her life. Just a few days, and now Sandy sat here in this Explorer as Ruthy's daughter-in-law. Paul was beaming a wide, unstoppable smile. This was not a plan. What he meant was it was not his plan. It was far more than he could have dreamed of this morning.

Susan seemed in good spirits, considering the circumstances. She sounded tired, but inside her mind she was calculating. She was doing what Susan does best: planning the rail and bank shots, trying the hard cuts into the side pockets, and leaving the straight-on, scratch-probable shots to the amateurs.

They rode up the elevator with Susan. The note she had left on her desk was gone. She called a number, said simply, "I'm back," then hung up and turned to them with the warmest grandmotherly voice she could muster. "They worry about me." She walked over to Sandy and placed a set of keys in her hands.

"These are for this office. I wouldn't hang out here too much, just in case, but I was the only one using it. Feel free to use it as you need when you are in New York. You had better go now. I have a cleaning crew coming, so it will smell like bleach and chemicals soon." She hugged a stunned Sandy, then did the same for an equally stunned Paul. She walked toward the apartment in the back to gather her things.

As she walked away, she thought, *Paul's accent is a ploy. Not natural to him anymore. How very clever of him.*

Had anyone watched her walk, they would have seen it in real time: the confidence in her plans, the ability to use anything to her advantage. At that moment it climbed her spine like a ladder. In private, once she stopped to gather her belongings, it settled back into place and reconnected. Home sweet home.

59

Hospital Honeymoon

AUGUST 5, 1994 – BELLEVUE HOSPITAL – NEW YORK CITY

Paul turned to Sandy and they shared a kiss. It was only their second, the first at the altar. To Sandy's surprise, Paul said, "We should go check on Roger."

"What? Are you sure? This is our honeymoon. I don't want to ruin the day."

"I know you," Paul said. "This is unfinished business and I appreciate you thinking of me first. But I want all of you and this would sit on your heart no matter where we went. Let's see Roger and then we will plan the rest of our short honeymoon. Besides, I have a place in mind for tonight, and after that we can figure things out."

Sandy kissed him again. "Come on. The sooner we check on him, the sooner we can go."

If only that turned out to be true.

After arriving at the hospital, they found armed guards outside Roger's room. They went to the desk and asked if they could see him.

"Oh yes, certainly," the receptionist said. "Sandy, right? You rode in the ambulance with him from the scene?"

"Yes, and this is Paul, my husband. We literally just got married."

"Oh my, congratulations! Just grab a seat and I will let the nurse know you are here."

Still in their wedding clothes, they sat and waited. A few minutes later, a nurse approached.

"I am sorry but I cannot let you see him right now. You are not family and we cannot locate next of kin."

"You will not," Sandy said. "It was just him and his mother and she took her life from her balcony several years ago."

The nurse hesitated, clearly uneasy.

Before she could respond, two uniformed officers approached along with one of the plainclothes detectives from earlier.

"Well, look who came back," Detective Haun said. "Hey, look, guys, it's our good Samaritans from the attempted murder yesterday morning. We were worried when you did not return yesterday. Oh, and how convenient you got married. Now our only other solid witness can claim marriage protections if this ever goes to trial."

"Hold on," Paul said. "We were here for an hour when Sandy came in the ambulance. We cooperated with your boss, Detective Davis, and he gave us permission to go on that trip with the understanding we would return. Knowing of course you are a highly trained detective; I can see your powers of observation have confirmed we did return and are here in front of you. As for the wedding, we did not plan it; it just came together at the last minute. And before you make a comment or joke about last-minute weddings, I want you to be aware I would consider that an insult to my wife."

"Calm down, calm down," the detective replied. "We just think the timing is odd."

"Well, show the lady a little respect," Paul said. "You don't know her at all."

"That is where you are wrong," the detective said, turning toward Sandy. "We know your name is Sandy. Do you know how we know?"

"Basic police work involving a computer and a donut?" Sandy remarked.

Detective Haun chuckled and then continued. "Good guess but no. Your name is the only thing that has come out of the victim's mouth since he arrived. He keeps saying, 'Sandy, why did you do it? Why did you come back? Sandy, how could you?' Over and over. Not conscious but talking. We would like you to come to the station."

Before Paul could respond, Sandy spoke. "What exactly are you charging me with? Being the last person, he saw before he lost consciousness and then muttering my name in a fever dream? That seems like a long title for a warrant. A judge would fall asleep halfway through the explanation."

The detective paused. "You are not under arrest. We just want to talk."

"And what are we doing right now? Smoke signals? Most people voluntarily walk into the station, where the police hold all the advantages," Sandy said. "We are not doing that."

Detective Davis came into view, making his way toward the group. As he approached and read the body language, his pace quickened. He heard Paul say, "Okay, it's my fault. I set the tone. Let's all calm down and start over. How about you get us into Roger's room with you, as long as we don't interfere with his care? If he wakes up, you can ask him directly."

Detective Davis saw the opening and took it. "Well, that sounds like a reasonable idea. We are helping you and you are helping us. That's how it should always be between the police and the public."

Which would have been the perfect transition had Sandy not spoken next.

She added, "And when you talk to him, you will learn something important. He was shocked to see me saving him because he assaulted me in 1979. Now think about his words again. 'Why did you do it? Why did you come back? How could you?' That sounds much more like a shocked apology than an accusation. Gentlemen, you can pick your jaws up off the floor. Let's go check on Roger."

Paul and Sandy walked hand in hand down the hall with the detectives and two of the officers.

When they reached his room, Roger lay connected to machines but breathing on his own. Sandy spoke gently to him. "Roger, I am back. I am here." She stroked his hand. "Just rest."

Paul felt his heart pound but he stayed steady. He pulled a chair close and helped settle her beside the bed. The detective attempted to question her about the assault allegation. Roger's heart monitor reacted instantly. Sandy kept her gaze on Roger. "Leave it. Let us get Roger stable first."

Paul was asked to step into the hallway with Detective Davis, who missed the earlier exchange and wanted to hear it for himself. Paul answered only the facts he knew; he did not speculate. Then Detective Davis asked the question he clearly most wanted answered. "If he assaulted her in 1979, why would she not run him over? Why save him?"

Paul breathed out slowly. "Her car is in a parking garage. You can check it. The hit-and-run was a black Suburban and she drives a Ford Explorer. And the deeper reason is simple, that is who she is. She survives. She overcomes. Forgiving is newer for her but she will grow into it. You or I might seek revenge. She has known where he lived for months. If she were a revenge killer, two things would be true: you would never have known it was her, because she would not have held him and ridden here in his ambulance. And had she wanted him dead, he would be dead, and you would have no idea she ever existed."

A nurse opened the door. "The doctor is on his way. The patient is becoming more aware and beginning to communicate."

The next several minutes were busy and focused. Roger's bed was lifted and tilted slightly. Still holding Sandy's hand, his heart rate was steady. His left eye did not move, giving him a macabre expression. His legs did not respond but the nurse reassured Sandy softly. "Do not worry about that yet. It is too soon after the trauma. He has several broken bones and nerve damage. The neurologist will do a scan today."

The nurse leaned closer. "Do you know anyone who can help him make medical decisions? We don't know his family situation."

"You should ask him while he is awake," Sandy said.

The nurse did. "Roger, can you answer a few questions?"

"Yes," he whispered.

"What is your last name?"

"Snow."

"Do you have anyone who can be your medical decision maker if you cannot speak for yourself?"

"There is no one. Just Sandy." He tried to turn his head toward her; only his eyes obliged him. One eye tracked while the other lagged. "I know I should not ask," he said, "but would you be my voice? You are the only person in my life I could trust not to pull the plug."

Sandy answered immediately. "Yes. I will sign whatever you need, and Paul and I will take care of you. But why me? Why trust me after what you did?"

"You knew where I was, and you came anyway. You could have let me die. You did not seek revenge." He raised his voice slightly. "Detective, write this down. It was not Sandy or the man with her. They saved my life. I know who hit me and for my own safety and for theirs, I am not going to tell you. You will never find the people who did this. Even I don't fully understand who they are or what they are up to."

He exhaled heavily. "If you will excuse me, I need to rest."

"Sandy, do whatever you feel needs to be done," Paul said. "I will be down the hall and will check back later."

He leaned in, kissed her, and left her with the man who once victimized her, trusting she was safe.

Detective Davis again followed Paul into the hallway. "Hey," the detective said. "Sorry. No hard feelings. It looked like one thing and turned out to be another."

"So now what?" Paul asked. "Do we get another 'do not leave town' warning?"

"No," the detective said. "Mr. Snow's dictated statement in front of two officers is enough to clear you. His statement cleared your wife of the hit-and-run and confirmed his assault on her from 1979. It is too old for criminal charges but she could bring a civil case. He is wealthy—he owns a penthouse near the Waldorf Astoria."

"Detective Davis, there is one more thing I think you should know. What you probably already know is Roger was accused of killing his mother but he was never charged. Apparently, a car horn was used from the same garage we were in today. The police, or perhaps the men posing as police who questioned me earlier believed Roger used the sound of a horn to startle her into falling to her death. We used the horn today to try to warn Roger. We could see the Suburban take off as soon as he stepped off the curb. I just wanted to put that out there in case it comes up later. Our only intent was to startle him back to the sidewalk. Instead, the sound stopped him in his tracks and that is when he was hit."

"As for Sandy going after his money, she will not sue him unless he hurts another woman."

"You will not need to worry about that," the detective said. "It seems his spinal cord was severed at S2. He will never harm anyone again. But I did not tell you that."

Paul shook his hand. "I never caught your first name."

"I never gave it," the detective said. "Most everyone calls me Detective Davis. Even my wife and kids do." He smiled. "Chances are you won't be here long enough to get familiar but my name is Haywood. You can call me Hay. It gets confusing in a crowd. Anyway, I wanted to tell you my second cousin, Scotty, says hello. When I saw your address come up as Caledonia, I thought now that's quite a coincidence. Scotty says you're a good guy. Says there was no way you and Sandy were here to hurt anyone. Scotty is solid. His boss is not. You should not trust the sheriff."

"I have that figured out already but thanks for the confirmation."

They shook hands. The detective walked to the elevator. Paul stood still for a moment. "When God closes a loop, He really does it with style," he whispered. "Momma, you were right. He is always good."

Paul returned to check on Sandy. The two uniformed officers lingered outside the door, more for her protection now than for Roger's. Paul stayed with Roger while Sandy stepped away to use the restroom and get coffee. She returned and gave Paul a long hug, easing the tension from his shoulders.

"I need to stay until after his surgery," she said. "I am sure the detective brought you up to speed, but I need to be here in case this first surgery has complications. He will be heading to pre-op soon."

"Well, Mrs. Matthews," Paul said, "I will be in the lobby if you need anything."

"Paul, you must be exhausted. You could get a hotel room and rest."

Paul smiled. "There is no way I am spending my wedding night alone in a hotel while you are here taking care of Roger. I will wait for the hotel until you can join me. Somehow, I love you even more than I did this morning."

He held her coffee while she settled in. She slid her hand into Roger's as he slept, his heart monitor showing a calmer, steadier rhythm. Under his breath, so quietly no one could hear, Paul whispered, "You and me both, pal. You and me both." He smiled and stepped out.

A few moments later, he heard Sandy's voice drifting softly down the hall. Conversations stopped. Machines seemed quieter. Visitors and nurses paused as her voice filled the corridor. It sounded as though the song was meant for everyone in that wing, not just Roger. The desk nurse swore she heard the harmonies, though of course that was impossible. Sandy was singing alone.

"Abide with me. Fast falls the evening tide. The darkness deepens. Lord, with me abide. When other helpers fail and comfort flees, help of the helpless, oh abide—with me."

60

Paul's Plan

SEPTEMBER 22, 1994 – PAUL'S HOUSE, CALEDONIA, OH

Information was growing fast but most of it was disconnected. People's names. Dozens of locations with no apparent connection to each other. Sandy was tracking down every mother and child who had passed through Suite 18, and the task was beginning to feel like sweeping sand off a beach with a corn broom. The group was small and controlled for a reason. No one was sure who to trust, so they kept the loop tight.

After a very brief three-day honeymoon, Sandy had her hands full helping Roger transition back to his apartment from the hospital and find a new normal.

Both Sandy and Paul agreed to stay focused. Sandy leaned in to screening and hiring caregivers. She was looking for someone to assist Roger with his ADLs, what the therapists called Activities of Daily Living, making sure his needs were being met. His wealth helped him adjust to his new limitations, but there was only so much comfort and care money could buy.

Paul's influence in Caledonia had waned during his relatively brief absence. Sheriff Clavell had been pleased during that absence and was not going to be happy when Paul returned.

Driving back into town, Paul spotted Scotty parked along Route 746, half asleep and waiting for speeders. Paul punched it from the posted 45 mph to an unmistakable 70, right past Scotty in his cruiser.

To his credit, Scotty woke up fast, flicked on his lights, fired up the car, and gave chase. To his shock, the car pulled over immediately and waited. In Scotty's entire career, no one had ever just pulled over. Not once.

He walked up with a little swagger until he saw the arm holding the driver's license out the window.

"Paul? What are you doing here? Uncle said you were in Manhattan and in deep trouble."

"Not anymore, thanks to you," Paul said. "I appreciate what you told your cousin about me. It helped."

"Any luck convincing him I scare easy?" Paul asked.

"Actually, yes. Want me to haul you in for speeding? That'll really sell it," Scotty said, a grin spreading across his face.

Paul grinned. "Sure, why not. Clavell will love it."

Paul left the car locked on the shoulder. Scotty even slapped the cuffs on him for show.

Before they walked to the cruiser, Paul said, "Hit me in the face. Hard enough to make my nose bleed."

"No way. That's brutality. I don't want to hurt you."

"If you drag me in bloody, the story lasts longer. Throw in a night in the tank for resisting and attempted assault on an officer. I swung at you, you ducked, caught me on the nose. Next thing I know, I'm cuffed and walking. Plays perfect. Then you interrogate me in front of Clavell through the bars. I'll drop some crumbs, you look like a hero, and we find out exactly who he's reporting to."

Scotty shook his head slowly, not to say no but more as acquiescence than answer. He eventually went along with it.

The plan started bumpy but it worked.

"Sorry about your nose," Scotty said, loud enough for the station, "but that's what you get for taking a swing at me. Strong self-preservation reflex, I guess."

"Now, since we went to all this trouble, the sheriff has questions. Cooperate, or he might leave the room and let me have another shot."

Paul fed them just enough. Scotty could tell some of it sailed too far into left field, but Clavell bought most of it.

Bryan Clavell leaned in. "So, where you been? Your house looks like it has been vacant for a month or so. I had to have some kids mow the lawn. Don't worry, I'll bill you."

"Well . . . none o' your business, but ah did end up in Manhattan," Paul said. "Ah help a man after one bad hit an' run. Spend hours wid de cops, hours in de hospital, an' den a few days in Jersey checkin' on an old friend. Look, Sheriff, ah ain' lookin' for no more trouble wid Scotty or he boys. Ah fixin' de house, flippin' it for cash, an' den ah gone fuh good. You ain' gon' see me again. How dat sound."

Clavell almost smiled. "Sounds good, Paul. Now, to be clear, no one's asking you to leave. You'll miss the Farmers Festival and the Firefighters Water Battle. We've got little league baseball games and even a historic bowstring bridge across the Olentangy. Someday they might even finish it into a park, if the politicians can ever figure out who should pay for it."

"Sheriff, I don't want trouble from Scotty's friends or from you. I know we started off on the wrong foot way back when, but if you're asking me to stay . . ."

The sheriff jumped back in, thinking he may have overplayed his hand. "Well, no offense, but you make people nervous with all your questions. Maybe it's best if you left. You know what they say, the sooner the better. I'll have Scotty get with Wayne over at the bank to help you find a realtor and sell the place. A property like that ought to go quick. By the way, did you ever find what you were looking for?"

Paul felt the room tighten. Clavell's pulse was up. Paul could practically hear the blood pumping. One wrong word and the surveillance would never end.

"Yeah," Paul said, real casual. "Yeah, ah did. Found one old box o' artifacts down in de crawl space. Ah gon' carry it by one local historian. De man live out pon a farm jus' outside town. Prolly nothin' but old junk an' clippins, but you know how it go . . . one man's junk, nex' man's treasure. An' wid all dem Bigfoot sightings up by de Great Lakes, tell me dat ain't somethin' Know-It-All Paul should look into fuh de radio show."

Now Paul threw all the cards on the table. The smile dropped off his face and his expression darkened. The silly grin and the folksy patois disappeared in an instant.

"It seems like crime is pretty high around Marion County. I thought the village police were here to handle things in the village. I'm sure you and Scotty helping out like this, being the welcoming committee and the chamber of commerce rolled into one, makes their job easy.

"I wonder if Mayor Overhill is on the same page. Anyway, I have the information I needed and I don't want any more trouble from you or Scotty and his guys. I'm heading toward Cleveland tomorrow. Warren Jones has also agreed to fix up the two smaller bedrooms and make a few improvements for a reasonable price. I'll get the house on the market as soon as Warren is finished. Might as well make some money on the flip. Won't take me long. Now, am I spending the night here or do I go back to pack so I can get out of the way earlier tomorrow? Your call, Sheriff. You hold the cards."

He watched Clavell's face. *That was the bait. He wants me gone, I can tell, but he also isn't sure I will go for good. I bet he tails me out of town.*

"Look, Sheriff," Paul said, easing the weight off the decision, "all I want is a good rest, and when I leave here, I never want to drive anywhere near Marion Williamsport Road again."

Scotty dropped Paul back off at his car and they shook hands quietly. Paul headed back to West Liberty. He pulled into the garage and waited. Eventually Scotty came by on foot and they sat in the living room with the lights off, enjoying some downtime. Paul told Scotty all about the wedding. Scotty walked back to his cruiser after a brotherly hug and wondered quietly to himself, *Is there anyone out there for me?*

61

Roger's Judas Despair

OCTOBER 10, 1994 – ROGER'S APARTMENT, NEW YORK, CITY

Roger would never walk again. The hit-and-run did its work. Sandy signed every release form as next of kin and had his penthouse apartment rearranged to accommodate his new lifelong limitations. With Paul's help, she hired a male nurse for around-the-clock care. Still, the weight of it all pressed heavily on them both.

In desperation, Sandy called Mattias.

"Hello, Mattias, it's Sandy. Yes, Paul and I are doing well. Listen, at the risk of being rude, we could use your help. We know how to care for Roger physically but his soul is way over our heads. His time is growing short. Can you come?"

Mattias agreed but with one condition: since Sandy and Paul were now married, they must be in full agreement. Forgiveness toward Roger now affected them together. When they readily accepted, Mattias arranged coverage for his flock and arrived a few days later.

He found Sandy and Paul exhausted but resolute. Paul would soon have to meet up with Greg and Melanie for several days of recon in Dublin and he needed to know Sandy would be all right in his absence. Not that she could not handle herself but this unexpected behavior from Roger really had her upset. That evening, after polite greetings and small talk, Mattias sat across from them in the living room of the same penthouse Roger inherited from his mother.

"So," Mattias said, "let's dive in. I'd like to meet with Roger in the morning when he's sharpest. But first, tell me what's really going on."

Paul spoke first. "He looks like a man set on punishing himself forever. Being kind doesn't come naturally to him at all. He sees God's light reaching for him but watches it from the corner of his eye, like he's slipping on sunglasses so the brightness doesn't show how much darkness is still holding on to him."

Sandy squeezed Paul's arm, momentarily overcome. "You sounded just like Ruthy," she said softly. "I've been missing her so much."

Paul pulled her closer as Mattias smiled warmly.

Sandy continued, "I have forgiven Roger, honestly and completely. But I can't find peace knowing he's heading into eternity like this."

Mattias nodded. "You're showing concern for his soul before you've fully settled your own. The Lord does work in mysterious ways." He leaned forward. "Show me the video he made."

Paul started the tape. Roger appeared on screen, his wheelchair now visible.

"Hello, my name is Roger. I have loved and lived a sinful life. I've been paid to do heartbreaking things. I have more kids out there than I can count. No one has ever loved me and I have never loved anyone. That is, until now."

He described how the very people he hurt most forgave him and saved his life. "They are the real deal, people genuinely committed to the gospel. If you write or email the addresses at the bottom of the screen, we'll send you a booklet and a Bible at no cost. It's too late for me but not for you. No matter what you've done, God can forgive you. Don't delay. Tomorrow is not promised."

Paul turned off the TV. The room was quiet.

Mattias exhaled slowly. "You're not overreacting. This is what some call Judas Despair. Judas knew the truth. He felt remorse. But he believed his betrayal was too big for the cross, so he hanged himself instead of asking for forgiveness. Roger understands sin and grace intellectually but he believes his own sins are irredeemable. He thinks God shouldn't save him."

The next morning, Mattias met privately with Roger.

Roger listened politely, nodding at the right moments. He openly affirmed the gospel was true and Christ's sacrifice was sufficient for any sinner who repented and believed.

"But I am not saying God can't save me," Roger said with quiet passion. "I'm saying God shouldn't save me. I'm not worth it. I'm ready to face my fate."

He pictured hell the way many casually do: an uncomfortably warm place, largely unpleasant but endurable. In his mind, his mother was already there, hosting bridge club with her eternal neighbors, serving cheap wine and poorly prepared catered meals. He figured he could handle it. He belonged there. Mom was waiting. Dad probably was too.

Mattias leaned in, his voice gentle but direct. "Roger, I'm going to ask you a series of questions. Are you willing to give me your honest answers?"

"Certainly. I understand you are friends with Sandy and Paul. I am happy to do anything for them."

"Do you believe the gospel is true?"

"Yes," Roger said emphatically.

"Do you believe Christ's sacrifice was sufficient?"

"Yes."

"Does God save sinners?"

"Of course, he does."

"Do you believe someone can hear and understand the gospel intellectually and even agree with it intellectually, but not spiritually?"

"That one I am not sure about. It is a very intriguing question. One inviting longer thought than a few seconds."

Mattias paused. "Last question: can someone have a distorted view of themselves, either by grandeur or by degradation?"

"Well, that is another good question. I think half yes and half no. The full answer will have to wait until another discussion. I have to get some more packages out today and then call my nurse to help me get ready for bed. May we talk again some other time soon? Will you be able to stay with us a little while longer? Your questions are intriguing."

As Mattias was almost out the door Roger spoke up "excuse me? Would you like to understand more about why I am the way I am?" Mattias spoke softly assuming Roger was speaking in softer more theoretical terms. "I think most of us would like that of ourselves. Some root cause other than sin."

"No, that is not what I meant. Let me give you something. Share it with Sandy and Paul if you think it's right."

Paul reached down to the left of his desk and Mattias heard four soft beeps, the kind you'd expect from a touchpad lock on a small safe. Paul came up with an envelope yellowed with age, the name "Virginia" written across the front.

"I found this in my mother's things. It is not an excuse or an explanation, just background and context. Have a nice evening, Mattias. I hope we talk again soon. "Later that day, Mattias closed the loop with Sandy and Paul.

"He believes the gospel is real. He even believes the offer extends to him on paper. But standing at the foot of the cross and saying 'He can save anyone except me, my sins are too great' is to tell Jesus His blood isn't enough. He doesn't see it yet."

Mattias rubbed his chin. "He also has a shallow view of hell. He thinks it's something he can endure. It's possible the brain injury is affecting his reasoning, so we should speak with his doctors. But at the root, this is a spiritual battle. We'll keep talking, keep praying, and trust the Lord."

Sandy's voice was tight. "He's on very shaky ground physically. He doesn't have much time."

"I'm not saying he does," Mattias replied gently. "I'm saying God's timing is not dependent on us. The same Lord who told a dying thief, 'Today you will be with Me in paradise,' is not short on patience or power. Even if Roger changes his heart at the very last moment, you may never see it. That's where trust comes in."

Mattias stood, weary but steady. "When Christ raised Lazarus, He didn't climb into the tomb and drag him out. He simply called him by name and Lazarus walked out under the power Christ gave him. We'll do what we can. The rest belongs to the Lord. Roger still has time. The question was whether he would use it to hang himself slowly or finally let the One who already paid the price carry him home."

"There is one more thing," Mattias said, reaching into his back pocket and pulling out the envelope Roger gave him. Sandy reached out and accepted the envelope with a trembling hand and an apprehensive look on her face. "I have not opened this or seen what is inside. Roger handed it to me today and hinted it might shed some light on why he is the way he is. He also suggested you might benefit from it as well, Sandy."

He exhaled, the weight of the day settling on him. "It has been a long, emotional day for this old pastor. I am going back to my room to pray, unwind, and maybe drift into a nap or something longer. If you need me for anything, do not hesitate to come find me."

Paul and Sandy said goodnight to the pastor, then settled onto the couch. Paul opened the envelope, and together they unfolded what looked like old memos or a historical journal summary. Sandy leaned her head against Paul's shoulder as they began to read side by side.

62

Origins: “Made” for Each Other

MAY 16, 1960, PHONE CONVERSATION (COMBINED ACCOUNT – A-FF ANALYST 259)

In the same spirit as the early 1900s “Best Babies” and “Fitter Families” eugenics contests, the Foundation launched the ROGER project. For fifteen days, births were occurring. “Roger” was never a person. R.O.G.E.R. was an acronym, a hypothesis entering its first live trial. If results proved consistent, the Foundation would scale it. Phase one.

R.O.G.E.R. (Recombined Offspring Generating Elite Reproductives) served as the pilot for the propagated series embedded in the Foundation’s long-range plans. Commissioned by Miss Veil, it ran parallel to the creation of her in vitro daughter, Sandy. Roger and Sandy were Foundation products, siblings in purpose rather than biology.

Two lab rats. One raised in a maze of praise and reward; the other in a maze of cruelty and survival. The program was simple: cultivate a pool of exceptional young men and women from collected children. Fifty men. One hundred women.

Before Dr. Mills, there was Dr. Ackman. It began with a phone call in 1958.

“Hello.”

“Miss Veil here. I have an assignment for you.”

Her voice was resonant and deeper. Her clipped words had a smoothness built in. The doctor had heard enough about her to be wary.

“How may I be of service?” he asked, crushing out a cigarette in an overflowing ashtray.

"I want you to compile exceptional health studies, physical appearance profiles, and pathology reports I will provide, sorted by group pod locations. I need fifty highly skilled, healthy males and one hundred women of the same caliber. Are you familiar with the Better Babies and Fitter Families initiatives?"

"Somewhat," he said, unsure where this was headed.

"You will lead the screening. Ages eighteen and older. I will handle the posters and fliers; you will select the participants. I will give you a list of traits and access to our physicians. You are looking for ideal pairings. Eliminate fifty women to refine the maternal pool. You are relieved of all other duties until selection day. Thank you."

The line went dead.

She chose him precisely for his arrogance and narcissism. When the contest concluded, the men were required to legally marry their assigned partners and the firstborn boy was surrendered to the Foundation. This was a variation on the Baby Moses protocols, the same machinery that would shape Sandy's fate: an engineered life without her knowledge. This is how Roger was chosen for her.

Over several years, contestants endured physical, mental, and psychological testing designed to eliminate the weak or empathetic. Blood, mucus, and every measurable trait were analyzed in the Addison-Foster Foundation labs.

Then came courtship. Fifty women were cut, leaving fifty men and fifty women paired by a compatibility algorithm Miss Veil designed. Virginia and her first husband ranked in the top ten. All top ten couples married and were encouraged to be fruitful and multiply. Families who produced girls returned to their communal homes. Families with boys advanced. Virginia and Roger won. They were paid handsomely. And then something unexpected happened, at least unexpected to the Foundation.

The plan was to take the money and give up the baby. But Virginia, exceptional in her own right, divorced her assigned partner immediately and kept every cent. She kept the child too. Miss Veil was impressed. The outcome was better than anticipated. Why not let nature and nurture work together?

So Sandy, a daughter Miss Veil had no interest in raising, was placed in a stable environment for ten years, long enough to reach early puberty, to which Sandy and ROGER were genetically predisposed, then thrown into hardship, danger, and survival. She endured the world's crucible, "nature red in tooth and claw," as Mister Foster loved to quote. She learned to hide her gifts: her intelligence, her beauty, her talents, everything that did not fit her philosophy of becoming a window.

Roger, by contrast, was raised to indulge his narcissism and sociopathic tendencies. He embraced his looks, intellect, charm, and cruelty. Like his mother, he loved nice things. She raised him to love them.

Miss Veil orchestrated all of it. The protocols, the contest, the nature and the nurture, all for one purpose: her grandson Gabriel. His parents were literally made for him.

63

Origins: Baby Girl

APRIL 7, 1960, MARION, OHIO (COMPILED ACCOUNT – A-FF ANALYST 259)

At a small hospital in Marion, Ohio, in 1960, a baby girl was born. The clinic staff had no idea how unusual her conception and parentage truly were. The mother arrived as a vagrant, escorted by a presumed Red Cross volunteer with a clipped German accent. Her name tag read Abigail Glut, RN.

Abigail explained how she and her husband recently relocated from Germany. He was an engineer hired by the world-renowned Marion Power Shovel Company. She was a licensed nurse at the Landstuhl Trauma Center and just moved from Kaiserslautern but she was not yet licensed in the United States. They arrived in Marion the day before and she signed up with the Red Cross that morning. According to her story, she found the pregnant woman in labor on the sidewalk outside the Palace Theater, across from the Harding Hotel where she and her husband were staying. Nurse Glut waited in the lobby to ensure the mother and baby were healthy.

The labor and delivery were natural. The conception was anything but. The technique used was unknown to the world at large and untested outside the walls of the Addison-Foster Foundation.

By any measure, this was an unnatural birth. It crossed lines. The only question was how many.

The method creating this pregnancy would later be recognized as a form of in vitro fertilization but not for another thirteen years. As usual, the Addison-Foster Foundation was ahead of the curve. Their technology typically ran five years ahead of national discovery. They had the money, the secrecy, and the freedom from oversight. They stole research, improved it, and buried anyone who asked the wrong questions. A foundation claiming to eradicate a genetic disease for humanitarian reasons earned enough goodwill to hide almost anything.

The young mother was an Unwanted. She was twenty years old, strong, capable, and screened personally by Susan. She was never assigned a name. She went through Main Landing, the rite given to wards of the Foundation. Her designation was NF330194 and she would never have anything else.

The young woman considered this an honor. She was told her number would be memorialized forever as a new version of Eve. It was manipulation, of course. Technically it could be true in some twisted context, but Susan never intended to release the designation. Protecting the mother's identity was essential to hiding the child's true parentage. This was no ordinary birth.

The mother was chosen for her medical history, her temperament, and most importantly her lineage. It was not uncommon for influential people to quietly terminate pregnancies conceived in secret or outside marriage. The Foundation capitalized on this. It increased the quality of the Natural Born. They collected from intellectuals, celebrities, athletes, geniuses, musicians, politicians, industrialists, and artists. Even in 1960, the free love generation had secrets to protect, and Susan knew how to exploit that.

The egg belonged to Susan Veil, now forty years old and leading the Addison-Foster Foundation. The egg was removed and inseminated in a petri dish with a sample from her lifelong protector, Gustav. They were unmarried and Gustav refused to conceive a child the natural way without marriage. Susan considered marrying him but ambition kept the idea on hold. Gustav would not budge, so this was their compromise.

The fertilized egg was implanted into the healthy uterus of the Unwanted female, designation number NF330194. Labor began on the 276th day after implantation. On April 7, 1960, a baby girl was born. It was not a joyous occasion. It was a moment of achievement. The celebration was for the success, not the child.

The baby disappeared the night she was born. A search was conducted, though many questioned how sincere it truly was. Most believed they knew exactly where the child ended up. She did not go home with NF330194. She went to a financially distressed couple who were paid fourteen thousand dollars to raise her as their own.

The Vanover's were thrilled. They loved the girl and the money. They named her Sandy, but when she was just learning to talk, she could not pronounce it. She would say DeeDee instead when asked what her name was, so as a toddler they called her Dee Dee most of the time. For ten years she lived with them, strong and healthy. In her ninth year she began changing from girl to woman far earlier than her classmates. She was teased and singled out. Her teachers and her neighbor Donna tried to reassure her she was simply an early bloomer. Donna and Mrs. Vanover taught her to dress modestly and reminded her that early beauty could cause problems but that was not her fault.

Donna always wanted a daughter but had three boys. Mrs. Vanover always wanted a boy. So Donna's son Danny often visited her mother while Sandy spent time with Donna.

When Sandy's father died unexpectedly, she and her mother carried on. Then, not long after losing her father, Mrs. Vanover collapsed from a heart attack on the living room floor. Sandy was ten years old and sat with her mother as she died.

After that Donna tried to adopt Sandy, but Sandy was prioritized into the Marion County foster system for reasons no one explained. When Donna tried to keep track of Sandy, the system blocked her at every turn.

Life grew busy. Her boys were growing and her husband traveled constantly. Over time she had to stop searching, though she never forgot Sandy. Donna likely wondered about her until the day she died.

For Sandy, the memories between her mother's death and her entry into foster care were gone. Susan Veil appeared at the Vanover home the day Mrs. Vanover died, posing as a psychiatrist. She guided the girl through her first tachypsychia event. She monitored Sandy's health for a time, reassuring everyone she was simply a normal child who had experienced trauma. In truth, most of the trauma came from Susan's overuse of hypnosis and experimental drug protocols. The goal was to remove Donna from her memory and her life. Someone swooping in and showing the child true affection would circumvent years of effort.

Sandy moved from foster home to foster home; each placement manipulated by the Addison-Foster Foundation. The goal was to sharpen her survival instincts and prepare her for her "special purpose," a phrase whispered under hypnosis.

It was all by design. Hardship was the mold. Pain was the tool. The missing months between her mother's death and foster care were erased. Her formal training ended and she was released back into the wild on her eighteenth birthday, April 7, 1978, her Freedom Day. Sandy was ready. More ready than Susan expected.

Killing the Vanovers separately to sever her attachments was, in Susan's view, necessary for the greater good. Hardship forged the traits she wanted. Killing Sandy's only aunt and cousin in a staged automobile accident served the same purpose. No one could swoop in and soften her with nurture or what Susan called "useless love." Donna would have been next had she continued digging. Susan hesitated only because Donna was well known in town. Too many deaths around Sandy would have drawn additional attention.

Instead, Susan used subtler methods. She manipulated Donna's husband's travel schedule through her Marion connections, keeping him away for long stretches. Donna was left with three active boys and no help. Eventually she stopped searching, though she never forgot. Susan used other methods to erase Donna from Sandy's memory.

Sandy buried her head in Paul's shoulder just long enough to gather her composure. Paul knew she was on the verge of tears but with Sandy that ship can sail very quickly. Paul didn't speak, he learned to let her absorb. He was doing the same but this information was not as personal to him as it was to her.

Sandy sat up, stood up, and in a very normal tone said, "Paul, let's put finding Donna's grave on our list for Scotty. He can find out quicker than we could. I would like to pay my respects."

Paul did not respond with words; he did not need to. He just put his head down and prayed for wisdom and direction.

As they were lifting their heads, a Siamese streak flew across the glass table and lunged at the window, landing on the same type of metal ledges he loved so much back at the LeVeque. With a satisfying slap against the glass, a group of pigeons bent to his will and scattered.

Sandy said, "That's right, you don't mess with us, right, R2!"

A satisfied "Yowl" came from the ledge, followed by another slap, and a new group of pigeons scattered in fear.

Satisfied, Roger walked past Paul and Sandy slowly, as if about to settle in and curl up with them. But pigeons are not the brightest bird and Roger does not tire of the game. Off he went again.

"Yowl." Slap. Pigeon chaos.

Paul started to laugh, a hearty, full-throated laugh.

Sandy gave him a look and said, "What's so funny?"

"That cat is just like you. He just picks on pigeons."

64

Up, Down, Up, Down, Emergency

NOVEMBER 11, 1994, DUBLIN, OH, NEW H.Q.

Sandy slid out of the water of the Scioto River as she had many times before. The time was 1:15 a.m., according to her all-black Swatch. The temperature was thirty-eight degrees, a cold November morning with a steady breeze. The moving river hovered near fifty degrees.

She tied off her black floating device and unzipped her wet suit around the neck to her fanny pack to make it easier to move.

Lefty said, Just focus and be cautious.

I will, Sandy answered silently.

Time to focus.

The light breeze against her wet face was almost unbearable. Her uncovered skin might be frostbit if she did not reach warmth quickly after she left the cover of the tree line. Months had passed since her last intrusion and she had no idea whether anyone was inside the complex tonight. She had a plan but the unknowns were many.

She pulled the fanny pack around to her front and unzipped the waterproof seal. She removed night-vision goggles and placed them on her head. She took out the nine-millimeter Sig Sauer and inspected it quietly. Satisfied it remained in proper condition, she inserted a magazine, racked it, and flicked the thumb safety on.

Still hearing nothing, she slid the pistol into the strap around her waist and pulled the cyclops night scope over her eye.

This is a lot better than covering one eye with my hand, she thought.

Sandy looked around, and once satisfied the goggles were working reliably, she headed toward the covered hatch to the lower level. The exterior lights on the property were already installed. She saw them on before. Tonight, they were dark. *Are they off or on a timer?*

The hatch was well hidden but she had used it before. It had been a while and she was unsure what alarms or surveillance systems might have been installed since her last visit.

She peeled back the carefully crafted camouflaged cover and slid the unlocked latch to the three o'clock position and felt the release of the two slide locks. The quiet hinge was a strong improvement. *They are dialing in on the finishing touches.*

Sandy focused and slid into the hatch on her stomach. She pulled her legs in and let her thin frame guide her downward. The hatch lid fell flat behind her. Thankful for the green glow from her goggles; without them she would be in total darkness. A three-foot-wide tunnel stretched out ahead. The tube was made of PVC, so it was somewhat slick, like a playground slide, and easy to shimmy through on the way down. Climbing back up was always harder.

She reached the bottom and hearing nothing, turned the handle and moved into the lower level. The hatch opened soundlessly and smoothly. *I wonder if they thought that through. If this were my home and covert lair, I would want it to sound like an ironing board opening.*

Inside, she paused again to listen. Before leaving this entry room, she noticed there were now uniforms hanging in a cutout in the wall. Sandy quietly turned a jacket, expecting to see an Enclave logo. What she saw were blazers embroidered with an "A-FF" logo patch.

Sandy broke the silence of the room unintentionally.

"Whose logo is that?"

Catching herself, she listened while she absorbed what this might mean. *Did Enclave get bought out? If this place isn't being built by EPS, then who is building it?*

She also saw some towels with the same logo. She dried off with one and put it into the exit tube to take with her when she left. She wanted to know more about that logo and how it connected to LIFE and EPS. Sure, they would miss the towel or then again maybe not. But it was nice to dry off.

Hearing nothing, she made her way toward the elevator. She had done this before but that was before the elevator was operational. She opened the mechanical room and turned the release valve to lower the hydraulic pump. A light sound emanated from the cylinders as the elevator lowered from the first floor to the underground level. When the sound stopped, she pushed the release valve lever back where it was and the pump motor kicked back on, ready to push the elevator up. Sandy hit the glowing red button and the door opened. Climbing into the now open and waiting elevator car, she pressed the up button. The elevator kicked on and carried her to the first floor.

Once on the first floor, she listened. She heard faint movement somewhere above. She moved quietly toward the stairs, weapon drawn, fully aware she was committing a felony.

At the top of the staircase, she saw light glowing from under a door at the end of a long hallway lined with rooms. It resembled a hotel, which made sense, since this wing held eighteen master bedrooms, each with its own suite and bath.

She crept down the hallway. The newly constructed facility was quiet. The floors were solid and did not creak. When she reached the door, the warm light beneath it felt inviting. She paused to listen. The room was quiet. Deliberately quiet.

Then she heard writing. A pencil across paper. A page turning with that familiar soft curl.

Before Sandy could decide what to do next, she heard a young man's voice through the door.

"You can come in. There is no sense in lurking in the hallway when we are the only ones here. Please come in, maternal donor."

Sandy eased the door open, pistol at the ready. Light from the room spilled into the dark hallway. When the door opened fully, she saw him.

He looked more like a young man than a fourteen-year-old boy. His voice was deeper than she expected. She half expected to find an agent. But this. She was not ready for this.

He sat at a large demilune desk facing the door. The room was far larger than she assumed from the hallway spacing. It was laid out like an apartment. This front room served as a living area. Further back, through openings in the wall, she presumed there must be a bedroom and bath.

Gabriel stood. He looked at the gun and said, "Now, Mother, you are not going to kill me. You had your chance in 1980 and you chose to let me live. So I doubt you came here to take my life. And I am grateful enough not to take yours. Please put the gun away. As I said, there is no one else in the house."

Sandy still had not spoken.

You cannot trust him, said Mister Right.

His advice was ignored. This marked the first time she did not respond to her inner voices. She did not want safe advice. She was too close to getting answers her inner counsel could not provide. She fumbled with the fanny pack, clicked the safety on, slipped the pistol inside, and zipped it shut. She fumbled because she could not take her eyes off Gabriel.

Motherly thoughts stirred within her. He has gotten so big. He is very handsome.

These thoughts collided with counterpoint questions. What is going on? Why is he here?

Gabriel walked around the desk and stood in front of it. Something unexpected hung in the air. Dangerous and far outside anything either of them might have imagined this meeting would be.

Sandy could not speak. No quick wit. No inner edge. Not even fear or anger. Only two overwhelming emotions rose to the surface: immense joy at seeing her son and crushing guilt for what she did. How could she have handed an innocent baby to predators?

"Now's our chance! I can't believe they have you here alone. Come on. We can leave together right now!"

Before she could continue, Gabriel stopped her.

"I am not a captive. This will be my new home. There is so much you do not know. Go home. Forget about it and just live your life. I am fine. You will see."

Sandy started to object but he simply said, "If you want to stay and talk for a bit, that is fine. However, I will not allow any more discussion about this topic."

Pushed off guard by those conflicting feelings of protection, guilt, and pain, Sandy closed the distance between them in a single movement. Before either could process it, her arms wrapped around him. Tears flowed as she whispered, "I am so sorry."

Gabriel stood stiffly, arms at his sides. He did not reciprocate, but he did not pull away.

In a detached voice, he said, "I have always wondered what a hug felt like. I have seen other people do it but have never experienced it myself."

Sandy regained enough composure to speak. "They have turned you into Mister Spock."

To her surprise, Gabriel laughed. And so did she.

As Sandy was leaving, Gabriel said, "Up, down, up, down, emergency."

Then he shut the door.

Sandy was confused for only a few seconds before remembering. The elevator code. She had forgotten that detail already. With the elevator now in service she would not have been able to get back to the lower level exit. He knew that. He was making sure she got out safely.

She went to the upstairs elevator doors instead of taking the stairs. She pressed the down button and waited. Once inside, she pressed up, down, up, down, emergency. The elevator dropped her silently to the lowest level.

Minutes later, she floated down the cold Scioto River, then rode her camo-painted bike back to her Explorer. She cranked the heat to warm her face and turned off her headlights to drop the bike back into the high grass for next time.

Campus Hippy spoke up. *You think there is going to be a next time?*

In the aftermath of finally meeting her son, with the realization he isn't trapped, he is participating, perhaps even planning whatever the end game is for these people, are we actually going to be adversaries? Then why am I doing this if he doesn't want to be saved? Like mother like son, eh, God? Point taken.

Sandy realized it in that moment. She did not rely on her inner voices as much as she used to. That hit harder than she thought it would. Like losing a childhood friend. *Not quite yet,* she thought *but the days are numbered. And I think that's for the best.*

65

Gabriel Goes to Law School

NOVEMBER 14, 1994 – OSU COLLEGE OF LAW, COLUMBUS, OHIO

True to the genius Gabriel was bred to display, he began law school at the age of fourteen. Having finished his bachelors and masters at Case Western Reserve in record time for that prestigious university, he began attending The Ohio State University College of Law.

Gabriel's first-year law school professor posed this question to the entry-level contracts class.

"So who can provide the most relevant answer to this scenario as it applies to contract law? Our situation is this: We are trying to evaluate if a local advertiser's offer establishes a legally binding offer or is simply providing an avenue for negotiation. What is the relevant doctrine, and what circumstances would have to exist, if any, for the offer made to become enforceable?"

The first student to speak up was in the front row. In fact, he was always seated in the first row. His name was Langford. Gabriel often teased that his own name screamed lawyer. However, he thought to himself, *Lang ford, now that name has mine beat by a mile.* Langford seemed to be the whole package. He was smart and handsome. His parents had money, and despite his pompous nature, he was likable when he wasn't kissing up to the professors.

"The question is begged, sir. *Harris v. Nickerson* and others establish the default: Advertising is generally assumed to be an invitation to negotiate, not a contracted offer and therefore not considered enforceable."

"Standard answer, Langford. Anyone else care to weigh in or do you all agree with Mister Langford?" the professor posed.

A young lady in the middle of the room raised her hand and the professor acknowledged her next. "Yes, Sally."

"It depends. What about *Lefkowitz v. Great Minneapolis Surplus Store*? If the ad provides quantity, price, and conditions of acceptance clearly, to a reasonable person it is legally binding under those circumstances."

"Well, both of you are right but these are memorized answers. Adequate, yes. But is there a more complete or comprehensive way to analyze this situation?"

Gabriel spoke, his fourteen-year-old voice resonating like a man's, though his frame had not yet reached full stature. "Sir, may I take this opportunity to work this out in the expository? I think I know where you are going. May I approach your question as a verbal exercise to reason this out rather than defining a singular answer. I find this helpful in all critical thinking exercises."

Someone mumbled but sufficiently loud for the class to hear. "Critical thinking? Which do I want? Oreos or Chips Ahoy with my milk before nap time?"

The professor spoke: "Well, I for one will enjoy watching this brilliant young man dismantle this problem and make a complete fool out of whomever made that remark. Remember this day when you work for young Mister Foster someday soon."

Gabriel began confidently but was cognizant of the importance of this moment. *This is my chance to prove I belong here.* "Professor, I believe the core issue you are raising is when does an advertisement cross over from a vague offer into something functioning as a real contract. To make this point easier to comprehend for my anonymous fan in the room, I will attempt to bring the Oreo and Chips Ahoy down to the lower shelf." A small murmur of snickering spread through the room.

"Most advertising consumed now is broadcast, either on the radio or on television. There are other forms, but I will use this as the illustration. They fall under a general 'Hey, check this out!' format. If the terms offered are vague, then how can one be obligated to them? After all, if the terms aren't clear, how can you argue they are binding? If the message is unclear, who can be prepared for action?

"So, to finally take the lid off that cookie jar analogy: low-definition ads are clearly invitations to bargain. Highly defined, less ambiguous ads are viewed as enforceable offers.

"After all, which one of us would feel good about responding to a highly specific advertisement only to find the details are incorrect? The more I contemplate this, the clearer the line becomes. Someday I hope to have kids of my own. When I give them a toy helicopter for Christmas and they are disappointed because it doesn't fly around the room like the advertisement on television showed, this violates trust. It is essentially a highly defined offer that does not reflect the actual experience for the consumer.

"I believe this example is very clear and can be used as a benchmark for quickly evaluating whether an offer is enforceable or merely an invitation."

With that last word Gabriel sat back down. The bell rang, people started filing out, and the professor said, "Gabriel, if you are not heading to another class, may I have a word with you?"

"Of course, Professor Samson. May I call you Professor Samson or do you prefer just Professor?" asked Gabriel.

This young man really has instincts, the professor thought. *Most students would not have thought to even ask. To people my age that was a shrewd and consequential question. This young man has something extra. I can feel it. Susan did not oversell his genius.*

"Oh no, Gabriel, Professor Samson is perfect. Thank you for asking."

They talked for hours. Gabriel used the time to dig deep and learn more about this man. The professor seemed unaware of how much he was revealing, verbally and nonverbally. At the end of the conversation Gabriel concurred with Susan. This was the right man to groom.

66

The Campaign Rally

SEPTEMBER 7, 1998 COLUMBUS, OHIO

The stage was covered with red, white, and blue balloons with ribbons. The sign above the dais said "Gabriel Foster and Howard Samson," and under those two strong names sat the campaign slogan: "Plotting the Course for Ohio's Future."

"Ladies and gentlemen, may I have your attention. I have the honor of introducing to you the finest young mind and young man I have ever been privileged to call a student. Today he is not here as a student. I am here to tell you I have learned more from Gabriel Foster in his four short years at The Ohio State University College of Law than from any other person in my life. This includes the professors who taught me, although I highly doubt any of them are here today."

Light laughter filled the air as Howard continued. "I first met Gabriel Foster just four years ago. He went on to complete law school with honors, but you may not be aware that the rules of the Ohio Bar Association prohibit Gabriel from taking the bar exam until after his twenty-first birthday. Well, the legal profession's loss is a big win for all Ohioans! I am so excited to introduce to you now. The soon-to-be youngest governor ever elected in any of the fifty states. My friend and student turned mentor. The one and only Gabriel Foster!"

The crowd erupted into a frenzy as Gabriel took the stage, waving both arms toward the audience and then embracing his running mate, Howard Samson, before stepping to the microphone. "Hello, Ohio! Now let me first thank my running mate, my professor, and my friend Howard Samson."

As the crowd settled, Gabriel stepped into his zone. He had the ability to analyze situations in fast-forward mode while the rest of the world ran slower. This was not magic or something supernatural. Gabriel had the rare, documented, and unique ability to release his own adrenaline at will. During this "mind pause," as he referred to it, he was able to map out the speech he was about to make and make it land in just the right place for this particular crowd. He was able to control his rare form of tachypsychia rather than having it thrust upon him by trauma like most occurrences.

"Now you all are aware of the Samson in the Bible, a powerful man until he allowed Delilah to cut his hair. Well, one look at old Howard here and you won't find a hair left on his head, but he sure has not lost his power!"

This friendly Ohioan vernacular was an affect. He would have never said "old Howard here" like he had just climbed out the window of the *General Lee*. He was adjusting his style but the crazy thing was no one ever called him on it. In fact, they seemed to like it.

They were running on an independent ticket, not because they could not secure a major party nomination but because they did not want one. They were the outsiders and they milked that title for all it was worth. The funding came from Gabriel's pockets with no donations at all. They were refused if offered. "I'm not for sale," he would often say. "Keep your money. I'll still fight for you either way." Ironically, when you talk dark money, you can't find much darker than the Addison-Foster Foundation.

The speech was long, but the highlights included: "We will not keep the status quo. Ohio has produced more presidents since the Civil War than any other state in the union and only falls behind Virginia by one. Ohio is the birthplace of aviation. It is home of the Wright brothers. We have produced twenty-five astronauts, far more than any other state. We walked on the moon first with Neil Armstrong, and we orbited the planet first with John Glenn, not to mention the Apollo 13 hero Jim Lovell.

"We excel in finance and manufacturing and so many other industries, not just now but throughout Ohio's long and rich history.

"Are you content with being in the heartland but never being the heart?" Cheers erupted. "Are you tired of having the coastlines of the country control all the power?" More cheers, much louder. "Isn't it time Ohio stood out!" The tipping point was reached. The crowd roared and waved signs for Gabriel in the air.

Gabriel waited and then continued. "Our plans are ambitious. Together Howard and I will take Ohio and turn it into the Heart of America. Ohio deserves better. You deserve better. We will make Ohio the center of finance, commerce, tech, and most of all we will lead in manufacturing again. Ohio will dominate in the next four years, and if you choose us twice, together we will make Ohio the new seat of power for America!" More cheering and waving of signs followed this last statement.

"One last thing. In the future we will need your help to make tough decisions together. I am asking for your vote now and your support, which I can already feel. Together we can shape Ohio into the new seat of power sitting under the desk of success in America."

After the speech he joined the crowd and formed a receiving line in front of the stage. In line stood a conspicuous woman waiting patiently. *She was here!* Why would she risk the consequences? Frustrated with her lack of concern for her own well-being, he continued to greet the line. No one would have noticed his frustration. He was far too polished to show it.

The woman finally reached the front of the line. She shook Howard's hand first and avoided eye contact with the flanking security detail. She wore a disguise of a large sun hat pulled low on her head and dark sunglasses. She looked like someone who was trying to hide by being seen, that is, just enough to appear to be hiding something. Her gaze was evasive and her actions furtive. When she arrived in front of Gabriel, she attempted to slip him a note from the palm of her hand. The attempt was sloppy and easily witnessed by the security detail.

She moved on into the crowd at the end of the row. Sandy looked back to witness the confiscation of the note as Gabriel handed it over to his handlers. After witnessing the confiscation, she turned into the crowd, removed her hat, and tossed it into a trash can. Speaking out loud to no one in particular, she said, "Well, no going back now! I think I will stop at the library and then catch a quick lunch somewhere nearby."

67

POV 3: Greg and His Team

SEPTEMBER 7, 1998, COLUMBUS, OHIO

"Yes. Reminder: no names," said a man's voice answering his private line. There were very few people Gabriel trusted with his direct number.

Greg.

"Understood, sir. Is it true there was a woman who slipped you a note at the rally?"

"Yes."

"What did it say?"

"Unfortunately, I never saw it. She made it too obvious. My security detail watched her put it into my hand. They asked for it immediately and I had no plausible reason to refuse. I rely on the 'crazy fan' defense when necessary but I never ask to see the content afterward. For obvious reasons."

Gabriel took control of the call. "Look, I do not trust Enclave. I am ordering you personally to keep this conversation between you and me and no one else. Do you understand?"

"Yes," Greg said, his voice clipped, the tone he reserved for radio traffic.

"She and her activities can be tolerated no longer. More accurately, they will not be allowed to continue. Everyone on this side wants her dead immediately. I do not disagree, at least from our larger perspective. I need her to disappear and leave us alone now. You and I will lose the ability to protect her if this stretches beyond today. She must be convincingly perceived as dead. Today."

"Sir, are you asking me as an Enclave agent or are you asking me personally?"

"I am not asking. Consider this a courtesy call. I know you are at the very least an acquaintance of hers. Beyond that, I do not want to know anything further. If you succeed, convince her to stay dead. Send her somewhere else. I do not care. If her death is not convincing, I will blame the failure entirely on you, after I have you killed to preempt your version of events. You cannot fail. You cannot alert her. She will not cooperate. I do not care how you achieve the result. If you fail, someone else will clean up the loose ends. You have until the end of the day. Are we clear?"

"Affirm."

The line went dead. Greg remained seated, the phone still in his hand. If he could get Sandy on board, this was survivable. She could disappear. Staying gone would be another matter. He would need help to change her identity yet again once the plan was in motion.

Greg picked up the phone again. "Enoch?"

"Yes."

"I have a job for you. You are the only one I trust and it has to happen today. I can only tell you what your role is; please do not ask anything else."

Once he brought Enoch up to speed without betraying the confidence demanded by Gabriel, he made another call.

"Benjamin, Greg. Listen, we have a special op today. Here is what I need you to do to help me set this up. This is need-to-know only and it comes from well above our normal chain of command. Now, before you comment, I think you should know one very important benefit to this assignment: If we can pull it off, it will be a big boost toward my retirement and your new career."

Benjamin jumped in before Greg could go on. "What do you need from me, sir?"

Greg said, "I knew you would react that way. I need you to pull in three agents. One will ride with us and the other two will be on tail duty. There is a catch. I want newbies, fresh faces she won't recognize but will understand she is being followed. I can explain the details later. Right now, I need you to get three agents and another Suburban and meet me in the parking lot of the Veterans Memorial building in half an hour. Can you do that?"

"Yes, sir, I can and will. I have to ask one question. Who is the target, and what is the objective?"

Greg answered, "The target is that woman named Sandy who has caused a lot of trouble for the Foundation. And the objective is to eliminate her and I will handle that personally. After all, I was her handler many years ago and she has been nothing but trouble. My orders are to handle it personally and they come from the top of the top, not just Enclave top, if you understand what I'm telling you without actually telling you. This is my chance to retire soon and yours to take over for me. I know you can do it, kid. You have impressed me many times. But this is my op and my way to the beach, so you will follow my lead. Do you understand?"

"Yes, sir. Thank you, sir. I won't let you down."

Greg considered using a payphone to call Sandy to give her a heads-up. He dismissed the thought every time it occurred. *The Lord will cover the details I can't. My duty is to do what I can do and He will do the rest. I will trust the Lord to work out the details.*

Well, thought Greg. *Gabriel is not wrong. She is smart and she is a threat.* Greg stopped and bowed his head to pray.

"Thank You, Lord, for this opportunity to save her life. I am a little fuzzy on the details. Lord, forgive me for not being honest with Gabriel and the agent. I know You admonish us to tell the truth. I am running fast and want to honor Your wishes in the midst of this urgent moment. Please grant me clarity for Your will in this situation. My heart's desire here is more for the state of her soul. She has wrestled with You for too long. Please draw her to You today. Your will though, Lord, always Your will. I will do my part but only You can bring about the result. Lord, selfishly I admit I pray Your result and my desire are aligned today. Lord, thank You for all You do, and I pray in Your name. Amen."

Greg called Melanie next and brought her up to speed. "Hello, honey. I have an urgent and unusual request and no room for error. Are you at the lab?"

"Yes," she replied. "What do you need?"

"I need a syringe with a sedative that can make Sandy appear to be dead and I need you to tell Enoch what to give her to bring her out of it. And I need it in the next thirty minutes."

"Yes, I can get you a dose of ketamine for her size and weight. I will get Enoch instructions on how to watch her overnight and help her transition out of it the next morning."

Before he hung up, she said, "Is there anything else I can do to help?"

Greg was about to say no and then changed his mind. "Can you use the key for her apartment and go now and retrieve her go-bag and R2? I can't get in touch with her right now for some reason. I know that is where she will try to get as soon as she realizes she is being followed. She probably won't have time to get there before this plays out."

"Certainly," Melanie replied. "I'll bring them to my place."

"No, please take them to Enoch. He has a place for her to lay low for a bit. It will bring her comfort to see R2 once this goes down."

Melanie replied, "I will take care of it. Be careful. I love you."

"Will do and love you too."

Things escalated quickly. The agents followed her to a Taco Bell on West Broad Street and waited for her to come back out. From there, everything accelerated. Greg knew Sandy would try to circle back for Roger and he knew she already had contingency plans. What he trusted most was she would not return to her apartment if she suspected they were already inside the building.

While Sandy crossed the bridge, Melanie was inside her apartment gathering Roger and his carrier. She pulled the go-bag from beneath the bed and checked its contents. Cash was still there. Everything she would need to disappear.

Melanie exited the elevator and headed toward the garage door when she heard someone shout, "Gun!" She did not wait to see what happened next. Roger was placed carefully in the passenger seat. The go-bag went into the trunk. Melanie pulled out in her Mercedes without hesitation and immediately picked up the car phone.

"Enoch, it's Melanie. I'm heading your way with her cat and the go-bag. I have printed instructions for you to help her come out of the Ketamine. They are in her bag.?"

"Meet me out the back door. I want to be in and out before anyone else arrives."

"Understood."

As Melanie drove back down Broad Street, she saw Sandy running through the rain, two men following her on the sidewalk. Every instinct told her to stop. To pull over. To intervene. She did not. If she did, everything would unravel. Providentially, Sandy did not see Melanie pass. Melanie turned left onto Pearl Alley.

Greg waited in the Suburban with Benjamin. They were angled across the corner of East Lynn and Northern Pearl, positioned to block access to Gay Street beyond them. The rain intensified into a near-solid sheet. He saw Melanie's white Mercedes enter Pearl Alley. Greg eased the Suburban back just enough for her to pass. He stepped out as she slowed.

Melanie rolled down the window. He took the syringe and slipped it into his jacket pocket. Their eyes met. No words were exchanged. He was Issachar. She was Dr. Mills. Agent Benjamin sat in the passenger seat, watching.

The third agent crossed Broad Street and took position at the crosswalk. Greg stepped aside. Melanie continued through. Melanie met Enoch moments later. The rain soaked them as she handed over R2 and the bag. She turned and left immediately.

Less than a minute later, Greg was back in position. The agent across the street forced Sandy into the alley. She scanned the space and locked eyes briefly on the SUV, though Greg knew she could not see him through the tint and rain. She found the dumpster and pulled garbage bags over herself.

Greg's heart hammered. He could not warn her. He had to play this clean. If she exposed him in front of Benjamin, the younger agent would not hesitate to shoot him and claim the credit. Greg knew the rule: *Speak first or lose control.*

When all five agents converged in the alley, Greg stepped out into the rain. One agent limped badly, blood seeping from his shoe into the pooling water.

"What happened to you?" Greg whispered.

The agent pointed toward the trash bags.

"Oh," Greg said quietly. Roofing nails. Of course.

A wave of paternal affection surged through him. He forced it down. As they approached closer to Sandy's position, Greg put his finger to his lips. The agents understood the gesture to remain quiet and increase their stealth. Greg's purpose was to give her time to finish praying. At that exact moment, she was praying; he could tell by the cadence of her muttering beneath the pile of trash.

Ruthy's words from eighteen years ago hit Sandy with clarity at the peak of urgency. Yet the urgency was not what was different this time. It was understanding. It was realization. It was comprehension, and most importantly, it was repentance. She no longer wrestled.

Greg heard no more mumbling and could not freeze this moment much longer. One more quick reminder to himself of his training: *Speak first or lose control.*

"Sandy, come on," a gentle voice said. "Hiding in garbage?"

As Greg and Sandy bantered back and forth at the end, they knew the other knew. At the moment Greg pushed the needle into Sandy's neck, the rain reacted.

Melanie was driving toward I-70 to head back to the office. Her wipers barely kept up with the heavy rain. Suddenly, the rainfall's intensity dropped so dramatically, as if she went under an overpass. There was no overpass. The change lasted only about five to ten seconds, and then the sky opened again and the rain fell, making a loud, startling thud on her windshield. She hit the hazard lights and pulled to the shoulder.

The clock in her car read 3:30 p.m.

68

Spy2K

DECEMBER 31, 1999, "Y2K" EVE – NEW YORK CITY

The world and all its experts saw Y2K as an internet protocol crisis. Gabriel saw something entirely different. His IP was not internet protocol at all. It was intellectual property and this moment was a singularity, a point in human history when everything he started and everything Susan already built could survive and grow.

From that singularity would come an event horizon, not in the cosmological sense but rather a point beyond which the Foundation's future could run forever. He had already rewritten the world once with his GPS technology, embedding quiet access points in every device carrying his code. But this was different.

This was the moment he was created for: a six-hour rolling window when the world's systems would blink, when safeguards would fall away, allowing the Foundation to reach and eventually, manipulate the very building blocks of life.

For months leading up to the rollover, governments and corporations had been racing to patch systems they barely understood. Temporary passwords were issued. Firewalls were taken offline for updates. Backup protocols were suspended. Entire networks were placed in diagnostic modes bypassing normal security. Hospitals ran parallel systems never meant to be exposed. Utilities relied on emergency overrides. Water treatment plants, dams, bridge controls, gas pumps, air traffic systems, early DNA archives including the Human Genome Project, and the first generation of digital medical records. All of this sat vulnerable behind half-finished patches and rushed fixes. It was the closest thing to a global digital blind spot the world had ever created.

Mankind has often tried to build a superior society by killing those who did not fit someone's version of the ideal. With this opportunity, DNA itself could be accessed and reshaped for advantage. No more killing. Meaning no more reason to kill. People eliminated before birth on a massive scale. A web-driven decision engine filtering potential births.

Now the Governor-elect for Ohio, Gabriel was on track for his planned destination as the youngest president ever elected. Gabriel believed he carried the fate of humanity on his shoulders, a weight Susan placed there long before he understood it.

Johnny Keys worshiped him, eager to please, eager to be useful. Gabriel did not trust him but he did not need to. He only needed Johnny to open the doors he could not reach alone. If Gabriel seized this singularity, the takeover could run on its own. If he hesitated, the Foundation's dream would die before it began.

Johnny had been working on the Y2K opportunity for the past six months. Gabriel asked him to lead the project personally. They were on the eve of the opportunity. Johnny sat drinking a cup of coffee and thinking back to the day Gabriel came into his office and shared his world-changing vision personally with him.

Just then Gabriel entered the "Spy2K" command center, as Johnny referred to it. That designation annoyed Gabriel but for now he needed Johnny happy and focused. Quietly, Gabriel entered the room and approached Johnny. He touched Johnny's elbow and guided him away from the others. The room was filled with terminals, each one running code that looked like a foreign language to everyone except the two of them. Gabriel stopped at a quiet corner station and brought up the sequence he showed Johnny earlier, the elegant framework Johnny had been building on for months. It was the kind of code that made Johnny feel like he was standing in the presence of a master.

"Johnny, I am afraid I am about to throw you a curveball. The only reason I would consider this is my utmost confidence in your ability to adapt to this serendipitous opportunity."

Johnny stared at the new lines on the screen and shook his head. "If we leave these loose ends in our new access, anyone could wander in. It opens our Veil Web to other traffic we cannot control."

"Johnny, picture two highways. The public highway runs on top. Every car is different. Every plate is registered. Every ramp on and off is marked and obvious. Every movement is tracked. That is the world everyone knows.

He tapped the screen. "Now imagine a second highway running right below it. Same entrances. Same exits. But down here there are dozens of off-ramps the public highway does not have. Places no one knows exist."

Johnny frowned. "But if the upper road is open, people might find their way down here by accident."

"That is exactly what I want," Gabriel said. "On the upper road every car is unique. That makes them identifiable. On our road every car is the same make, same model, same color. If you were doing something you wanted to keep quiet, which road would you choose, and what car would you drive?"

Johnny hesitated. "The dark one."

"Exactly. And the more people who wander onto that road, the safer we are. Their chaos hides our purpose. Their noise covers our signal. Let them build their little kingdoms behind their curtains. Let them think they discovered something forbidden. While they chase shadows, we move freely."

Johnny swallowed. "So, the loose ends stay."

"They stay," Gabriel said.

Epilogue

Lights, Camera, Distraction

JANUARY 28, 2001 SUPER BOWL SUNDAY TAMPA, FLORIDA. RAYMOND JAMES STADIUM

Gabriel looked straight into the camera.

"My name is Gabriel Grant, your governor of Ohio. The new heart of the USA. At eighteen the youngest governor ever elected. I have my whole life ahead of me." He held the camera for just a beat. "But like millions of other Americans living in the shadow of Huntington's disease, I have no guarantees. That is why I made you a promise. And where I come from, that means something."

He paused, the easy smile breaking through.

"Now, since I am the governor of Ohio, I have to admit I am rooting for the Ravens tonight." He raised a hand before the words were fully out. "Now hold on before you storm the studio. I know there is still a lot of Cleveland muscle on that field. We take pride in the athletes, not the owners in the box."

Susan stepped in beside him, composed, a trace of warmth at the corner of her mouth.

"I am Susan Vael, Chief Extinction Officer of the Addison Foster Foundation. Right now, Huntington's disease will be with us for another fifteen to twenty years. Fifteen to twenty million lives still waiting for a cure. These are families. And these are ugly, protracted deaths that do not have to happen."

Gabriel turned toward her briefly, then back.

"Susan's team believes we can do it in five. Together this could be the largest medical mobilization in world history. But we cannot do it without you."

Susan, steady and direct.

"We are not asking for much. Just visit the website at the bottom of your screen. Request your free Do Not Accept kit. A little swab does the job. Not hard. Won't even hurt. Send it back. Postage is paid. Your DNA stays anonymous. Your contribution does not."

There was a commotion off camera. Susan turned, genuinely surprised.

"Oh my. Look who is here."

Ethan Driver walked into frame, still in his stage clothes, the halftime show barely behind him.

Susan laughed. "You guys really rocked it out there tonight. What are you doing here?"

Ethan grinned at the camera, all swagger and zero hesitation.

"I am looking for one of those Do Not Accept kits. For me and the boys on the bus." He pointed at the lens. "Let's do this."

Susan touched her hand to her heart. "Wow. Thank you, Ethan."

Gabriel brought his hands together in three clean, unhurried claps. The kind that meant it without making a show of it.

Driver caught it, turned to Gabriel, and gave him the rock and roll nod. Chin up, two fingers to the temple, a slow point back. The kind of gesture that said, we are good, you and me, without a single word.

Gabriel, looked back to the camera, quiet and certain.

"Huntington's kills over a thousand patients every year. We can wipe this family killer out by 2005. And we won't stop there. This is just the beginning."

Susan, spoke to the lens.

"Won't you help us today."

About the Author

Dan is a lifelong entrepreneur, musician, and storyteller who has spent many late nights chasing ideas. A published songwriter and committed Christian since childhood, he has served in multiple roles within the churches he's been a part of. He and his wife, Kyra, his high school sweetheart have three grown children and seven grandchildren.

Dan served as vice president of operations for the Ark Encounter from its pre-opening planning in 2011 through the COVID shutdown in 2020. He now works full-time while managing a large venue and preparing to launch a new corporation built around a digital advertising platform scheduled to debut in 2026.

Throughout his life, Dan has helped with church plants, written music, and stayed busy in every season. Now with the encouragement of his family he adds fiction to the mix, crafting novels reflecting his love for the Lord, his family, and the power of a good story.

Acknowledgements

I want to thank my wife Kyra for enduring the words "I was just researching . . ."; my daughter Marisa and my son-in-law Spencer for their encouragement; and my youngest son Colton, without whom this story would never have been told.

Finally, thank you, Lord, for my overactive imagination and for Your unending mercy and grace to me, a sinner.